DOWNWARD SPIRAL

Detective Laura Warburton
Book Four

By

JAY DARKMOORE

Also, by Jay Darkmoore –

Horror
The Space Between Heaven and Hell
The Space Between Heaven and Hell – The Shadow Man

Thrillers
Det Laura Warburton Series

Left for Dead
Breaking Point
Deadly Silence
Downward Spiral
The Reckoning

Stand Alone
I See You

Short Story Collections
Tales From the Inferno Volume One
Tales From the Inferno Volume Two

Compilations
Into the Nightmares

Novellas
Lorna – A Dark Romance
The Night Shift

Dark Fantasy
The Everlife Chronicles – Hunted
The Everlife Chronicles – Conquest

Nonfiction
The Jobs F****d – Secret Diary of a Police Officer

"And they shall be made to crawl on their bellies to enter the kingdom of darkness."
-    Dante Alighieri's *Inferno*

Never miss another book and become part of my exclusive community where I host giveaways, behind the scenes content, and much more.

Sign up at www.jaydarkmooreauthor.com

For my aunty Jayne, who always encouraged me to chase my dreams, the power of nature, and for our nights drinking whisky and singing Black Sabbath.

DOWNWARD SPIRAL

LAURA

FIVE MINUTES BEFORE THE OFFERING

Laura shakily took the mobile phone from Catherine and swallowed dryly. The agony in her neck from the attack rose again, like trying to force down a ball of barbed wire. Why was *he* answering Jeremy's phone? *Gabriel.* The man they had been searching for. The man who had strangled her to within an inch of her life. Laura knew it could only mean one thing. They were already too late, and Jeremy was dead.

Burnell, Francis, and Catherine looked at her with bated breath. Francis worked on the computer, desperately trying to locate the call's location. Laura couldn't wait any longer, so she put the phone to her ear. Heavy breathing permeated the receiver.

"You cut me," his grainy, gravelly voice whispered down the receiver. "The lamb fought back." Laura checked Francis. He caught her eye, gesturing for her to keep him on the call as long as possible. She racked her head for what to say. If she taunted him, he would end the call. If she lay down and rolled over, he would end the call, and they would be lost.

"You underestimated me," Laura said, forcing through the rising pain in her throat. A beat of silence. Laura felt like her nerves were being pulled taut. The sound of keyboards rattling. The rapid clicking of the computer mouse as Francis worked. Burnell pressed headphones to her ears, listening to the call. Catherine's eyes turned more and more bloodshot, as the sound of his voice rocked her to the core, bringing back the memory of the gunshot and the heart-breaking despair that came with it. "Where is Jeremy?" Laura could almost hear Gabriel's lips crack into a sneer.

"The final offering."

"Gabriel," she said, "no one else has to die." A sinister laugh cackled down the phone. Laura had to steady herself as her legs turned weak. A laugh that chilled Laura to the bone. A laugh that meant someone else was going to lose their life, and there was nothing Laura could do to stop it.

"There is no death, only transcendence," he said. "I am offering their flesh to the Lord, and you are the heretic who is trying to stop me. But I am chosen, and no matter what you do to my earthly prison of flesh and bone, I will transcend all and be welcomed into the arms of my Lord for completing my work in His name."

"Thou shalt not kill," Laura said, trying to buy more time. "It's the most fundamental commandment." Laura looked at Burnell, who was mouthing something to her.

Don't piss him off! Laura swallowed hard. It was like walking on a thin sheet of ice. One wrong step, and it was all over. One wrong word. One wrong inflection. She was done, and more people would die. She had to be careful. So careful. Like feeding a cobra a live rat without gloves and blindfolded.

"Again," Gabriel said, his tone gravelly and hoarse. "The condemnation of humankind is the work of the Lord. And I am his sword. I rain his vengeance upon thee, and thou shalt quiver in his wake." A shuffling of weight, the sound of chains rattling, the distant caw of a bird. Laura focused on it, closing her eyes, trying to picture where he was.

But then she heard his voice, and everything changed. "Listen to the sinner beg for his life." A moment of silence. Movement. The sound of a heavy door being pulled open.

"...Laura..." Her eyes snapped open. The team's attention was focused on her.

"Jeremy," Laura said. "Just do whatever he says. We will find you. We will help –" Gabriel's voice cut her off.

"In this chamber of hellfire, the flesh will be cleansed, and dust will return to the wind." Laura tried to stop it, but the bubbling anger rose too quickly.

"You sick, stupid motherfucker!" Laura screamed down the phone. Burnell snatched the headphones from her head and stood up quickly, moving to Laura to take the phone from her. She was losing it again. The ice beneath her feet was cracking, and they needed to pull her away before it shattered.

"The final offering," Gabriel continued. *"The truth shall be revealed at last."*

"Give me the phone," Burnell barked, thrusting out her hand. Laura pulled away.

"Gabriel," Laura said quickly. "You don't need to do this."

"Secrets rot the ground we bury them in," he said. "You know what secret you hold. You know what sin you have committed."

"Gabriel, you fucking psychopath!" Laura blasted.

"Laura, phone, now!" Burnell raged.

"Enough of the games. Enough of the riddles. Where is Jeremy?"

"Laura!"

A hiss of laughter.

"Come find me," Gabriel said. "Ensure you're alone," then, a chill ran through Laura's bones as he uttered, "I will be watching you. You have one hour." The call went dead. Laura screamed down the phone into the silence. She eyed the phone like it was a hissing rattlesnake and threw it across the room. Catherine barked. Burnell wailed. Laura pressed her hands to her ears.

"Enough!" Francis boomed, rising to his feet. The women stared at him. "This is what he wants! He wants us to fight amongst ourselves!" His voice bounced around the MIU office. "Like it or not, we have no choice but to play this game. We tried going against what he said last time, and three officers are dead." Burnell's face dropped, the sound of the explosion still fresh in her mind. "He is in control. He is always one step ahead. And he has Jeremy. But Jeremy is still alive. There is a chance that we can save him."

"What do we do?" Burnell stuttered. "We can't let him call the shots!" Francis took a deep breath.

"What choice do we have?" he said, the waters of defeat running deep in his voice. "We find out where he is. The call locked onto a location—nothing too specific." Francis turned to Laura, desperate for answers. What was on the call?"

"I heard a bird," Laura said meekly. "A cawing of some kind."

"Like a crow?" Laura nodded.

"I think so."

"Okay, so he's near woodland. What else did he say?" Laura tried to make her mind still, like trying to grab an out-of-control Walzer.

"He said something about fire and cleansing." Francis moved back to the computer and pulled up the telecoms map. He pointed to the screen.

"There's a crematorium in this area. Shafer and Son's. It's abandoned." Laura felt cold ravish her.

"Crematorium?" She said, mouth turning dry. Horror wrapped her face. "He's going to burn him alive." In a flash, she grabbed her coat and went for the door. Francis moved to her, taking hold of her arm.

"You aren't going alone," Francis said. Laura continued to move toward the exit. Francis grabbed her arm.

"I have to," she said, moving away.

"Are you listening to me?" Francis urged, his voice breaking. "I said you aren't going alone!" Laura shook her head and stared at Francis, her eyes brimming with hate.

"You thought I murdered someone, and you left me to

rot in that cell for hours," she seethed, words laced with knives.

"I saved your life," Francis said.

"You abandoned me first, remember?" She snatched his hand away. "I go alone," Laura said, adjusting her coat. "There's enough blood on my hands already." Laura's gaze met Catherine's, who was sitting on her chair with her head in her hands. "And I am so, so sorry," Laura said, trying to stop the tears from breaking through. Catherine didn't answer. Instead, she stood up and, like a violent wind, disappeared out of the office.

"I can't let you do this on your own," Francis said. "I have to come with you." Laura gave him a tight smile.

"Like you said, Francis. What choice do we have?"

Outside, the cold air slapped Laura as she pushed through the back entrance. Catherine was sitting in the corner, smoking a cigarette. She turned as she heard the door slam closed. Her eyes were red with pain.

"I'm sorry," Laura said. "So very sorry." Catherine nodded. A nod that said everything that needed to be said.

"I loved him," she croaked.

"I know you did," Laura said, tears breaking free. "But it was just sex. Nothing more on my part. If I'd have known what was going to happen…" Laura felt like someone had driven a knife through her heart and was twisting it. She stepped towards her car, and then Catherine said something that stopped her in her tracks.

"Why does everything you touch die?" Laura didn't

answer. She didn't need to turn to see the hate in Catherine's eyes. She could feel it boring into her already. Laura pulled out her keys and got into her car, and she drove like the Devil himself was chasing her.

Laura eyed the large iron gates before her as she pulled into the crematorium car park. A thick and rusted chain coiled around the rungs like a dead snake. It had been cut open. The engine idled. The clouds were a mattress of grey over the horizon, and tombstones peppered the dull grassy hills that stretched on and on.

Laura collected her thoughts. She was walking into a trap. She knew it. But what other choice did she have?

She cracked the door open, and her foot crunched on the white stone beneath like loose teeth.

Her phone buzzed. A text came through from Jeremy's number.

Leave your phone. Your radio. Your car keys.

Laura clenched her eyes shut. This was suicide. She was walking to her own death. She unstrapped her radio and placed it on the car seat. She did the same with her phone and then finally her car keys. She eyed the crematorium sign.

Safer and Son's Crematorium - Where the Earth Meets the Heavens.

She was in the right place, and Laura Warburton slipped through the parted jaws of the gate and ran down the path leading to the large old brick building in the distance. Her breath escaped her lips in ghostly wisps. The silence was uninviting and the murder of crows that perched in the skeletal trees cawed at her, begging her to turn away and to save herself from what was awaiting her at the end of that lane.

She got to the building and peered through the cracked glass. She couldn't see anything. Only uninviting darkness that grew teeth. Laura depressed the lock on the large doors that were ordained with depictions of devils, flames, and the heavens.

She swallowed dryly. As soon as she stepped into that black, there was no turning back.

The door creaked open. The air was permeated with the pungent scent of dampness, rot, and death. The scent so thick Laura felt like she was choking on it.

She moved through the dim. Spiders had made their homes in the corners of the ceiling. Old tables had been overturned. Vases shattered with long dead flowers, like black, withered bones, littered amongst glass shards. Chipped paintwork revealed grey bricks, like dead flesh stripped away by vultures. Ghosts watched her as she moved. Laura's foot kicked old papers and empty bottles that rang out into the quiet.

She continued to search, checking room after room. An old chapel that had long been abandoned still had the faint aroma of incense. She checked another room, which looked like an old office. Rats and spiders scurried on the ground as she pushed open the door, which scraped on the hard, concrete flooring.

"*Help…*" She stopped. Fear gripping her in its icy grasp.

"Jeremy?" Laura called out to the void. Her voice twisting, reverberating, and coming back to her like an atonal quartet of lost souls. She continued to move. Quicker this time. Thrusting open doors and peering into the black, she finally found a door that had a stone staircase that descended deeper into the belly of the building. The walls were donned with old black-and-white picture frames of faces with dead eyes that stared at her, their features almost completely consumed by rot. She took a deep breath and descended down into the dark. With each step she ventured deeper into the maw of the beast. A steel door was at the bottom of the staircase. She pushed it. It was heavy but came away. She stepped over the threshold. Then, she saw them.

Two furnaces. Both looked aged. Both with their mouths sealed shut. Laura raced to one of them, peering through the small port hole in the door. Jeremy was sitting inside. His body crunched up, folded in half. His clothing stripped from him. His bare form laid out for the world to see. His face bloodied. Two of his fingers missing. His body brutalised, marred with red. Was he sleeping? Or worse? Laura furiously banged on the glass, but he remained still. Her voice barely audible through the iron tomb.

In the furnace next to him lay another body. Her heart tore in two. Jason lay face down in a pool of blood, dead, because of her.

She stepped away from him, not wanting to look at him any longer. She saw it then. On a table next to the white walls.

A radio with a note taped to it and the word 'TALK' scribbled in rough handwriting. Gingerly, she moved and picked up the console.

"I'm here," Laura said. Static escaped from the console. She looked around her. There were no other doors. Just two furnaces and pipes-lined the ceiling. Dials fed into the iron chambers like arteries feeding a heart. At the top of the walk, fixed into place, was a timer stuck at five minutes. There was nowhere for Gabriel to hide. He wasn't here, and Laura was right.

This was a trap, and she had walked right into it.

"Where are you?" Laura said into the radio again, trying to fight the rising fear in her chest. "Gabriel, I'm here! I'm here! Now talk!" The sound of the furnaces running. The lights hummed and flickered to life, bathing her in artificial radiance. "Gabriel!" Laura screamed. "Gabriel, talk to me!" A voice crackled through the radio.

"Welcome, Laura," his voice said, "to the final offering."

"Gabriel, let them go. Let them go right now!"

"Anger. I love your anger," he said. "It's what defines you. But what happens when your anger consumes you? Blinds you? You step away from the light and fall into darkness. The two men you see. Jeremy Marriot. Jason Hughes. They will burn if you fail. Their sins cleaned away by the flames. Jason has long departed this world, thanks to you. But Jeremy? He is very much alive. In a few minutes, you will listen to his screams, and that symphony will forever be a reminder of your failure to save him. To save those you care deepest about."

"Gabriel!" Laura shouted down the radio. She moved to the furnace door that was holding Jeremy. She had nowhere to run. No back up. No bargaining power. She was lamb in the lion's den, and she had to play by *his* rules. "Okay," she said, defeated. "Tell me what I have to do."

"The task is simple," he said. "Confess. Confess, and you will walk free from here unharmed. Only when the truth is repented from the sinner's lips, will the soul truly be free."

Laura furrowed her brow.

"I don't understand."

"Search your mind. Uncover the dirt on the secret you hold in your heart. Unearth the defiled corpse from the rotting ground you buried it in. You are both killers. Confess, and this shall be over."

Mary, Laura thought, and then looked at the furnace holding Jeremy. *I knew it. But what about me?*

"Celine? Is this what this is about? I killed Celine because she was going to kill me! It was self-defence!" Laura begged. Her eyes filling with pain. "I have nothing to confess!" The gravelly laughter echoed through the receiver again.

"No," Gabriel said. "You know *who* I am talking about. The one who haunts your nightmares. I know what really happened. And so… do… *you.*" Laura heard the furnaces coming to life. She saw Jeremy stir and the horror in his eyes as he opened them. "You have five minutes," Gabriel said. "Confess. Confess, or watch him burn." Laura heard Jeremy's voice and saw his hands banging on the small port hole of the oven. She saw the counter on the wall start to count down. Then, through the radio,

"Let the offering commence."

CHAPTER ONE

LAURA

FOUR DAYS BEFORE THE OFFERING

"I can't get my head around it," Laura said as she crouched over the remains of what she thought to be a woman in her twenties. "How can someone wear those shoes with that dress? I mean," she turned to Jeremy, who was standing there with a cup of coffee, his face turning the wrong shade of pink. "No wonder she's been murdered. With those flats on this terrain? You wouldn't ever expect to get away." Jeremy rolled his eyes.

"I don't think she expected this to happen, ma'am," he said, stepping out of the way of a CSI investigator who was taking photographs. "I don't think she dressed for a *what if I get dragged into the woods, get killed and then set on fire,*' type of scenario." He looked around him, his shoes sinking into the thick dirt under him, slowly sinking into a blanket of rotting leaves. Laura inspected the cadaver closer.

"She's been dead for a few hours," Laura said. "Her blood has begun to pool on her underside, so Liver

Mortis has set in. Rigor Mortis looks like it's been and gone."

"How can you tell?" Jeremy said, not wanting to look any more than he had to. The nightmares of the Butcher's victims were becoming too much to handle. He didn't want to add to his collection of horrors.

"Skin still has its elasticity. I reckon with the cold; it may have sped things up. Given how she was dressed, she was on a night out. Plus, she has some stamps from bars on her hand."

"What makes you think it's one of the Butcher's?" Jeremy said. Laura took out a pen from her coat and lifted the girl's upper lip. As she suspected, some of her teeth had been removed. A trademark of his work. Jeremy stole a glance, then turned away. As much as he *had* to see it, it didn't mean he *wanted* to. He held himself tighter as the winter wind cut through the skeletal trees.

Laura touched her gloved hand to the cadaver, lifting her head. Moving away her long brunette hair that was matted in leaves and dirt. The bruising had come out around her neck.

"She was strangled," Laura said. "Strangled and dumped. I think he started removing her teeth while she was still alive."

"That's his M.O.," Jeremy said. "He likes to cause pain."

"Yeah," Laura said, still crouching. She looked around them, as if trying to find the answer in the wind. "But why leave her here? Compared to the others, she's barely been mutilated at all." She realised how fucked up that sounded as soon as she said it.

"And that's a bad thing?" Jeremy queried.

"No," Laura said. "Just odd. Serial killers follow patterns. Height. Weight. Hair colour. Ways of execution. But this guy? He isn't playing by any rule book I have seen. He's unique, and that's what makes him so dangerous." Laura let out a long breath, stood up and moved to one of the CSI officers taking photos. "Seize her clothing as standard. Do what you do, and then let me know if anything comes back. Fingerprints. DNA. Anything that we can go off." The officer nodded, then moved to the dead girl. Laura wasn't hopeful. There wouldn't be anything to go off. There never was. Every death they had been to, three of them so far, was different, and there was never a trace of any DNA left at the scene. No evidence meant no questions to give to the press that were running the story all over the news twenty – four hours a day. Laura's face was plastered all over the media. The Butcher was winning, and the police were losing, and everyone knew it.

Laura listened to the sound of the river running through the woods, mixing with the singing of the birds that stayed home for the winter months. A robin perched on the tree where the girl had been left.

"Right," Laura said. "Are you going to get fucked by the press this time, or am I?"

"You're being flippant again, aren't you, ma'am?" Jeremy said. Laura smiled.

"I am being flippant, Jeremy," she said. "Because this is body number four, and we have nothing to go off." They moved up the embankment back to the path, holding onto the trees for support.

"So, you want me to take on the press this time?"

"All I'm saying is I'm getting a little raw. The press aren't gentle with me." Jeremy let out a morbid laugh.

"Sure thing," he said. "I could do with a little rough play myself these days."

They reached the top of the hill. Francis was just past the outer cordon and taking a statement from the dog walker who found the body. It is always a dog walker. If she was a serial killer, that's exactly what cover she would use. However, that meant she would have to buy a dog, and she very much doubted Bagpipe would allow that to happen.

Catherine was on the phone, relaying the findings to the senior command team looking at the incident.

"We can finish up here and then head back to the station," Laura said. "We need to look at this from a fresh perspective. CID are doing their part, but there's only really you and Francis on the unit. Catherine is back, which is great, but I am again seeing her with crosswords on her desk when I walk in. She should have stayed on the drug squad. Plus, with her new boyfriend…"

"The accountant?" Jeremy said breathlessly. The short walk up the hill taking it out of him. He had said he was going to start losing some weight, but then he and Mary got into difficulties, and now he was eating more and not sleeping either. Laura nodded.

"Yeah," she said, then did air quotes. "Jason, *the accountant*. Definitely a cover story," Laura had met Jason. Met him more times than she would ever admit to anyone. Certainly Catherine. If only she knew the truth. "Have you seen him?"

"He came with Catherine to the house once," he said, cheeks flushing red. "Mary made them some food. I was working in the back room. They stayed for a little while. Catherine was dropping off some paperwork for me."

"So, you know he doesn't exactly *look* like an accountant."

"And how does an accountant look?" Jeremy said, smiling.

"Not like he spends all day in the gym. Only numbers that guy counts are the reps on his bicep curls."

"Well," Jeremy said. "Catherine seems happy. Plus, after the Weaver case, she specifically requested to come back and work on the unit again."

They moved to the outer cordon. Francis was still talking to the person who found the body – a dog walker in his fifties. A springer spaniel on the lead with a ball in his mouth, begging to be let loose to chase squirrels. They both moved to him, and Laura leaned down and stroked the dog. Francis turned to her. His face lit up.

"Hi ma'am," Francis said. He eyed her and felt the cold cut through him. "Are you not cold?"

"Roasting," Laura said, barely taking her eyes off the spaniel.

"I was walking down here," the walker said, "and Miles," he gestured to the good boy with the ball, "he came back with a shoe. I thought *well, that's odd*. So, I looked down, and I saw… well, I thought it was a mannequin at first. I had never seen anything like that around here before. So, I got a bit closer, and I saw her face and her burned clothes and arms. I tried to get down to her, but my knees can't take it these days, so I…"

"Get on with it," Laura interjected. The old man's eyes widened, his bushy eyebrows rustling in the wind. She held out her hand. "Detective Inspector Laura Warburton, head of the Major Investigation Team. Sorry to interject," she said. "But we could do with getting your statement down at the station." She turned to Francis. "If you can take him down and get one off him?" He had a look of bewilderment on his face.

"Actually, ma'am," Francis said, "I was going to take one here and help out with the scene?" Laura didn't blink, and Francis felt the heat from her stare frying him alive. "Or I could head back to the station and take one there…"

"Good idea," Laura said. Francis closed his notebook with a purposeful slam.

"Right," he said, returning his attention to the dog walker. "Mr Walters, if you could please come with me? I will take you back to the station."

"But what about Miles?" He said, his sausage fingers pointing to the ground where there was now no longer a dog. He turned and looked, only to find Miles had slipped his lead and was chasing a squirrel. Walters called him back, and Miles returned with what can only be described as a Celtic headdress of ferns, twigs, and leaves nestled into his fur and ears. Laura smiled.

"I think he's had a good time already today," she said. "Take him back to the station and take his statement."

Francis and Mr Walters moved back to the opening of the woods. Laura overheard Mr Walters say, *'She's hard work, isn't she?'* And Francis' diplomatic reply of *'You get used to her.'* Laura watched them go with a smile on her face. It was nice to know she hadn't lost her touch.

CHAPTER TWO

LAURA

CSI worked their magic of facial recognition, and the dead girl was revealed to be Kacy Milton, age 19. She had been arrested for petty shoplifting, and her mug shot gave a positive hit. The wonders of modern technology.

Laura checked the stamps on Kacy's hand. The most prominent one from a rock bar in Wigtown named 'The Boulevard.'

They drove there, and Catherine went to do CCTV enquiries from some of the other bars in the local area with a picture of Kacy. Laura pulled up outside the bar. The remnants of vomit still on the pavement at the foot of two sealed black doors.

"Looks like a wild place," Laura said, regarding the vomit. Jeremy scrunched up his face.

"Looks like they're closed."

"We'll have to knock extra loud then," Laura said before cracking open the door. They were parked on double yellows, so Laura put the hazard lights on. She saw a traffic warden eyeing them up from further down the street. She flashed her badge, and the warden moved on.

Jeremy knocked on the doors to The Boulevard. A knock so weak they wouldn't rouse a sleeping toddler. Laura rolled her eyes and pulled out her baton and slammed the butt against the wood. That knock was so loud it could wake the dead.

"Do you have to?" Jeremy said.

"Do you want to come back when it's open?" She said. "A police officer walking into a bar filled with drunks?" Jeremy didn't answer, and that was enough for Laura.

Seeing no signs of life, Laura went at the door again. Fiercer this time.

"I'm coming!" A voice called from inside. Satisfied she had made her point, Laura put her baton back in her coat. A moment later, keys rattled, and the doors opened an inch to reveal a short man with a goatee and messy black hair. His face was heavily pierced, and his breath was more rancid than the stench of the stale booze that emanated out of the gap.

"What?" The owner blasted. The expulsion of breath nearly curling the officer's toes in their boots.

Laura flashed her badge, and the bravado vanished.

"Police," Laura said.

"I don't know anything," the owner said.

"You don't know what I want to ask yet."

"Well," the owner scratched his wiry beard, flakes of dandruff falling away like snow. "What do you want?" Laura smiled.

"First, to get out of the cold and come inside." The owner eyed the two of them like a dragon protecting its treasure. After a moment, he unlatched the door, and Laura and Jeremy stepped inside.

They walked down a narrow staircase. Their feet sticking to the vinyl floor. The walls were painted black, donned with band memorabilia, graffiti, and old records. Laura had been into some shitholes before, but this was top of the list. The pool table looked like an angry rottweiler had chewed on it. The optics behind the bar were rusted, and the bar itself looked more unloved than a pair of old socks left out in the rain. She wouldn't drink in this place if she were paid to. She wouldn't even take tap water. Fuck it. Not even bottled.

"So, what can I do for you officers?" The owner said. He rested his arm on the bar. Laura thought he may now need a tetanus shot. Jeremy pulled out a picture of Kacy.

"We want to see if this girl here last night." The owner leant in and squinted in the dim light. He shook his head.

"Never seen her before." Laura noticed a furrowing of his eyebrow. As quick as lightning and it was gone. But she saw it.

He's lying.

"She had your stamp on her hand." Jeremy continued.

"Yeah, and? We were busy last night." He said. He glanced to Laura and Jeremy. "Why? Is she hurt?"

"Just answer the question," Laura interjected. The sight of booze was making her skin itch. She wanted to down a bottle so badly, and this lying fat prick wasn't making it any easier. "Where is the CCTV?" The manager scratched his chin and then his balls. Laura grimaced. She didn't know if she was imagining it, but she was sure she could smell him. "What's your name?" Laura said.

"Kyle," he said. "Kyle Netherland."

"Okay, Kyle," Laura said, growing impatient. "Where is your CCTV?" Kyle straightened and moved past Laura to behind the bar. Laura wasn't imagining things. She *could* smell him. Fuck. She could *taste* him it was that repugnant.

God get me out of here.

She thought she should mention his aroma, but that would be impolite. She was in his home, after all, and she had already woken him with her banging her fist on his door. To tell him she could close her eyes and wouldn't be able to tell the difference between him and a steaming pile of shit was nothing short of bad manners. *But fuck me!* Laura thought, as she followed him behind the bar, *have a damn bath in something other than cat piss.* Kyle continued to talk, whilst Laura nodded, trying to stop her eyes from watering. She looked down under the bar. Among the glasses, she spotted small snap bags containing white powder. Kyle clearly had a little side business going on.

Kyle pushed open a door at the back of the bar, and they moved through a tight corridor. The air turned desperately cold, like all warmth had been relinquished from the space. She saw her icy breath leading the way in front of her. Jeremy tightened his hands around his body.

"Jesus," he said, blowing hot air into a tight fist. "It's freezing down here." Kyle turned, his hand resting on a door that said 'Office,' written in crude marker pen.

"I keep the heating off. It helps keep costs down."

Can't pay the gas man with drug money, can you? Laura thought. Before she stepped across the threshold, she noticed something hanging from the ceiling.

"What are they for?" She said, eyeing the instruments with a morbid curiosity. Kyle peered his head around the corner. His bulging lips parted. He was missing most of his teeth.

All that drug money and you can't afford toothpaste.

"Meat hooks," he said, almost proudly. "This place used to be a butcher shop back in the day. After I bought it, they relocated to a farm. More space."

"More space indeed." Laura eyed the hooks. They were tarnished with years of bloodletting. She wondered how much meat had hung off them. How many dead carcasses had been hanging there, crimson dripping off them? Pattering on the floor on everyone below.

"Ma'am..." The voice cut through her macabre train of thought. Jeremy was holding himself tight, desperate to get into the office. "Can we?" Laura pulled her eyes away from the meat hooks. She nodded.

"Sorry," she said. "Mind wandering." *I was imagining a dead animal hanging from the hooks. Or a woman with her ribs torn out like a bloodied angel. Her blood raining down on me.* "C'mon."

Inside the office, Jeremy spotted a small desk side heater and turned it on quickly, rubbing his hands like he was trying to start a fire and thaw himself out. The office was a shit show of record keeping. Piles and piles of paper that had browned and curled at the edges. Drink orders. Half empty crates of beer. A waste bin that was overflowing with takeout wrappers and drinks cans. Even the flies didn't want to lay their eggs there.

Kyle pulled out a chair that looked like it had had bites taken out of it. Brown fluff pushing through, like a burst wound left to fester and rot.

"Sorry about the mess," Kyle said. "I wasn't expecting company."

Ever? Laura thought, but instead she did that thing that cops do when they walk into a place so filthy that even the rats didn't stay long.

"It's fine," she said with a tight smile, trying to not inhale the noxious odour that was emanating from the waste bin. Her eyes were starting to burn. "I've seen worse." It wasn't a total lie, but this was a contender for gold.

Kyle sat in the chair, which groaned under his weight, and turned on the computer. It looked so old the Mayans could have used it to track when the world would end. Kyle clicked through different screens until they got to last night, which he fast-forwarded. Laura passed him the photo of Kacy.

"Have a proper look this time," she said. Kyle regarded the photo, then took out some glasses from his desk and leaned in.

"I think I remember her, actually," he said.

I knew it.

"Anything in particular?" Laura said. Kyle thought about it, scratching his wiry beard.

"She was drunk." Laura rolled her eyes. *No shit.*

"Anything else?"

"She was *really* drunk," he enunciated.

"So, I assume you stopped serving her and called her a taxi? Duty of care? Licensing laws?" Laura snapped, awaiting the response. Kyle could feel the heat from her scorn. The small room seemed to close in around him.

He shifted his weight. His silence told her everything. "Just play the footage," she said, her patience already wearing thin. Bar owners, like it or not, had a duty of care. You can't serve someone when drunk, and you must ensure all in the establishment are safe. Given the copious amounts of cocaine he possessed, it was evident that his priorities did not lie in protecting the vulnerable.

The footage played. Thankfully, it was in colour. At around two in the morning, the bar was really ramping up, and Laura had to get closer to the monitor to get a good look. The stench coming from Kyle was unbearable.

"Say," he said, quietly. Laura pursed her lips.

"Yeah?"

"You want a drink later?" Laura tightened her jaw.

"I don't drink," she said.

"Food then?" She eyed Kyle.

"I just really, *really* want to watch this footage, if you don't mind," Laura said, dragging the words out. Her glare so chilling, Kyle felt his balls shrivel up and crawl inside his body.

The footage continued. Laura stabbed the monitor with her finger. "There she is," she said. Kacy was there, stumbling and falling all over the place. She was dressed in the same summery clothing that she had been found in. Such a shame. Little did she know she would soon be dead and discarded in the woods. She had a life. Probably at university studying her passion. Dreams. Ambitions. And someone had taken it from her. Someone had snuffed out her life before it had even begun.

Kacy fumbled and stumbled on the bar, pointing at

someone serving drinks. A fat hunk of filth with a wiry beard and missing teeth. The same fat hunk with missing teeth that Laura could smell right now. Kacy was shouting at him.

I knew he was lying. She turned to him.

"You said you didn't remember her?" Laura said. "She looks pretty unhappy with you?" Kyle's face flushed red.

"The amount of shit I get in a night. I don't remember all of it." He was still trying to lie. What wasn't he telling her?

The footage continued. Kacy grabbed a drink from the bar and hurled it at Kyle. He then gestured off camera to a member of the door staff. A huge hulking bouncer marched over, dressed head to toe in black, with a beanie cap.

The doorman grabbed Kacy. She screamed at the doorman, pointing to Kyle and then elsewhere in the crowd. A melee ensued, and Kacy was dragged out of the bar to the cheers and jeers of the other members of the public. Kyle switched to the street view CCTV camera, and Laura watched Kacy walking down the street. Not soon after, she turned down a side street. Kyle sat back in his chair.

"That's it," he said.

"Did she come back?" Jeremy asked, suitably thawed out enough to do his job. Kyle shook his head.

"Burn it off for me," Laura said. "I'll need the CCTV." Kyle shook his head.

"I can't do that," he said. "I don't know how." Laura bit her lip. She had had enough of this guy and his attitude.

There was a reason he didn't want them to have that CCTV. Laura moved into Kyle's face. Her teeth an inch from his.

"You better stop fucking lying to me," Laura hissed. Kyle's eyes went wide. Laura glared at him like a starving dog guarding a meal. "You know that girl. More than you're letting on. Why was she so angry at you?"

"I told you," he said, trying to stem his panic. "I don't know. Maybe she wanted to screw my brains out and I said no. Kids these days."

"The CCTV, now." Laura ordered. Kyle continued his tirade.

"Get some booze down them and think they can do what they want. I tell you, the number of young whores that come walking through these doors." Laura dived over the computer and snatched the power cord out of the wall. "What the hell are you doing?!" Kyle said, rising to his feet.

"Seizing the console as evidence," Laura said. "You said you don't know how to work it, and I need that footage." Jeremy stood behind her, dumbfounded. He didn't know whether to help Kyle or Laura.

"Under section nineteen of the Police and Criminal Evidence Act..." Jeremy stuttered.

"We're taking it!" Laura interjected, pulling the console free. "You can raise a complaint later."

"You can't just take my stuff!" Kyle barked, grabbing at the console, his fat fingers fumbling with it. "You pigs think you can do what you like!" He eyed Laura with rage. "Fucking dyke." Laura's eyes went wide. She let go of the computer monitor and shoved Kyle against the desk, making the papers fall onto the floor, dust exploding into the air. She grabbed Kyle around the throat, her teeth bared an inch from his face, and grabbed a fistful of his pecker and balls. Kyle let out a tight squeal, his brow bursting with sweat. His clenched eyes were on the verge of tears.

"Listen here, you fat disgusting cunt," Laura hissed. Kyle squirmed, his manhood being crushed in her hand. "I saw the coke under the bar. Not enough to get you for supply, I'm sure. And I doubt it's even good stuff. You don't have money to pay dealers. Just have enough to wash yourself in the sink once a month." She squeezed a little tighter. A small whimper escaped Kyle's trembling lips.

"Please…" he winced. Laura crushed his nuts a little tighter.

"Now, I am taking that computer, and I won't bring you in for possession." She leaned in closer. Kyle's hot breath came out in staggered intervals. "You caused this," she spat.

"I didn't do anything," he cried.

"Yeah," she said. "You know exactly what you did." She released his boys from her grip, and he crumpled to the floor, holding his jewels.

Outside, Laura took out a cigarette and inhaled a deep lungful. Jeremy stood behind her, tightening his coat, clutching the CCTV console underneath his arm. She watched as cars lazily trudged along the main road, splashing dirty puddles towards her. The smell of the bakery a few doors down emanated through the polluted air. A bus pulled up to the curb opposite, and people piled out. Their eyes were glued to their smartphones. Music playing in their ears. Laura wondered how their lives would change if they stopped and looked around for a moment. Maybe fewer bad things would happen? Maybe they would help those around them instead of being trapped in their own self-absorbed worlds? She smoked again, holding it inside her, not wanting to breathe in the putrid stench of the world. A world where it was *me first.* The collective. The helping of someone else. That could burn. She felt Jeremy's eyes like daggers in her back, trying to find a vulnerable spot.

"What?" She said. Jeremy moved towards her, the console under his arm wrapped in a crudely taped up bin bag.

"Excuse my language, boss," he said, "but what the fuck was that about? He showed us the CCTV. Why the rest of it?" Laura turned to him.

"Really, Jeremy? What use were you in there? We're supposed to be partners, and you stood there with your dick in your hand and did nothing." Jeremy was taken aback by the comment.

"You assaulted him," Jeremy said. Laura chewed on the word.

"I am up to my fucking neck in it, Jeremy. I have bodies piling up and no suspect. I have coke dealing dick heads trying to keep evidence from me, and I have my detective sergeant crying because it's a little cold in the cellar, telling me how to do my job." She shook her head with disdain. Laura watched Jeremy shrink by a few inches. She let out a long breath. "You saw how his face changed when we showed him her photo. You also saw how he reacted when we watched the CCTV, and when we wanted to take it. There is something on that computer he doesn't want us to see, and I think it has a lot to do with Kacy." She slipped into the driver's seat. Jeremy placed the computer in the boot and got in the passenger side. "Make the call to forensics," Laura said. "I want this computer fully decrypted by the end of play today." Jeremy took out his phone and called digital forensics.

"Six week waiting list," he said.

"Tell them if they don't fast track it, they can answer to the Home Office. God knows they love the police not doing their jobs properly." Jeremy did.

"They'll pick it up today," he said. Laura nodded a *well done*. Jeremy hung up the phone.

The January rain patted on the windscreen. Laura fired up the car and let it idle for a moment.

"Sorry," Laura said. The apology caught Jeremy off guard. "I'm just up against it," she said. "I shouldn't take it out on you." Jeremy sniffed.

"It's okay," he said. "My mind is elsewhere at the minute, anyway." Laura pursed her lips, then turned to Jeremy.

"How are things with you and Mary?" The silence between them now was so thick it could choke a man.

"We're getting through it," he said, his throat beginning

to close. "I want to work things out. We have a meeting next week with the marriage councillor. I didn't go home last night," he said. "I stayed at the office and then fell asleep in my car." It sounded tough for him to say, like he was trying to drag a car out of mud using nothing but his teeth.

"Jesus," Laura said. "Sorry to hear that," she said. "Anything I can do? Do you need some time off?" Laura chewed on her nail, awaiting the response.

"No," he said. "We're too busy. We have too much going on right now."

"Jeremy," Laura bit, stabbing her finger towards him. "You are no good to me if your mind is elsewhere. Take it from me – The job doesn't give a damn about you or your family. They care about numbers and arses on seats. If you died tomorrow, you would be missed for a week, and forgotten in two. There would be someone else doing your job by the end of the month. If you need some time off, then take the time off. We will manage." Laura felt her heart pick up. She didn't know if she was still speaking to Jeremy or reflecting on her own experience with the police force. She dedicated her life to a career that treated her as a means to facilitate the lives of those above her. "So, you need time off?" Although a moment of quiet filled the line, Laura could almost hear the straining and fighting that was happening in Jeremy's mind. He was a man, of course. And men were not good at asking for help. Throw in that he is a police officer. Throw in that he has been one for most of his life and is close to knocking on retirement's door any day now. His mind is like a locked box filled with scorpions intent on destroying each other. He might say that he is fine, but any man sleeping in his car in the middle of January wasn't doing fine by any meaning of the word. "Right," she said. "I'm making the call. You finish what you need to do today, then I'm going to sign you off for a little while. No buts." There was another beat of silence, and then Jeremy cleared his throat, and his stoic façade began to crack.

"I just don't know what I have done..." He said, the emotion rushing out. "We have been so happy for so long," he said. "So happy. She has supported me in every way possible, and she is the love of my life. And now she hardly speaks to me. I thought something was going on. We haven't had sex in months. Hell, it might be over a year. I know we're getting on a bit, but nothing. She hardly even kisses me. It's been like this for a while, but I just kept putting it down to maybe I was working too much, and she was angry with me, but things have been so busy with all the shit we've been dealing with." Laura nodded. She was listening, but also putting pieces together. Him throwing her to the wolves. Betraying her. Backstabbing her for a promotion. It made sense now. It wasn't about Laura. It was about his wife. He wanted her to respect and love him again. Show her he is powerful. He is the man. That he wasn't a failure. That he was something worth loving. And even though what he did fractured Laura's trust in the man so much that she could never look at him the same ever again, it made her understand. Understanding was the first step in helping someone and acknowledging the pain they caused you and themselves, then growing and moving past it. "I think she's having an affair," Jeremy said. Laura felt her body flush with heat.

"What makes you say that?" She said.

"I don't know. Just a feeling," he said.

"You should confront her about it." Jeremy let those words sink in.

"You know when something just doesn't feel right? She's secretive with her phone. She's always coming home late stinking of booze. When she thinks I am asleep, she slips downstairs and spends time by herself. When I go down, she seems just to be sitting there in the dark, holding her phone in her hand. She denies anything is going on. Pair that with the not touching me, despite my best efforts … and my God Laura, I'll spare you the details, but I have tried." Laura was thankful for the details being redacted from his breakdown. She could fill in the gaps herself. "I asked her about it. She lost her head and told me to get out, and I haven't been home since. I either stay in my car, grab a hotel, or stay at work. Said she doesn't want me near her. Says she doesn't love me anymore. Twenty years, Laura. Twenty long years." He let out a long sigh. "So yeah," he said, lowly. "My mind is a little elsewhere at the minute." Laura forced a smile. Not because she didn't feel for him, but she had learned it's safer not to feel anything.

"I'm sure you'll get through it," she said. "You should go home. Have a talk with her." Jeremy nodded. Laura let out a long sigh. "Maybe you're right," he said. "I just need to see her."

Back at the station, Laura walked into the MIU with a round of coffees and placed them on her desk along with her coat. Jeremy walked in, holding the security console, and placed it on the desk.

"Right," Laura said, regarding the computer. "Forensics are coming to fast track the computer. I think there's some dodgy shit on there, so I want someone to volunteer to go through it later." Francis raised his head.

"How dodgy are we talking?"

"Fifteen to life," Laura said. Francis smirked.

"Yeah, sure. I have nothing to do tonight, anyway. Joys of single life." Laura smiled and passed out the coffees. Catherine had her computer open, displaying a plethora of gruesome crime scene photos, but under her desk was a copy of a magazine with a half-filled crossword. She noticed Laura standing there, and then she noticed she was looking at the puzzle.

"Hi ma'am," Catherine said quickly, trying to focus on the case file and not the puzzle that had been left out.

"To lose employment, nine across," Laura said. Catherine furrowed her brow. "*Dismissed,*" she said, then pointed to the crossword on the floor. "Don't let me catch you doing a crossword on work time again," Laura said. Catherine's face flushed red. Laura moved to the front of the office.

"How was the statement?" Laura said to Francis.

"He was insistent on bringing the dog inside. I told him

he was going to get me sacked, so he agreed to leave him in the car with the window down."

"Smart choice," Laura said. If there was one way to bring a police station to its knees, it was to let a dog loose in the office. "Okay," Laura continued, taking a sip of her latte. "Walk me through it. What have we got so far?"

"Three victims so far," Francis said, looking at his notes. "Two men. One women. Different backgrounds. Builds. Ethnicities."

"Kacy is number four," Jeremy said from behind.

"If she is one of the Butcher's," Francis said.

The Butcher. The name was like a dull knife across Laura's bones. Coined by the press because of how he brutalised his victims before killing them. Leaving them alive for as long as possible before they died of shock or blood loss.

The first victim was Martin Keller, a wealthy businessman who had more assets than she could shake a stick at. He had funds tied up in offshore accounts and even crypto currency. No evidence of money taken. Meaning that the motivation for the crime wasn't financial. He had been found with his head in a vat of liquid gold that had since solidified around his head. His hands had been removed. Judging by the serration marks on the body, the CSI determined he had been alive when it happened. Alive and conscious. The serrations in the flesh and on the top of the bone suggested that a blunt blade was used, like a butter knife or a trowel. It was as if the killer wanted to inflict as much agony and torture on the victim before they died. They even found traces of adrenaline in some old IV bags found at the scene. It had taken hours for him to eventually die. His vocal cords had been severed. He couldn't even scream.

The next was Mariette Ayer. A prostitute and drug user from the most deprived parts of Wigtown. She was found hanged by the neck by her own insides. Her genitals were mutilated, and needles were sticking out of her pelvic region.

Then there was Gordon Wood. A man so large that the undertakers needed to have a wall taken down to get him out. He had been tied to a chair with barbed wire and forced fed food until his stomach burst. A large table filled with food and drink laid out in front of him. A blender and funnel were found next to him, meaning when he couldn't eat anymore, he had been forced fed. His legs were filled with sores from sitting for so long. His arteries and veins clotted. CSI said he must have been there for days. Maybe weeks before his body finally gave out.

Then there was Kacy. Nineteen years old. White and a student on a night out. Nothing fit. Nothing matched up.

"Okay, everyone," Laura said, gesturing to the coffees. "Get caffeinated up. It's going to be a long night."

The clock struck eight in the evening, and Laura turned her computer off and began packing up. Jeremy eyed her.

"You're off?"

"Indeed," she said. "My therapist said that I need to

make some time for myself outside of work, so I am taking her advice, and I am taking a few hours to myself. I'll see you tomorrow. If anything comes up, let me know. But only if it's urgent." Francis raised his head, looking at the mounds of paperwork and evidence they needed to get through.

"You can't be leaving?"

"I haven't stopped recently. You go through the evidence. I'll have my phone on me in case anything comes up. I can feel myself getting a little…" She made a disgusted face, "burnt out. So, I'm going to go for a run, watch some shit TV and have a bath so hot I could boil vegetables in it." Jeremy nodded.

"Sounds brilliant," he said, trying to hide the bitterness in his voice. He waved goodbye. Laura moved to him and passed him a piece of paper. Jeremy regarded it and opened it up. "What's this?" He said.

"It's time off work," she said. "Only a few days. You can ask for more if you like. Finish up here, and then we won't bother you until you're ready to come back." Jeremy felt a ball forming in his throat.

"Thanks," he said. "But I don't need –"

"Jeremy," Laura stabbed. "This isn't a request. Take some time off and get things sorted with Mary." Jeremy soaked it in and nodded.

"Okay," he said, gesturing to the console. "I'll let you know what we find."

"Let Francis do it," Laura said with a wink, moving for the door. "Unless it's urgent, it can wait until tomorrow."

Laura moved along the car park, smoked a cigarette,

then got into the front seat. She took out her phone and opened her messenger app.

It's me. She said, then waited for the WhatsApp ticks to turn blue, and for him to start typing.

Same as usual? He replied. Laura chewed on her thumbnail.

Be at mine in forty minutes. She held her breath, waiting for the reply. She knew she shouldn't, but she did anyway. He replied, and she felt a rush of heat consume her. She didn't know if it was excitement, or guilt.

I'll see you there.

CHAPTER THREE

LAURA

Laura walked through the front door and hung her trench coat on the wall hook. The place smelt of lemon. She had done a thorough clean. Something she had been meaning to do for a while. But it seemed pointless when she never had company. Sure, Jeremy and Francis would stop by here and there. Even Catherine had been known to drop by to pass her updates on a case they were working on. But it was never anything more than that. She hadn't had any *real* company since Celine.

Until she met *him*. And *he* wasn't just anyone, and *he* stayed for more than just a bite to eat. She liked her home being clean for when he arrived, and then scrubbed both the home and herself when he had left. Call it pride. Call it washing away the filth of her day. The filth, and the guilt. The guilt of him. It made her feel less dirty inside.

She moved to the kitchen, nearly tripping over Bagpipe who was lying splay on the ground as she walked in. The damn cat was pitch black, lying on a light kitchen floor, and she still didn't see him. She cursed and then continued to the kettle, where she made herself a strong black coffee and forced it down her throat. It was going to be a long night, and as dirty as she felt, she couldn't ignore the excitement that was rising in her stomach.

Laura had a quick shower, shaved herself smooth, and

dried herself off. He would be here soon. She took out her lingerie from the wardrobe and sat her naked arse on the bed. She went for a deep purple on black underwear and stockings set. The purple like wisps of lavender smoke emanating from a pit of coal. He enjoyed the colour, and she did too. She had used red, and even green before. But the purple was her favourite. He helped with the cost, of course. The price tag didn't matter much anyway, especially when he was peeling them off with his teeth. She rolled up the stockings and clipped them onto her corset. It was tight but good quality. Applying a little makeup – nothing much: some dark rouge lipstick, topped off with some black mascara – she finished by fluffing out her wavy red hair, so it fell loosely over her shoulders. Then, she slipped her feet into her black heels and marvelled at herself in the mirror.

Her stomach was toned, but not shredded. Skin smooth and smelling of roses. He liked roses. Especially enjoyed devouring hers. She turned in her mirror. Her arse was firm and rounded. Perfect for a mouth to gorge on it.

Her phone went.

Outside.

She bit her lip.

Come in. I'm on the bed.

A moment later, the door went, and she began playing the music from her phone to the Alexa in the bedroom, like a siren's song calling to the sailors. But instead of sharp rocks, there was a beach of earthly delights.

She heard him coming up the stairs, and she dimmed the lights and made sure the candles were positioned in the right places. She lay back on her plush bedding. The pillow devoured the back of her head. Her legs fell open, spreading wide. The first thing he would see when he got to the top of the stairs was her lying on the bed, the flickering of candlelight, and her fingers massaging her bare pussy.

Laura played with herself, groaning gently. Her nipples were stiff, and her body tingled as he walked up the stairs. Just as she thought, his eyes devoured her.

Come break me.

"What took you so long?" She whispered, her nails dragging against the headboard of the bed. He moved in, filling up the space. His hair was short and prickly. His shirt was tight against his body. He had come straight from work. He hadn't had a chance to get showered or changed. Laura preferred him like that. Something about the smell of a man after a hard day's work. Something primal. Raw.

"I've got to make my girl wait, haven't I?" He said, his voice deep. The flickering candlelight danced in his pale eyes. He threw down his coat and moved to the nightstand, unbuttoning his shirt. Laura's fingers worked quicker. The sight of him made her pulse and her body writhe.

"Fuck me," she whispered. Ignoring it, he continued to unbutton his shirt, then stripped it off like a second skin, revealing his wide back and boulder shoulders. Moving to her, she watched him take his time, teasing her. He loved it, and she knew he did. He sat down on the bed, it depressed under his giant frame. His stubble was salt and pepper. He ran his hands over her legs and caressed the insides of her thighs. He looked at her working, a grin spreading along his face. "Fuck me," she said, barely containing the lust that was brimming inside her. She had been thinking of him all day. After a tough day at the office, she got to have him for the evening while his girlfriend was working on the case.

He looked at his body. At his lips. That flesh she wanted to bite. That back she wanted to claw. "Fuck me!" She blurted.

His hand collided with her face, and she stopped massaging herself for a moment. He gripped her cheeks and scrunched her face together.

"Bad girl needs to wait," he said, leaning in closely. He held her gaze. Her eyes were wide. He looked at her hand playing between her legs. "Don't stop until I let you." He snatched his hand back, slapped Laura across the face, then returned his grip around her throat. Her breath quickened as she continued to pleasure herself. She was close. So. Fucking. Close... to cumming. "Keep going," he said, as he stood up off the bed, listening to her symphony of ecstasy slip through her clenched teeth.

He slowly unbuttoned his pants and let them slide to the floor as he watched her. He was hard. She could see the fabric of his boxers fighting to contain his cock. She wanted that throbbing meat inside her. She wanted him to fill her up with every inch. Laura rubbed, then slipped her fingers inside her dripping pussy, dragging her nails across her breasts with her other hand.

He moved to her again and grabbed her around the

throat. Squeezing the sides, making those nerves come to life. They locked eyes.

"Faster," he whispered, his mouth an inch from hers. His breath was hot on her face. She was getting closer. So close she could barely contain herself. He could sense it. The flushing of her skin. The quickening of her breath. "Don't cum until I say, or you get nothing else." He felt her body twist. She was driving off the edge with her foot on the gas and the brake.

"Please…" she whispered. "Please, I'm begging you." He shook his head.

"Keep playing with that little cunt, but don't cum until I let you." Laura rolled her eyes, groaning loudly. He took his hand from her neck and placed it over her mouth. She scrunched her eyes shut. He took her hand and put it in his mouth, licking between the fingers. Tasting her. Tasting how good she was before sliding his fingers inside. She was tight around his fingers. Tight, wet, soft, and quivering. Her body begging him to let her go over the edge. He found all the right spots and began working, listening to her body. Listening to her breath. Bringing her right to the edge of euphoria, before pulling back. She groaned under his hand. Her nails found his shoulder, and she dug in deep. He grabbed her hand and forced it to the bed, pinning it with her wrist. "Bad girl," he whispered. His face cold. His eyes like stone. A monster that couldn't be tamed. Him her master, and her his loyal servant.

He worked more, edging her closer and closer each time. But she knew not to go too far. If she did, he would stop and he would leave, and she wouldn't see him for a week. She knew the price of taking her pleasure before he gave it to her. Before he allowed her to have it.

She groaned louder as he worked faster, fucking her with his fingers, using her body. Exploiting it. *Using* it for his own enjoyment. He leaned in. "Are you ready?"

"Yes," Laura groaned. He worked more.

"What's the magic word?" He whispered.

"Please. Please let me have it." He kissed her lips. His touch sending an explosion of heat that ravaged along her skin.

"Okay, baby girl," he said. "Because you're so good." She let that pent up raw lust loose. She grabbed at him with her free hand, reaching up and sinking her teeth into his shoulder, stifling the scream of sheer heaven, as stallions of endorphins rattled their hooves along her flesh, racing through her bloodstream. She screamed as her pussy quivered and clenched around his fingers. A long moment of time suspended on a cloud of bliss. She heard him laughing softly to himself. "Good girl," he said, pulling himself out of her.

She fell back to earth. He stood over her, Laura breathing heavily. He took off his boxer shorts and discarded them. He stood proudly before her. Hard. Throbbing. Ready to take her.

He pounced onto the bed, grabbing her hips and pulling her down to him. Like a wild beast, he tore her lingerie apart like tearing a ribbon from a birthday gift, her body naked on the sweat-soaked sheets. His hand collided with her jaw. "Fucking whore," he hissed, venom percolating his words. He meant it, too. Laura could taste the hate in those words.

"Use me like a whore then," Laura barked. In retaliation for her outburst, his hand found her throat and pinned her to the bed. A greedy man with a greedy heart, to consume all that he touched. To devour every part of her until he was done.

He enveloped her. Devouring her. Laura felt every hard inch of him thrusting. His pelvis hammering against hers. Laura's melody of ecstasy built, until the crescendo erupted. She felt that rush of euphoria consume her. Her breath was heavy, her nails carving into his back. He erected and pinned her arms against the bed. "Fuck me harder," she demanded. He obliged. Laura lay on her back while he fucked away every thought she had. Every feeling. Every single thing that came into her head that wasn't about how good this felt. He did it all. Taking away every ounce of pain she had ever felt. Every kind of worry. Agony or impulse that was destined to destroy her. She didn't want to feel anything else other than the breaking in her spirit that was happening with that fleshy hammer that was pounding away at her.

He grabbed a fistful of her hair and pulled her towards him, forcing Laura onto her knees. He slapped her ass, and she relished the sting. He grabbed her by the hips and entered her again. Laura's back was a blank canvas to be painted red with his hands. He pawed her. Felt her. Devoured every part of her. She took it. He ravaged her from behind, and Laura buried her face into the bedding, gripping hold of the bedsheets so tight that her knuckles turned white. She felt him going faster. More frenzied. His grunting matched her stabbing moans before he dug his fingers into her hips so tightly, she could feel every indent on her hipbones.

He came hard. They both did, in unison. Came so hard they shook the earth. Laura quivered and spasmed wildly. She bit the pillow as she felt him fill her. The thrusting slowed and died away, and in the absence of flesh colliding, she could hear his heavy breathing. She could feel the droplets of sweat on her back. He finished inside her. She told him *not* to do that, but when the build-up was *that* good, she would take a pardon.

He retracted himself from her and fell onto the bed. He looked up at the ceiling. The sweat on his brow glistened in the flickering candlelight.

"God," Laura said, taking in a deep breath and lifting her head from the pillow. Her hair stuck to her face, resembling a bush that had been in the middle of a hurricane. "I needed that." She rolled onto her back and stared at the ceiling. The fixtures of the room cast shadows that stretched and danced above them. He didn't respond. He sat up, wiping the sweat from his brow. Running his hand over his shaved head. The strands ejecting the moisture into the air like running through the morning dew on grass.

"I don't want to do this anymore," he said. Any passion Laura felt in her body shrivelled and died away. He always fucked it up when he opened his mouth, which is why she preferred him when he was eating her out.

"You turn me on and do that to me," Laura said,

crawling out of the bed. "Then you open your mouth, Jason." Laura moved into the bathroom and sat on the toilet. She pulled off some toilet paper and cleaned herself before standing and looking into the bathroom mirror. She fixed her hair and checked the damage. He had done a number on her arse. It was red, raw, maybe even bruised. Sitting would be tough tomorrow at the office. She stared at herself in the mirror for a moment. Observing the wrinkles on her brow that seemed to become deeper and deeper. The crow's feet under her eyes getting more and more pronounced. The bags under her eyes were pulling so tightly, she wondered how she could keep her eyes open. She had stopped drinking, yet she had just found something else to destroy herself with.

He was Catherine's boyfriend, and he was fucking his girlfriend's boss while she was at work catching a serial killer. No two ways about it. This was messed up. And that was why Laura loved it so much. She could have had anyone else. But he was forbidden. He was damaged, just like her. He was the only thing that made the nightmares go away.

The images of the corpses that got pulled out of those abandoned warehouses. The pictures of her on the front of the newspapers that were circulating around social media. Tabloids that she was a failure. A drunk. A religious maniac who dismembered and disembowelled his victims, making them eat themselves and nailing pages from the bible to their bodies. Anyone would crack under this pressure, and if she couldn't drink and had to sleep with someone else's boyfriend so she could keep her head on straight, then so be it. She didn't feel bad. She simply didn't feel anything.

She heard a knock at the door.

"Laura," Jason said, his voice sounding deflated. "Can we talk about all of this?" Laura moved to the shower.

"I'm getting a shower," she said. "You can stay if you want, but I might be a while." She listened, and after a minute, she heard the bedroom door close, followed by the front door slamming. The force of it rattling the house.

She was alone again.

What if he tells Catherine? It was the first thought that always came to her mind. He wouldn't tell Catherine. He loved her, or at least he said he did. Laura didn't care if he did. She was responsible for her own feelings and actions, not anyone else's.

The way he called her a whore. The anger in his voice. He meant it. So why did he keep coming back? He didn't have to come and see her, yet he came every time. Laura used him to block out her own thoughts, so what was he using her for?

CHAPTER FOUR

JEREMY

Jeremy watched Francis and Catherine working away on the case. He could barely keep his eyes open. The long nights of sleeping in his car and his unwillingness to go home were taking a serious toll on him.

He got up and stretched himself out, feeling his bones click and muscles tighten.

"Time to pack up for the night, guys," Jeremy said. "We've been on a few hours longer than normal. Get yourselves off." Catherine and Francis looked up from their computers in unison, then spotted the time. It was midnight. Each of them gathered their belongings and left the MIU, leaving Jeremy alone in the office.

He looked around. Seeing the coast was clear, he moved over to Laura's chair and sat in it for a few moments, savouring the power that the chair represented. He would never make inspector again. Not while Laura was around. But, God, didn't he want the power it brought. He had been the inspector of the MIU, if only for a short time, while Laura was causing mayhem. And somehow, she had once again found her way back into this chair, despite everything. The thought made him rack with envy. How come she got to call the shots? She was an alcoholic, and he didn't believe for a minute that she had actually stopped drinking. He figured she had just become better adept at hiding it. Plus, she had gone home early during a major investigation, while the rest of the team were working away trying to get the job done. Jeremy felt the arms of the chair. Imagined his name on the desk instead of Laura's.

He stood up, forsaking his usurped throne, and headed for the door. It would be another night in his car again. But what was it that Laura had said to him? He needed to go and talk things through with Mary? Try again? As much as he hated to admit it, she was talking sense. Her therapy must have given her some nuggets of wisdom. Plus, he couldn't handle another night lying on that cramped back seat.

Avoiding the problems in his life weren't making things better. In fact, they were going to be the end of him.

He went into the main office and walked past the response sergeant, saying hello to him as he did.

"Burning the midnight oil?" The sergeant said.

"Yes," Jeremy replied. "This fucker won't turn himself in, will he?" With that, Jeremy moved into the locker room, grabbed his coat, and moved into the car park.

The inside of his car was beyond filthy. Take away wrappers. Old coffee cups. Even a bottle on the back seat filled with piss next to his bag of dirty clothes he had been using as a pillow. He was living like a slob. He needed to go back home, and God dammit, even if Mary didn't want to speak to him, he would demand he stay there. The house was half his, and he couldn't live like this any longer.

The drive wouldn't take long, so he decided *not* to message Mary that he was coming home. She might lock the door and leave the key in, so it would be a nice surprise when he arrived home in the dead of night with a bunch of flowers, a raging hard-on, and a fist full of apologies.

He found a twenty-four-hour service station and bought the only bunch of roses that weren't decaying. He paid in cash, and hell, even bought himself a chocolate bar to treat himself. His cholesterol levels were high, but one chocolate bar wouldn't kill him. He hoped not, anyway.

He pulled up to his home address and killed the engine. The house was, as expected, in darkness. Jeremy stepped out into the silent street. The full moon was glowing in the night sky, hanging like a spotlight shining down on his life. However, what Jeremy didn't know was that as he turned the key and stepped into his marital home, his life was about to change forever.

The hallway light vanquished the dark away. He walked into the kitchen and placed the flowers down on the kitchen worktop. He eyed the glass of wine next to the sink and rolled his eyes. He felt his heart sink. She wouldn't even be awake. She would be in a drunken stupor upstairs. He felt deflated. He checked the waste bin, and there, as suspected, was an empty bottle of red wine. This was a mistake. He shouldn't have bothered coming home. His wife was lost to him. Lost to the bottle, and he had only himself to blame. Maybe that was why he had such disdain for Laura and her drinking? He saw the same weakness in her, her addiction, that he now saw in his own wife. Both women thought him to be inept. To be useless and less of a man, and both had their issues with the bottle.

He would sleep on the couch tonight. He wouldn't disturb her. They could pick up where they left off when he was free from work, and Mary wasn't drinking. He had thought about sending her to rehab, but he knew *he* was the problem. The drinking was just a symptom of his failings as a husband.

He scooped up the waste bin bag and exited out the back door. Using the glow of the kitchen light, he navigated down the flagged path flanked on both sides by grass and carefully planted flowers that had since withered and died from lack of care and attention. A feeling he knew too well, and that would easily translate into his own marriage. It was somewhat poetic, and he would have dwelled on it if, when he put the bin bag into the dustbin, it didn't bow and split onto his feet.

Jeremy cursed, crouched down, and sifted through the mix of old food and empty bottles of wine. He eyed one piece on the ground—something alien, an affront to his home and his life, something that should never have been there but was staring him in the face.

A condom wrapper.

He pinched the offensive item between his fingers. His body flooded with heat. He stared up at the dark bedroom window that overlooked him, like a black mouth laughing at him, exposing the deceit and treachery that had transpired in his absence.

I think she's having an affair, he heard his voice say to

Laura in the car earlier. Then her reply -

You should confront her about it.

He didn't know how fast he moved back into the house or how loudly he stormed up the stairs. He only realised what was happening when the bedroom light was burning into his eyes, the beating of his heartbeat in his head, and the silence after his wife stopped screaming as he crushed her windpipe with his bare hands.

SIN

Daylight broke before the latest lamb finally gave her last breath. I was rushed. I was impatient. My Lord was begging for flesh. She was unplanned. The girl in the woods. But you found her quickly. Spawn of the Devil, with hair like fire. You found her, and now you're looking for me.

I still have more to give. More offerings to make before I reveal myself.

There is one close to you. One who I must break to draw you closer to me. Away from the light and into the dark.

CHAPTER FIVE

LAURA

THREE DAYS BEFORE THE OFFERING

In the morning, Laura got up early and went for a run around Pennington Flash, the local nature reserve. She hadn't been back there since the Straw Man killings, where she was confronted with a dismembered heart with a candle and a picture of her and Ron staring at her. The thought made her shudder, but it was the quietest place to go running first thing in the morning. So, with a heavy heart and memories of last night, she got dressed in her running gear, scraped the ice from her car, and drove to the location.

She checked her phone. No missed calls and messages. No new deaths overnight, which she was thankful for. She knew she would be walking into a shit storm later. At least she knew how bad it would be before she got there.

She set out running down the dirt paths, her breath hot in the freezing air, and her mind running faster than her legs.

Somehow, the press hadn't found out where she lived,

and she owed that to both having no friends outside the unit, and having *no friends outside the damn unit*. She took a different way home each night, sometimes completely circling back the way she had come to make sure she wasn't being followed. She told her team this and anyone else she happened to bump into when they were hounded by the press that were loitering outside the station all hours of the day. If there was one thing that the media loved more than a juicy story about a sadistic, psychopathic killer, it was showing the public that those who were charged with the honour of protecting them weren't doing their job.

If someone was following her or managed to find their way to her home, then she knew it could only come from someone that she knew personally, which only meant a handful of people, meaning that she would flush out that rat and snap its neck with her boot. She was feared, and the sound of her name made even the most powerful men's ball sacks shrivel. She was not one to be fucked with, and with her mood as foul as it was today, her shit list was growing ever larger.

Laura slowed to a stop as she finished the loop and approached the car park. She pressed the timer on her watch and regarded her time. She had set a new personal best by some time. Anger, it would seem, was useful at times.

Exercise was the best thing for someone if they were having a shitty day. Laura firmly believed that if people got outside in the sunlight and moved their bodies a little more, it would cure nearly all depression and anxiety.

Something about being outside and challenging your body to do something you didn't think it could do did wonders for her. She needed it. If she couldn't move herself in the morning, there would be no telling what awful state she would be in. She might even start drinking again. That was the thing when you were an addict. You were never *not* an addict, and it was imperative she remember that. All it took was one drink. One slip off the wagon, and she would be right back to where she had spent so long running away from.

She stood by the reservoir's lapping waves.

It had just gone six in the morning, and the flickering of the winter sun was slowly creeping over the horizon. The clouds drifted lazily across the grey sky. The water by her feet was black. Laura couldn't remember the last time she saw the sun. It seemed so odd. So preposterous, but the more she thought about it, the harder it was to remember the feeling of the sun on her face. Her life had become perpetual darkness, and it had no signs of stopping.

She took out her phone and checked the news. Same old. Her face was everywhere, and the most insulting tabloids were about her ineptitude.

Good morning world!

She checked WhatsApp. Jeremy was online. She called him. It went to voicemail. She tried again. Why was he up so early? She went to message him but decided not to. He was off sick. She didn't want to bother him any more than she needed to. She began walking back to the car. Her legs had become stiff from the run, and then the sitting still, and she grimaced with each step. The car park was quiet. Not another soul was around her, yet she couldn't shake the feeling that she wasn't alone. Someone was watching her.

She surveyed the empty space. Nothing moved in that mist and gloom. The dark space that moulded into the trees stood like skeletal figures, their bony hands reaching over the walkways feeding into the maw of the thicket of the surrounding wood, ready to grab hold of someone, drag them into the darkness, and peel the skin from their bones.

She slipped into her car, feeling safer wrapped in its metallic shell. She put the key into the ignition, but the sense of anxiety overcame her again. She looked in her rearview mirror as she drove further away and out of the car park. Even as she got onto the main road and joined the rush hour traffic, she couldn't escape the feeling of those eyes on her.

Little did she know, it wasn't the first time he had been watching her.

And it wouldn't be the last.

Laura walked into the main office with the cold still clinging to her bones. She hardly felt it. Under her coat, she was toasty like she had been walking through the fires of hell, but her face told another story. Her cheeks were glowing. Her nose was running and chilled to the point one could tear it off and she wouldn't feel it. Her hair was windswept, like a fox tail over her face.

Francis greeted her as she walked through the door and

shook the cold from her. She took off her black trench coat and placed it on the back of her chair. A sense of Déjà vu came over her as she stared at the Starbucks mug on her desk. At one time, it had been her own mug, and it had been filled with vodka. The rest of the team would have been working away, like they were right now, heads in their work, cracking the cases that needed cracking. Saving lives from behind a desk. Unbeknownst to them, their commander and chief was getting shit-faced not ten feet away.

But that was the old her, however, and as she sat down and took a drink of the cappuccino Francis had retrieved, she didn't miss the bitter aftertaste of spirits or the masking, lying, and deception that came with them.

She was proud of her team. She had held them together at times when they, and the world, wanted to rip them apart. And they had done the same to her. Even if some of them would have loved to see her breaking into pieces and her swept under the carpet, never to resurface again. But that was the past, and her therapist, after Clara Weaver, had told her in order to move forward in life, she had to stop the weight of her past from holding her down. She thought it was some new-age wacko bullshit. What is trauma but a reminder of whom to and who not to trust? But with that, Laura found that weight was crushing her body and spirit, and alcohol was what she found to make the rock bottom seem a little warmer.

"Thanks," Laura said.

"No problem, ma'am," Francis said. Francis looked at Jeremy's empty seat. "Where's the sergeant?" He said.

"Jeremy has been given some time off. He's getting a little stressed at the minute." Francis chewed on his pen.

"I was getting worried," Francis said. "He hasn't been looking too good recently."

"Exactly," Laura said, and that was that. Not another word on the subject. Laura wasn't completely clueless. Jeremy had stabbed her in the back and twisted the knife, and she had insisted that he call her 'ma'am' at all times. She knew he was still gunning for her position, and he would likely stab her in the back again. Her signing him off was more opportunity than necessity. If he was out of the way, then he couldn't derail her investigation. Sure, she let go of the past, but she couldn't forget the snakes she let into her life, and how close they had come to consuming everything she had. She let it go, of course, but that didn't mean that she would forget it.

Never forget those who at one time wished to destroy you. They are counting on it.

"I have the report from the forensic team about the barman's computer," Catherine said, standing and moving over to Laura's desk. Francis joined them as Laura fired up the file. Hundreds of thumbnails from a hidden camera showed up. Dates spanning months. Years.

Laura flicked through the different images, clicking on them one by one. Women using the bathroom, taking drugs, and falling asleep half-dressed on the toilet. Even one giving a blowjob to a bouncer in exchange for a bag of cocaine. Laura felt sick just watching this stuff.

Then, a truly disturbing video came on. A young woman

was passed out. The camera time stamp was only a few days ago. She didn't recognise her at first. She was missing the leaves in her hair and the burns on her skin. But then she recognised the black flowery dress. It was her. It was Kacy. Laura looked at her coffee.

I wish I had the vodka now.

She was in the bathroom stall. The angle of the hidden camera catching it all. It had been secreted in a ceiling tile, pointing down to the cubical.

Kacy got off the toilet and stumbled into the cubical wall, then fell back onto the toilet and began laughing to herself. She took something out of her handbag that was by her feet. Her summery dress flowing. She didn't belong there. Not in a place like that. By the sunken look in her eyes and how easily she dug her house keys into the bag of cocaine and snorted it, she had been doing it for a while. Laura knew an addict when she saw one.

"Is this it?" Laura said, pointing to the footage. Catherine shook her head.

"There's more." Her tone suggested something sinister was going to happen, and within a few seconds of the footage rolling, Laura knew exactly what she was referring to.

The door went, and Kacy recoiled back. A man walked into the cubical. It was Kyle. He pinned Kacy against the cubical wall. His hands pawing at her dress. Kacy lashed out. Laura could see Kacy's silent scream erupt on the footage, and the manager smothered his big hand over her mouth and forced his free hand up her dress. Kacy bit down on his hand as hard as she could, and the manager released her. She ran out of the cubical and out of frame. The bar manager shook his hand, sucking at the blood that poured out of it. He looked directly at the camera; his face washed out. He was sweating. Probably coked out his head himself. He picked up Kacy's bag and moved out of frame. The footage ended. Laura sat there in suspended silence. She could hear that silent scream in her head. The face of Kacy as Kyle tried to defile her. Tried to rape her.

"That explains the bag of cocaine behind the bar," Laura said lowly. "It also explains why Kacy went back to the bar and why she was screaming at Kyle. He walked out of there with her handbag and pretended like nothing had happened." Laura sat back in her chair, the image of what she had just seen burning into her mind.

"What do you want us to do?" Catherine said. She pulled her hair back and tied it into a bun. They both locked eyes, and Laura knew she wanted the answer that was on the tip of her tongue.

"Lock the fucker up."

Laura took great pleasure in listening to the sound of the officers smashing in Kyle's door. He was dragged out in his underwear. His wife standing there, wondering why the police were dragging her husband out of their home. She enjoyed, sadistically, telling her exactly what he had been accused of. She wasn't allowed to do it. He was an adult. But she figured that the more she knew, the more likely she was to get the hell away from him. She screamed at Laura. She screamed at the officers and then raced out of the house to where the cops were, batting and hitting the window of the police car, screaming every insult, every foul utterance, every incoherent wail of disgust that she could muster. Her spittle slapping against the glass, and the terrified face of her husband staring back at her, knowing his life was over.

The officers dragged the wailing wife away, and Catherine took her inside and had a talk with her. A few hours later, Laura interviewed Kyle. He opted to have a solicitor. The same solicitor she had had the pleasure of speaking to the previous year when she interviewed Mark Johnston for the Straw Man murders. She was more than happy to see Laura and congratulate her on bringing the real killer to justice. Laura didn't share the mutual feeling and regarded Caroline Brown with a sense of apathy.

In disclosure, Laura showed Caroline everything they had. She didn't hold back. Caroline watched from behind her laptop computer screen like she was watching a scary movie at the cinema. The more Laura showed her of her client's debauchery, the more her mouth dropped and the closer her hands got to her face. By the end, Laura thought about handing Caroline the number to her therapist.

"I don't care what my client says," Caroline said once the footage of her client's actions had finished. "Send him to prison."

The interview started, and Kyle opted to go 'no comment' to all questions. Laura tried to hide her smirking throughout the interview. There was frankly nothing he could say in his defence. Every video. Every statement from other girls that had come forward detailing the sexual assaults they had been the victims of. The traces of their bodily fluids on the clothing that was found in his home from the fast-track forensics. Even photos of the girls passed out on the cubical floor were found on his phone. He had done this before, many, many times, and not all of the women had gotten away.

"Do you have anything to say?" Laura said, wrapping up the interview. Kyle looked like watered down shit. He shook his head, and he knew he was going to prison for a very, very long time.

The interview ended, and the silence that consumed them wasn't just deafening. It was enough to choke them. Laura bundled her papers and computer as she walked Kyle back to his cell. They would need to go to the CPS for charging advice. But it was just a formality. He was never going to be able to hurt anyone again.

As Laura got back in her car after reading the seventeen charges of rape, sexual assault, voyeurism, and more, she had a feeling of satisfaction running through her body.

There was more to do. There was still the *Butcher* on the loose. Although Kyle Netherland didn't murder Kacy Milton, he contributed to her death in so many ways, and Laura was happy that he would never see the light of day again. That the women of Wigtown had one less predator to worry about. It was a small victory in the grand scheme of things. But in the world of policing. Of good vs evil, you took whatever win you could get.

CHAPTER SIX

JEREMY

Jeremy stared at his wife's body. Reciting the events that had happened over and over. He thought about running. Packing a bag and vanishing into nothingness. He could board a plane. Draw out every penny he had. Go on the run. But he thought against that. They would find him. He knew how the police worked. NCA. Interpol. He wouldn't survive two minutes as a wanted man. So that left him back to square one. Staring at the woman he murdered with his bare hands.

The sun was high in the sky, and he sat staring at her body. She lay entangled in the blankets. Her naked body, strewn in the bed, bedcovers like an unwrapped meaty present. What had he done? He had completely lost his mind. Blind rage had taken over him, and now it had destroyed him. She had betrayed him, but he would pay the ultimate price. Her eyes were open, staring out into the bedroom like two vacant windows. The windows to the soul, but with nothing left inside. She had gone, and only her flesh remained.

He approached her tentatively. Maybe he hadn't squeezed too hard? Maybe he had knocked her unconscious? Maybe she was just too scared to move? Maybe he had just paralysed her? Maybe she was still breathing, and he could throw her down the stairs and make it look like an accident? She had been drinking, after all. A flicker of hope came to life in his heart, withstanding the winds of fear and anguish that were storming in his psyche.

"Come on, baby," he said, kneeling on the bed. "Come on, now," he touched her face. He moved her head and brought it to him, her dead eyes looking back. Her lips had turned pale. Her skin was cold to the touch. It's not true when they say a body feels as cold as ice. The cadaver simply settles to room temperature. But it's the emptiness of the vessel that chills us so, and as Jeremy touched the woman whom he had spent the last twenty years with, that pickaxe of realisation crashed through his heart. "Oh, no…" He whispered, retracting his hand like he had placed it into a fire. Holding it close to him, as if death was infectious.

Her neck twisted, causing her spittle, thick and stringy, to pool onto the bedding. Jeremy stared at the offending nodule of mucus and blood. He felt his eyes begin to burn with tears and sleep deprivation. He stood up and moved away, recoiling at the sight. Jeremy cried and screamed, calling her a whore, a bitch. A traitor. His legs went from under him, crashing to his knees, lost in his anguish. Shouting, touching, pleading with her to breathe. To move. To get up and walk out of the door and to never see him again. He would sell his soul for that to happen. Offer everything he had for her to let out a breath and sit up.

But she never moved. She lay there like a doll, her eyes

suspended in horror, that the last thing she saw in this world was her husband choking the life out of her.

Jeremy stood upright and began slapping himself. He pulled his phone out of his pocket. He hovered over the keypad, ready to dial 999. To call for help. Turn himself in. Beg for forgiveness. His blood went cold, and his legs felt like they had had cement poured into them. He couldn't call the police. Laura would be able to smell something was amiss the moment she walked into the home. She was good. Too fucking good.

He needed to do something. He would be eaten alive in prison. Being locked up with all of those you have spent the past two decades putting behind bars. He would be beaten. Tortured. Have his fingernails pulled off. His teeth extracted. His skin flogged and bones bleached. He had heard stories of what happens when a cop goes rogue. He couldn't handle that. No. He had to do something. He needed to figure a way out of this.

Jeremy paced the bedroom.

Think, mother fucker, think!

He was signed off sick and work knew that he was having issues at home. His absence wasn't suspicious, which meant time was on his side. But he had to make every minute count. What had he learned over the years? What were the pitfalls that meant he caught the killers? Could he stage it? DNA wasn't a problem. His wife was in his bed and their house. His DNA would obviously be here. What about witnesses? He had arrived home in the dead of the night. He said goodbye to the sergeant who watched him leave, and there was CCTV at the garage where he bought the flowers. Nothing unusual. He was on his way home to buy flowers for his wife. But what about the delay in calling the police? He could fix that.

He went downstairs to the kitchen cupboards and took out a bottle of brandy. The sun was high in the sky, and he stared at the outside like an animal in a cage. He could run. Pack a bag and never look back. But just like before, he knew he wouldn't get far. If you were wanted for murder, the police always found you.

Always.

Which led him back to square one. How did he make this look like an accident? But then, a darker thought appeared in his mind, sprouting like toxic mushrooms in the dark.

He could make it look like someone else did it…

He would do the work today, and then tonight, he would move the body. He would cover his tracks and then call the police in the morning and report her missing. But once he started on this path, there was no turning back. What he had to do was unthinkable. He had to take what he was about to do to his grave…

He checked himself in the mirror, peeling off his shirt, and saw scratch marks that had drawn blood on the back of his head, his arms, his hands, and his back. He didn't remember her putting up such a fight. Through that blur of fury, he didn't remember anything at all.

He felt his stomach begin to churn and the taste of vinegar in his mouth. Mary had blood under her fingernails. Which meant he had to do something about it…

He moved to the fridge and thrust it open, taking a long drink of brandy and pulling a face of war. He was feeling a little buzzed now, his gums turning numb. Fuelled by fear and adrenalin, his body went into autopilot.

He stepped out into the back garden. His neighbours didn't have CCTV. For once, Jeremy was thankful that they had ignored his advice for so many years.

He went into the shed and stepped inside. He looked around frantically, pulled off the pair of hedge cutters from the wall, and went back inside.

Using the bedsheet, Jeremy dragged Mary into the bathroom and placed her in the bath.

Holding her hand in his, Jeremy brought the snapping jaws of the hedge cutters across Mary's fingers. The sound of the bones crunching was sickening, and it took all of Jeremy's might not to throw up the contents of his stomach. The blood leaked out lazily. Thick and black. Already beginning to coagulate. Mary stared at him. Her face devoid of colour. Her eyes turned to bowls of white milk. When done with one hand, he worked on the other, removing every finger, a knuckle at a time.

He looked upon her, trying not to see her as a person, but more an object. A piece of furniture that was broken and needed dismantling. So, he returned to the shed and took out more tools: a hammer for her teeth. A blow torch to turn her eyes to jelly. A box cutter for her flesh. He had to brutalise her to the point where she was not only unrecognisable, but that no one would ever think him to be responsible. That no one of sound mind could inflict so much pain on another human being.

He worked on her until the sun sank below the horizon and the night took over, as Jeremy said goodbye to his old life and was welcomed into the life of the dead.

As the hours passed, Jeremy sat there, staring at the mutilated flesh of his wife. He couldn't falter now. He was already in too deep.

Jeremy pulled out some plastic sheeting from the back of the shed and hauled Mary onto it, being careful to wrap her so that nothing spilled onto the floor. Gathering the limbs, shards of bone and stray flecks of flesh, and taped it all up together like a fleshy Christmas present. He took out some black insulation tape and placed it over his car registration. He decked out the boot of his car with more plastic to be on the safe side.

By the time anyone found her, which he hoped would be at least a couple of days, then the animals and bugs would have taken what was left of her.

He got some lighter fluid and matches. He stared out the front door, checking the coast was clear, before hauling Mary's body into the boot. He stopped a moment to catch his breath.

You can still turn back now, the voice in his head whispered. *You can call the police. Turn yourself in. It isn't too late. If you go through with this, then you are damned.*

Jeremy left his phone inside the house still connected to the Wi-Fi. Ensuring his alibi for later.

He drove in silence, the hum of the engine blocking out his thoughts.

His first stop was to hide the body. He decided on the local reservoir, Pennington Flash. It was large enough that he could hide Mary, but busy enough that no one would suspect a car coming and going in the middle of the night. It was a popular spot for young lovers and for prostitutes to bring their clientele. There was plenty of wildlife, too, that would help *dispose* of her. Once he hid the body, he would head to another location and burn the evidence.

He pulled into the car park. The air was still, and the night was thick. He steered clear of streetlights peppered along the car park. He knew from his investigations that there weren't any CCTV cameras, but he couldn't be too careful.

Jeremy parked and stared at the darkness of the wood in front of him. It was a place to bury secrets. A place to lose yourself in.

He cracked open the door. The freezing January air slapped him fiercely and nearly took his breath away. He took in a deep breath and opened the boot of the car. Mary's twisted body looked back at him from behind the blood-soaked plastic sheeting. Her mouth twisted in a deadly sneer.

A silent scream that never ended.

He sucked in a deep breath that chilled his teeth. Mary's bloodied clothes in a pile in a separate bag disposal later. He donned his gloves, and put the plastic overall over his coat, and slid her out onto the ground.

He heaved up Mary's dead weight, his heart pounding in his chest. His face swelling with blood. It felt like it was going to rupture as he staggard deep into the surrounding wood. There, he placed Mary down and unravelled her naked body into the mud and leaves, throwing the crumpled plastic sheeting into the dirt. He looked at her, drenched in moonlight. Her skin was the colour of quicksilver. The bare bones of the trees encased them, like bony fingers closing around him, forcing him to sit with his treachery until the sun died and the moon turned black.

He unscrewed the cap of the white spirit and the kerosine and poured it over Mary. The smell was sharp, and it burned his eyes, along with the tears that he was trying to fight back. He took out a match and struck it. It hissed and exploded in his shaking fingertips before calming and settling into a bright bead of blue and yellow. He looked into the dancing fire, and he swallowed hard.

"I'm sorry," he whispered, before throwing it onto his wife, and watched as the hungry flames of his crime began to consume her, and the life he had once lived.

Back at the car, Jeremy stripped down to his underwear, and placed them in the boot along with the plastic sheeting, and then closed the boot.

He drove in silence and found himself heading to the derelict part of town. Old abandoned warehouses and buildings that were still needing to be renovated but had sat like empty skeletons for the last twenty years. The home of squatters and drug addicts. He turned off his headlights and drove into one of the compounds. It was deserted. Not a car in sight. He parked away from the entrance next to a large disused container. He stepped out into the cold, which bit his exposed flesh, and pulled open the heavy doors of the container to look inside. There was an old mattress in there, and some needles on the floor. He would have to be careful where he stepped, but the mattress would make for some good kindling.

He dragged the bin bag filled with the evidence and tools of his crime, and placed the mattress over it, nearly screaming at the rats and spiders that expelled from their home. He lit it and watched as the flames ate his crime away. He felt calm flood over his worry, like a hot blanket over cold flesh on a winter's night.

Stepping out, he got into his car and watched as the smoke poured out of the container. The police never got called around here, and it wasn't uncommon for people — kids mainly — to set fires inside these containers. He dared a smile. A wry smile. He was going to get away with it. All he needed to do now was to go home, clean the car, clean away any evidence, and scrub himself fresh. He would call the police and report Mary missing, and they would believe him. The words that would leave his mouth would be lies, but the tears that would fall would be those of pain and truth.

Jeremy felt it under his bare foot. He looked down to discover Mary's bloodied pyjama top had fallen on the ground out of the bag. In a snap, he grabbed it, clenching it in his bloodied hands. He couldn't go back to the container fire now. It was burning hot, and he would get soot on him, which meant more evidence to clean. He could dispose of the garment elsewhere, but for now, he needed to get away quickly.

He pulled the car away from the container and the derelict compound when he felt a bolt of fear rattle through him. There was another car pulling in—even worse, a car he recognised.

Oh, fuck, he thought. It wasn't just a car. It was Laura's car, and there was someone in the passenger seat.

CHAPTER SEVEN

LAURA

Laura pulled into the disused car park. The LED lights of her Audi gliding along the rolling black asphalt, shining on old shipping containers and the boarded-up building in the centre. Her heart was in her throat. She could have fucked Jason in her home, but that was becoming boring. She needed her next thrill. A new high. Something to really get the blood pumping.

She pulled around the back of the old warehouse. The shutters were pulled down like tape over a screaming mouth. The windows were boarded up with graffiti tattooed on them. The brickwork seemed ancient, and a large chimney pushed out of the top. It was quiet. It was abandoned. It was perfect. Somewhere she could scream, and no one would hear her. There was something both sexy and sinister about that.

Jason was staring out into the black. Laura put her hand on his leg, and he turned to look at her. Her face lit up by the centre console.

"Exciting, right?" Laura said. "Get to be a little naughty again." Jason smirked. His eyes were a deep green. His eyes, along with his muscular arms and defined jawline, were what made her want him. He was forbidden. The thing she couldn't have. It was sordid. *Wrong.* But she couldn't help it. Couldn't keep away.

She hadn't ever intended on their affair. But like a lot of these things in life, it just happened. She had met him when he came into work one day to drop something off for Catherine. He caught her eye too, and they shared a pause between each other. A moment that was hidden from the rest of the unit. Something only they could feel. Only they could see. Like electricity passing through them. Time stood still for what felt like an infinite moment, like someone had sucked the air out of her lungs and pressed the pause button on her heartbeat. She didn't love him. She had given up on love. This was sex. He left the office that day, and Laura placed him in the back of her mind, burying herself in her work. It was a few days later when he came back into the office to hand Catherine some lunch. She was happy for her, that she had found someone so caring. He left, and Laura couldn't stop herself. She made her excuses to head outside for a cigarette and to pass him her number.

"In case you need anything," she said, her hand lingering on his palm. He could have said no, and that would have been the end of it. But he took it. Those eyes luring her in, like a Venus flytrap. The nectar was so sweet, despite the dangers. That night was the beginning of their arrangement.

He was her new drug. He made her forget. Forget about Ron. Celine. The job. *Life*. But when he was gone, and she was alone, she felt the pain and self-loathing return. Their arrangement wasn't for him. It was for her. It was purely selfish, and Laura neither cared nor wanted to care.

She had given enough of her life and sanity to the world. It was time she took something back for herself. Even if just for a few moments.

It was the fix she desperately needed to forget what she had done.

To forget the secret she had convinced herself never happened.

"How does this look?" Laura said as she pulled up next to a container tucked next to the wire fence overlooking a woodland. Jason leaned in and touched his large hands to Laura's face. Their eyes lingered for a moment, and then he grabbed her face in a vice between his fingers.

"Shut the fuck up," he spat. His hand reaching down to his fly. He unzipped and pulled himself out. His cock hard and proud. "And do something useful with that mouth of yours."

Jeremy studied from afar. Laura, and someone else. A man? What was she doing here? Then the feeling of dread ran through him. Had they followed him? Were they coming to get him? He should run. Run back to his car and drive away quickly before they noticed him. Drive back home, grab a bag and make for the airport. But he continued to watch, eyes fixated on the headlights like a deer dazzled by the lights of a speeding HGV.

The driver's side door opened. Jeremy swallowed hard. *This was it. They're on to you, and you're too soft to do anything about it.*

Laura was being dragged by her hair. Jeremy felt a flare

of panic shoot through him. Was she being attacked? What the hell was going on? He should do something. Make a distraction. Shout out. But he stayed. Was he a witness to something? Was he a witness to Laura's death?

If she goes away, a dark thought whispered in his mind, *you will get away with everything* … he slowed his heartbeat, and he watched from the dark.

The man holding her hair was a brute, and Jeremy couldn't make him out from where he was standing. Laura thrashed back; their faces locked together. They were … kissing? What the hell was she doing? The man turned her around and grabbed a fistful of her hair, before he pushed her over the bonnet. Laura's arms spread widely over the metal. He ripped down her jeans and pulled his own down, too. Was she being assaulted? Jeremy cursed the heavens for his predicament. If he intervened, he would go to prison. If he didn't, he would watch something terrible happen, but he would be free.

The brute grunted as he entered her. A long moan that filled the empty space between them. Laura responded in kind. Each powerful thrust of his hips released a stabbing jolt of ecstasy.

I'm watching something I shouldn't be watching, Jeremy thought, unable to pull his eyes away.

He could feel himself growing hard in his underwear. He was watching his boss get fucked out in the open, and it was his sordid secret viewing.

But as he watched, his eyes adjusted to the dark, he discovered he now had something greater than a secret.

He had leverage.

It was Jason. Catherine's boyfriend. Catherine's boyfriend and Laura, Catherine's boss. He could end her with this. Finally, cast her out of the MIU, or even the police entirely, leaving him to fill the void and take her place…

She is the reason he went home last night. The reason he did what he did. Laura was the problem. The catalyst. How many times had the world set on fire because of her? And here she was, with not a care in the world, in the arms of her friend's partner. She was truly a rotten apple, and he would cast her out of the bunch before she could infect those around her. He stopped his dizzying train of thought.

To expose her would mean he would have to admit he was here, now, watching her. Exposing the affair meant questions, and questions led to prison.

He looked at her car. Her half-naked frame splayed across it. When he felt all was lost, opportunity presented itself. He had a twisted thought. A sinister thought that would save him from prison and put Detective Inspector Laura Warburton out of the frame for good.

Laura felt it building. His thrusts almost breaking her. He was big. He was powerful. He didn't hold back. She wanted him to know how much she was loving being fucked by him. She called his name. Called out to the Lord above. The grip on her hips tightened, burying his fingers into her skin. This wasn't lovemaking. This was raw. Animalistic. Their euphoria building together, until it erupted in unison.

"Fuck!"

They stopped; their breath heavy. Laura could feel the sweat on his hands as he ran them down her back, her legs quivering, her hair sticking to her face as she parted it away from her eyes. He folded in two, resting his head on her back, his body heat steaming into the night. He kissed her back. Laura lifted up, pulling her pants back around her waist.

"I needed that," Laura said. "You know how to make me forget about work." She took out her cigarettes and lit one, taking a lungful of the noxious toxins and expelling them. She watched the blue threads weave and disappear into the black sky. "What have you been doing today?" Laura said, trying to fill the void.

"Working," Jason said.

"At your *accountancy*?" Laura said, laughing.

"Why?" He said. "Do you really care?"

And with that, the euphoria dissipated like the blue ribbons from the cigarette. She felt the guilt and shame wash over her again. What the hell was he doing with Catherine?

She pulled her coat tighter around her, sitting on the car bonnet next to Jason, looking up at the sky.

"What do you think is up there?" He said. "Do you believe in God?" Laura rolled her eyes. He got like this often after they screwed, and it was the reminder of why she would never take things further with him. He got sentimental. It made her skin crawl.

"I wish you talked as good as you fucked," she said and

turned to him. His eyes were glued to the black canvas above.

"I mean," he continued, as if Laura hadn't even spoken. "Do you think there's a purpose to all of this?" He said, looking around with his arms open, gesturing to *this* being the very fabric of existence. "What happens when we die?" Laura rolled her eyes.

"We are born. We die. We become worm food. The cycle repeats."

"You can't just believe that," he said. "If that's all that happens, then why do people not just go crazy?" Laura threw her smoke to the floor and stubbed it out with her heel.

"Because I'll lock you up, and you spend the rest of your life in prison. That's why." He turned, a stern look on his face. In their passion, he was the dominant one. But outside of it, Laura wore the pants of their … relationship? Was that what was happening? A power dynamic? Was this becoming a *thing*?

"If God doesn't exist," he said, "then what is stopping you from ending it all right now? What's the point of living if it has no purpose?"

"Because," Laura said, then trailed off. "Just, because…" She let the silence creep back in. Laura was expecting a remark of some kind. But the look in his eyes said something else. The glistening streetlights from the faraway road, the moonlight that consumed them, the ruffling of the gentle wind on his cooling body—in his gaze she saw something deeper.

Pity.

He thought she was just a stupid slut with a fucked-up brain.

Only half of that was true.

"Why am I even doing this?" She blurted, shaking her head.

"Because you can't help being normal," Jason said, staring right out in front of him. Those words were the ignition to the bonfire in Laura's mind. Her mouth fell agape. He continued. "You don't want to live in this world knowing that you aren't anything special. That's why you drink. Why you're screwing me. Because you are destructive, Laura. Like the scorpion and the frog. You can't help it. It's just in your nature." Laura stared at him. For the first time in her life, she was stunned into silence. She didn't know where to even begin, like someone had found the cassette player of her consciousness and took a hammer to it.

"What the fuck did you just say to me?" She stammered. "You think you're better than me? Is that it?"

"I *know* I am better than you," Jason said, barely any emotion in his words. Laura slammed her palms down on the bonnet.

"I'm not the one cheating on my girlfriend. I'm not the one who is sneaking out and making excuses to come to the middle of nowhere and screw her boss on her car bonnet. A fifty-thousand-pound car bonnet, I may add. Have you ever touched anything as expensive as that? What do you do for a living? A fucking *accountant*? Please. Bet you have an *Only Fans* or some shit. Probably dragged up by some emotionally unavailable mother, which is why

Catherine bores the life out of you, but *I* get you ravenous." Laura drew in closer. Her mouth spitting swords. "You don't get to judge me, you understand? I have helped countless people in my career. I'm *the* queen bitch. You couldn't begin to fathom what I have been through. So, before you start judging me and my choices, why don't you look in a God damn mirror and sort your own shit out?" Jason let the words fall into silence, which was then filled with Laura's furious breathing. He sucked in his breath, then stood up.

"I feel sorry for you," Jason said, moving to the back of Laura's car and grabbing his jacket. "Don't call me," he said, throwing his jacket over him and walking away to the compound's entrance. She watched him stride away.

I feel sorry for you. The words sinking into her stomach and shredding her insides open. She bit down, then chased after him.

This wasn't over yet.

Jeremy watched them move further away, lost in their own battle, before moving to Laura's car.

"You've got some fucking nerve!" Laura screamed, grabbing a hold of Jason and spinning him on his heel to her.

"You are beyond repair," Jason said. "And you can't treat people like this!" The stone of his exterior was cracking, and the pain was leaking through. The streetlight over them cast his face in deep shadows. "You don't get to judge me, either. I love my girlfriend. I love Catherine. But you? I don't know what it is. I hate you, but I can't keep away. I can't help it. When I go home to her, I feel dirty. Filthy and disgusting. That's why I fuck you so hard. It's a *hate* fuck. I hate you, Laura Warburton. What you're doing to me. Doing to my life. It *isn't* right."

"So, walk away then," Laura spat. She wanted to feel something for him—pity, pain, remorse—but she couldn't. She couldn't let herself feel, couldn't let herself be vulnerable, not again. She had locked those feelings so far away she had forgotten where she had even hidden the key. They were lost to her now, and that was where they needed to stay.

She looked at him. He was chewing on something, chewing on some words that she didn't want to hear. If he said them, then things would have gotten so much worse for them. But then they slipped through his gritted teeth, and nothing was going to be the same again.

"I love you." Laura clenched her eyes shut. What had she done?

"Don't…" she said. "Don't say that. You're emotional."

"I said I love you, and you won't even listen to me. I love you, Laura. I love you." He raised his hands, his fingers curled like a dead crab. His hands shaking, like he wanted to throttle her right there in the street. "But I fucking loathe you too." Laura tried to remain composed, fighting back the feelings of pain that were threatening to breach her resolve.

"I'll take you home. It's a long walk back. You'll take

hours, and Catherine will be worried." She touched her arm on his. He threw it off like a rattlesnake.

"And now you care about her all of a sudden? You didn't care when I had you bent over on your expensive fucking car." He stepped back. The distance between them was less than a meter, but it might as well have been an ocean. "You don't care about me, do you?" He said, his words laced with venom. "You don't care about anyone but yourself." She could see the pain on his face. A man who was stripped of his flesh and bone, and just his vulnerable essence, laid out for her to poke and prod.

"Just," she said, a lump growing in her throat like a tumour. "Just get in the car. We don't have to talk. Let me drive you home." He looked out into the blackness. The empty street. The wagons that were parked up with their curtains drawn. He shook his head.

"Goodbye," he said, and he began walking.

Laura watched him go. She turned back to the warehouse, leaving Jason behind her. She put her hands to her head and grabbed a handful of her hair and dug her nails in tight. She closed her eyes, wanting the thoughts to stop. For them to just stop for a second. She crumbled to her knees, her breath coming out in short vicious stabs.

"I can't do this anymore," she whispered to herself. "I can't live like this."

Her phone rang, breaking her downward spiral. She pulled it out. The screen lights harsh on her eyes. It was Francis. She put the phone to her ear, stifling her cries. "Francis…" She said. He sounded panicked.

"Ma'am," he said. "There's another. He's got another

one."

CHAPTER EIGHT

LAURA

Laura drove to the location like a bat out of hell. She was twenty minutes away from the scene. She would get there in ten. Francis was on the hands free.

"What do we have?" Laura said, speeding down the empty roads.

"We got something through to the station," he said.

"Why were you still at work?"

"All I do is work. Anyway," Francis said, getting Laura back on track. He was driving too. She could hear the force radio in the background. "We got a cassette tape through, addressed to you. Where are you? I tried your house?"

"I'm out. Doesn't matter where," Laura said, dismissing the question. "What do you mean, addressed to me?"

"Yes," he said. "I don't know why. So, I played it. The voice said –"

"Do you have it there?" Laura said.

"I have a recording of it."

"Play it," Laura said. "Let me hear it." Francis sounded like he was fumbling around, and then the sound of a crackly voice came through the receiver.

"Hello, detective." The voice said. It was male. Thick and gravelly. Distorted. "You found my parcel in the woods. You have found my other offerings. I have another for you. By the time you are listening to this recording, you will have roughly one hour to save her.

Pride is the worst of all sins, for with it, it comes with lies. Lies to the world. Lies to yourself. And worse, lies to the Lord Divine. I would like to offer you, Laura Warburton, the chance to redeem your own sins by saving others that are lost in their own depravity."

"What does he mean, *redeem your own sins?*" Francis said.

"Shut up! I'm listening!" Laura barked. The recording continued.

"Broadcasting over the internet right now is a woman in a box. Her name, Rebecca Shaw. A woman who has made a following of millions from her story of being a survivor. A triumph for women around the globe. Endorsements. Sponsors. Hundreds of thousands of pounds for a façade of altruism and strength. When in reality, she is a drug addict, her children have been placed into care, and she is still living with her abusive partner.

The question I have to you, Laura Warburton – will you do the right thing and make this woman suffer and pay for the parasitic message she has pushed out into the world? Or will you save her and allow her sins to go unpunished? Let the offering begin." The recording ended.

"What the hell was that?" Laura said, her foot pressing harder on the accelerator.

"I was going to ask you the same thing," Francis said. "How does he know you?"

"My face is all over the news, Francis," she said. "We've

played right into his hands with this, and now he is making a game out of it." Laura checked the sat nav. She was a few minutes away. "How do we know where this girl is? Or if she's still alive?" Her phone buzzed.

"I just sent you the link to the live stream. We've managed to pinpoint where it's coming from. A construction yard for a new rehab and domestic violence refuge centre. Rebecca Shaw was due to be the one that cuts the ribbon when it opened." Laura pressed the link.

Her screen lit up to Instagram. The face of a woman. Her eyes are puffy. Her eyes bulging. The only light coming from the phone in her hand, squinting, trying to read a piece of paper. She was inside a box of some kind. Laura felt her stomach churn. Thousands of views. Comments going haywire.

"The police can't stop me," she said, crying. Holding onto her throat. She was suffocating, and it was being broadcast to the world. "The world will burn. The sinners will perish. Blood and death. The wrath of the Lord. The Alpha Omega." She was crying. "My life is a fraud. My world is as fake as my smile. My sins are yours now." Laura pressed on the accelerator harder. She was less than a minute away. She could see the cranes. The flashing lights of police vehicles. The drone of the helicopter above. "Detective Laura Warburton," Rebecca said, as she began to choke in her airless chamber. "You didn't save me." The stream went dark as Rebecca dropped the phone. The feed still going, broadcasting her body as it began to spasm and twitch, as she clung onto her throat and banged on the sides of the box.

"Laura…" Francis whispered.

"I'll be there in a few seconds. Get that girl out of there, now!"

Laura pulled up to the construction site. Spotlights blaring on a pile of rubble. Officers diving in, pulling away bricks and dirt, sandbags, and barrels. Laura raced up, falling, stumbling over the mess. She grabbed handfuls of bricks and dug. Francis appeared by her side, along with Catherine. They dug and dug. Rebecca on the livestream, still twitching.

They dug for what seemed an eternity until they found the dirtied lid of a box. As they cleared more rubble, they found it to be a coffin nailed shut.

"Give me something to open this!" An officer rushed to her, as Laura screamed for them to pry the lid open. It came away slowly at first, then splintered and cracked. Laura looked on the live stream. She saw daylight. They were in the right place. She dived in, wrapping her hands around the lid, and heaved with all her strength. The lid came away, and there, lying inside, was Rebecca.

Laura reached down with Francis and another officer and hauled Rebecca out. They placed Rebecca on top of the coffin lid. Laura put her ear to her mouth.

"She's not breathing!" Laura said. She crouched down and began CPR. Pressing her hands into Rebecca's sternum. Feeling ribs creak and snap under her palms. Rebecca's eyes open. Staring at her like vacant windows. Her lips were a dull pink. Her body was limp as Laura pressed down on her. "I need a defibrillator now!" Laura screamed. Other officers came in and took over. They used a defibrillator on Rebecca and shocked her. No heartbeat. Laura fell to her side, exhausted. Shocked. In pieces, as they continued to work on the dead woman. Praying that she took a breath. That she could be saved.

But they tried and tried, and when the paramedic arrived on scene, he declared her time of death.

All while the world watched via live stream. They saw the Butcher had claimed another victim, and the police were powerless to stop him.

SIN

The lawyer in his high tower. The hands he used to shake on those filthy deals that hurt so many. I removed them. The tongue he used to spread his lies. Severed. His mountain of gold consumed him and took his breath. The greed of this man destroyed lives, and in the end, his treasure consumed him.

The disease spreading whore who would fill her veins with filth so not to feel the pain in her heart. The pain the Lord gave her as her gift. A gift to be cherished, like the wise words from the Bible. She denied the pain by numbing herself from it, spreading filth with her rotten flesh, tempting married men into her bed. Destroying lives. Stealing from hard working businesses to feed her addiction. Her rotten body strangled the life out of her in the end, and her heroin swam through her body as she begged to live. She had a life filled with potential, and only when it was going to end did she finally want to embrace it. A waste. A pity. An offering.

The glutton who spent his life abusing his body. The body what was forged in the image of the Lord, yet when I gave him all he could have, he didn't want it, so I forced it down his throat.

And now, Laura Warburton, the Devil with the hair of flames, do I offer you another? One of deception. Of vanity. Of lies. One who spreads her vile message of rot into the world, claiming she was a fallen angel reborn, when her soul was as black as her clipped wings. Using social media to corrupt the world around her. Making money from her deception. Those around her praising her narcissistic image. An image I will shatter like a brick to a mirror, and the whole world will see it.

And they will see you too. They will see you on your knees with tears in your eyes, and they will see you fall.

Let the offering commence.

CHAPTER NINE

LAURA

TWO DAYS BEFORE THE OFFERING

She was in a black room with no windows or doors. A small light emanating from the darkness from the lantern in her hand. She called out, but her voice seemed to echo into the void before completely vanishing. The air was biting, and she could see the plume of ghostly smoke escaping her lips as she breathed. Stepping lightly on the ground. A light mist dancing around her legs.

She moved slowly, wandering through that blackness. She heard crying coming from somewhere. She froze solid. Fear gripping her into place. Laura looked around the empty space, turning on her heel. Each time she moved; the crying followed her. The sound drawn out. Stretching, like a violin string being played with a razorblade.

"Hello?" Laura called, almost afraid to speak should the darkness grow thicker and begin to choke her. The crying continued, stretching from the distance yet somehow so close. Laura went to speak again, but no noise vacated her mouth.

The crying began again. Except this time, it wasn't from the outside. It started low, like the slow rising of a volume dial. One long moan of horror that grew and grew in her mind. She could hear it inside her skull. She dropped the lantern, and the glass smashed, sending ripples of blue and white flames along the ground. The heat that blasted from it freezing, chilling her bones so deeply she feared they would shatter into smashed ice along the mist.

The horrific cry continued. A desolate mourning, like a drone of a mother at her child's funeral. Laura collapsed to her knees. The ground under her was soft and cold. Pressing her hands to her ears so tight, but the crying drone grew louder and louder.

Finally, it stopped. Cut away like the severing of a rope. She opened her eyes and saw the blue flames around her still dancing lively. Carefully, she listened to the empty space.

Then she felt the warm stickiness on her hands. Laura looked at the palms in the blue light. Thick crimson painted her skin. The blots and smears dripping into the mist around her. The wrinkles of her fingers. The lines along her flesh wriggling, moving in front of her eyes.

A groan again. Except this time, it was coming from her own lips, and beneath her, lying on the ground, were the mutilated remains of Celine. Laura reached down and pulled her into her. Tears, hot and salty, running down her cheek and into her mouth. Celine's mouth opening and closing like a drowning fish. Water pouring from her lips. Face drained of colour. A whisper broke free from her. Raspy. Choking.

"You could have saved me."

"I tried," Laura said. "I tried so hard." Celine's arm snapped from the mist and gripped hold of Laura's tricep. Laura saw the knife in her own hand, driving into Celine's body, over and over. Laura screamed. Blood pouring free, dousing her in fiery red.

Celine's maw a twisted toothy grin. Her eyes eating away to reveal two hollow wells of death. Laura screamed. She screamed and screamed as she gouged and cut.

"You could have saved me," Celine hissed, as her skin fell away from her face in thick clumps. "Murderer."

Laura snapped awake like she had had acid thrown on her sleeping body. Where was she? She wasn't in her home. This wasn't her bed. It was so dark. So cold. Was she buried? Was she in that airless box like Rebecca had been? She sat up and looked around her. Under her. She was on a couch. The walls were unfamiliar. A door in front of her. The nightmare still clinging on to her sanity.

The word began to come into focus. A poster. A bookcase. A table. She touched herself, staring into the darkness around her. The world slowly bleeding to life.

After the body had been retrieved, she drove back to the station to complete the paperwork. To collect evidence. To command the troops. She was on autopilot. Running on empty. Jason. The deaths. Celine. The nightmares. Fucking. No drinking. Stress. Panic. Betrayal. Worry. It never ended.

She had a terrible headache. She remembered that much. A headache like someone was sawing her skull open and filling it with marbles, then shaking it. She went into the *Quiet Room* for a lie down, and she must have fallen to sleep.

The nightmare came back to the forefront of her mind, and Laura felt the tears, hot and salty, finding her mouth.

"I'm losing my mind. I'm losing my damn mind." She whispered. What time was it? She checked her phone. It had just gone seven. At least she wasn't late for work for a change. She had a tonne of missed calls. None from Jason.

The thought of his name was like a sobering slap to the face.

Laura unfolded herself and got to her feet. She stepped out of the Quiet Room and walked through the dark and through the doors to the main office.

The overhead lighting was harsh, and it burned her eyes. The place was a frenzy. Senior officers moving to her, greeting her as she walked past. Eyes on her from officers. Her clothes were still filthy from digging out the girl at the construction site. She didn't need a mirror to know she looked like she had crawled out of a grave herself.

"Morning," she said, as she moved towards the MIU office. At the foot of the door, she saw Superintendent Bill Bennett standing there. His bushy eyebrows were intriguing, like two arctic fox tails.

"DI Warburton," he said, "a word, if I may?" He looked her up and down, his voice laced with disdain. Laura knew that 'a word' was a pseudonym for 'a royal arse kicking.' Just what she needed after two hours of sleep.

They slipped into a side room, and Bennett closed the door behind them. Laura took a seat.

"How are you, after last night?" He said, sitting opposite her.

"Tired, sir." He sat back.

"You look like shit," he said. What a way to make a girl feel good about herself.

"I didn't go home last night. I slept in the Q Room." He eyed Laura up and down. Her messy hair. Her dirty clothes. Her sunken eyes.

"I'm going to come out and say this, and I don't care if you get upset," he said. Laura primed herself for the next question. "Are you drinking again?" Laura snapped her eyes to him and gave a firm –

"No, sir."

"Do I need to find someone else for the job?"

No one else could cope with this fucking job.

"No, sir."

"Good," Bennett said. "The press is breathing down my neck, and I will give a statement on your behalf. However, in the future, you should answer the questions, not me."

"Understood, sir," Laura said, too tired to fight.

"We have another situation," he said. "I need you to be on it like a fly on shit." Laura felt something in her mind begin to crack.

"The girl from the construction site?" Laura said. "I had CID do some digging," then regretting her poor choice of words, rebutted – "they're seeing if there's any match on fingerprints with the notes. We found the victim was reading off a script of some kind. Very *Old Testament,* so we have no doubt this is the Butcher again. We're looking into Rebecca Shaw's background. Her recent movement, etc. We found that her kids were in care, and she was in a violent relationship with a man who had beaten her black and blue and went to prison for it. Her online platform started as a place to spread love and positive relationships, all the while she was living as a fraud." Laura shook her head. "The lies we tell the world to hide our true selves." While Laura was talking, Bennett's eyes were widening. He reached his hand over and pressed his finger into the table.

"No, Laura," he said, his voice grave. He furrowed his bushy brows. "Have you not spoken to your team this morning?" Laura remembered the missed calls. She had been looking for Jason's name and ignored all the others. She shook her head, dreading what the revelation was about to be divulged to her.

"No, sir. I haven't." He sat back and folded his hands. He took in a sharp breath.

"It's Jeremy," Bennett said. "His wife. Mary. She's missing, and it doesn't look good."

CHAPTER TEN

LAURA

Jeremy's house was a two up, two down with a garage. It was detached, with a large front garden, a conservatory, and a larger garden at the rear. Outside was a white CSI tent and three bodies walking around in overalls, masks, and gloves.

Laura pulled up to the outer cordon.

This can't be happening, Laura thought as she stared at the officers outside Jeremy's house. *Whoever the Butcher is, he is targeting me and now, those I work with. But why?* She stepped out of the car. The cold air was a slap to the face.

The place was a circus for the press. Officers standing at the cordon with reporters trying to ask them questions or shoving cameras into their faces. As soon as Laura slammed her door shut, like a dinner bell ringing at the zoo, the journalists converged on her like hungry wolves, screaming at her. Throwing questions at her. Touching her. *Violating her.* She had to get to the cordon quickly before she shoved a microphone up someone's arse.

She got to the police tape and ducked under, like she had entered a sanctuary in some zombie movie. She approached one of the officers.

"Get that cordon moved further up," she said, breathless. "We stay at this one. Give us some space between us and the press."

"Yes, ma'am," the officer said, then pushed the press back and rolled out more 'POLICE—DO NOT CROSS' tape. This gave them more breathing room, and Laura needed all she could get right now to avoid suffocating. When she was done, she went back to the officer.

"How long have you been on guard?" The officer's eyes narrowed at the question.

"Four hours," he said.

"Four hours and you haven't had a sit down or been relieved for a minute to stretch your legs?" The officer didn't reply, trying to remain stoic. Laura shook her head. "Where are the other officers?"

"We only have a few of us," he said. "We need more down here." Laura nodded. She looked around and saw Francis standing at the front door to Jeremy's home, speaking to a CSI officer.

"Francis!" Laura barked. At the sight of her, his face turned from grave to downright desolate. He moved to her, looking back at the vultures with cameras screaming for a statement of some kind.

"I can't believe it," Francis said. "Mary. Looks like she just upped and left in the night."

"Jeremy didn't call it in right away?" Laura said, a scowl in her eye.

"No," Francis said. "He said he didn't want to jump the gun."

"Your wife just vanishes in the middle of the night, and you don't think that's weird?" Francis shrugged.

"People are just people, Ma'am. We don't expect the

worst all the time." Laura considered that, then tossed it onto the pile of bullshit she was accumulating. She pointed to the Ford Fiesta on the drive.

"Is that her car?" She said.

"Yes," Francis said. "That's why the boss is all over this one. After last night. He wants a full investigation launched in case..." He trailed off.

"In case she's dead," Laura said bluntly. Francis choked on the words.

"Yes," he said. "In case she's dead. The Butcher is targeting *us* now. He's playing games with us."

"Brilliant," Laura said. Francis shook his head.

"Jesus. Mary. Mary, fucking Mary." His eyes were on the floor. Laura looked back at the cop on the scene guard.

"Do you have your kit with you?" Laura interjected. "A coat and radio, at least?"

"Why?" Laura pointed to the officer.

"Get your gear and give this officer ten minutes to stretch his legs and use the loo." she looked at the cordon on the opposite end of the street. "Then do the same with the officer down there. I'm all for police work, but we have to look after the troops for that to happen." Francis held her gaze, then looked back at the officer. His head cocked to one side so much that Laura thought it reminded her of a hanging man. His mouth was open just as wide. His eyes glazed over a little, too.

"Of course," Francis said, taken aback. Francis moved back to the car and opened the boot, pulling out his gear and his radio, strapping it on. It wasn't often you saw someone in suit pants, shirt, tie, and body armour, but it was nice to humble someone now and then. Even the bosses had to practice their close combat skills and arrest and handcuffing skills every year. Not like they needed it from behind the desk. But it was a nice reminder – You may have a star or crown on your shoulder, but you still have some shiny bracelets on your belts and need to know those magic words. You were always a cop. Despite what came afterwards – Superintendent. Detective. Whatever. You were a police officer first, and a politician second.

Laura took out her phone and opened Uber Eats.

"Do you take sugar?" She said to the cop, whose breath was frozen and pushing through his blue lips.

"Sorry, ma'am?" He said, leaning in.

"Sugar in your coffee?" Her eyes met his. Her trench coat flowing in the gentle wind. The sound of Francis' shiny boots clicking on the ground behind her.

"Oh," the cop said. "No, thank you." He smiled. "Sweet enough." He turned and gestured to the other officer across the way. "Sam takes sugar, though." Laura clicked some buttons.

"Done." She turned to Francis, who was taking up a position on the cordon. "I've got a round in. Be here soon. They've been paid for. I'll call up for some more bodies so we can rotate the scene more." She turned to the officer. "Ten minutes, and then I need my detective back. Okay?"

"Yes, ma'am," the officer said with a nod. Laura went to move away. "Sorry, ma'am?" The cop said. Laura stopped and turned. The wind picking up and freezing her face.

"Yes?"

"I know it might not mean a lot coming from me," he said, "but I think you did a good job yesterday trying to help that girl. Just a shame it ended the way it did." Laura felt a flood of warmth rush through her.

"Thanks," she said. "It is. And yes, it means a lot."

What would normally be a home filled with love and care was nothing short of desolate. It was as if the feeling in the room itself had changed. Like the air and joy had been sucked out of the walls and the space inside had been filled with a heavy weight.

There is an old belief that tragedy stains its surroundings. Like death and pain were infectious. It's the reason some people believed a house was haunted, or that there were spirits living inside the walls. Why people couldn't sleep at night in a new home, or a home that was centuries old. The essence of the pain and hatred that had infected the walls bled out of it, and the inhabitants would suck it in, and it would turn them rotten. Why you had to declare a death in the last few years when moving in. Because of that energy. That *pain* could still leech onto someone and make them go mad. The never-ending cycle of horror and bloodshed. Laura felt that energy now. The home felt sick.

She had been to Jeremy's home before, only a couple of times. Popping by after work for a glass of wine. Maybe even come round for a meal in the evening when she was feeling a little overwhelmed. He had his flaws, of course. But whatever flaws he had were offset by the loving nature of his wife, Mary. She was a kind woman. A woman whose smile warmed even the coldest of souls. A woman whose energy could lift a person and unravel the chains that their mind had constricted them in. Mary's presence made you be able to breathe again, and now that she was gone, that feeling of suffocation lay heavy on Laura's chest reappeared as she stepped through the front door.

"What have we got?" She said to a passing CSI officer, as Laura took out some gloves that were placed on a small table by the side of the door. Outside, she could hear Francis talking to other officers, doing the rounds, and relieving them, and then a short time later, a bicycle turned up with a holder filled with coffees.

The CSI officer pulled down her facemask. She was blonde. Blue eyes. Around twenty. Possibly fresh out of university. Her figure, although Laura couldn't make it out properly underneath her overalls, looked firm and yet round in all the right places.

"No signs of forced entry," she said. The home was laid out simply enough: a small entrance that fed to an open-plan living room with two couches, a coffee table in the middle, and a television that was hooked onto the wall above a speaker and some photographs. To Laura's right was a dining room, and then a conservatory that led into the back garden. Dead in front was a staircase that went upstairs to the bedrooms. Two beds. One master. One spare. Laura remembered Jeremy telling her they had bought the house over twenty years ago. He meant to fill the home with children, but there were complications. After failed attempts at IVF, Jeremy and Mary decided that the room would consist of several things: an office. A music room. Even a small library. But over time, they would swap and change the interior before they regurgitated it, knowing that what they really wanted it to be inhabited by would never be fulfilled. A child. Something to call their own. Like someone drinking salt water when they're thirsty. There is only so much you can do before it rots you from the inside out.

After a few years and a lot of heartbreak, they stopped trying and turned the room into a hundred other things. But that empty space in their lives would forever remain there—an empty space that could never be filled.

So, Jeremy threw himself into his career. Mary did whatever she did—floristry, working at the local supermarket, even running a book club. But they never moved on from that ache. They realized that they would never hear small footsteps running around the house. Laura realised that the pain she felt inside these walls wasn't hatred or malice. It was grief.

"What's your name?" Laura said to the CSI officer..

"Roxanne, ma'am," she said.

"That's an odd name," Laura said. "Where's Jeremy, *Roxanne, Ma'am.*" Laura cracked the joke, but Roxanne didn't respond. The girl was wallpaper.

"He's through the back, in the kitchen, being spoken to by officers." She leant in. "He's in a bad way." Laura nodded. *No shit*, she felt like saying, but managed to remain somewhat professional. She held Roxanne's gaze for a second longer than she should have, falling into her eyes. Roxanne's lip curled inwards at the sides. Laura pulled herself away.

Stay professional, she thought. *You have enough on your plate without trying to get someone in bed.* Laura looked around the home from where she was standing.

"Thanks," Laura said, and moved away.

"Say," Roxanne said. "Aren't you Laura Warburton?" Laura felt her skin prickle. Was she going to ask for a damn selfie?

"Unfortunately," Laura said. "But if we could keep the *'I'm your biggest fan,'* out of this for the time being?" Roxanne was taken aback by the comment. She nodded.

"Of course." She said. "Time and place."

"Time and place indeed," Laura said dismissively. She took out her notepad and scribbled some notes. Roxanne leaned over.

"What are you writing?"

"Notes."

"What kind of notes?" Laura furrowed her brow and her jaw tightened. She put the pad on the table, the pages falling closed.

"Well," she said. "Let's see." Laura moved into the dining room and looked at the table. She pointed to a small smudge. "The four chairs are all pressed up against the table, except one," Laura pointed to the chair on the right-hand side of the table. It was slightly off centre. "One person was eating last night, which makes sense because Jeremy has been having issues at home, and has been sleeping in his car, so it's unlikely he came home and had a meal with Mary. So, I imagine that's where Mary sits. People often sit at the same place at the dinner table.

On the couch. Even the side they lay on the bed. It's never discussed, it just happens. So, she was sat there, and judging by the coaster that is on the top of the pile, the round indent on the bottom with a crimson tarnish would make you think that this was an evening meal and that Mary had been drinking red wine." Laura moved to the light switch on the wall near the hallway leading to the stairs and bedrooms. "If you look here," Laura said, pointing her gloved finger to the light switch. "We see a small smudge of red wine." Roxanne looked closely. It was faint, but definitely there.

"How on earth did you see that?" Roxanne said. Laura let out a little laugh.

"Trust me," she said. "I could find wine anywhere. I would probably tell you what type it is." Both shared a morbid laugh.

"But what does that mean?" Roxanne said, looking at Laura like she was back on her first day of the job with the world in her eyes and hope in her heart. Laura let out a short breath.

"Well, it would mean that Mary didn't eat alone last night, and Jeremy drinks brandy, so it means Mary wasn't drinking with Jeremy."

"Very good," Roxanne said, her voice filled with amazement. But I don't get it," Roxanne said. Why do you think she wasn't alone? We haven't seen any signs of a break-in, and you said yourself that there was only one chair pulled out on the table?" Laura closed the distance between her and Roxanne.

"Because you don't drink wine at the table having a

meal alone. If you're alone, you drink it watching TV, or in the bath. Wine at a meal is a social thing. Now my guess is that if Mary had someone here, that they would have known each other."

"You mean to tell me she didn't just go missing?" Roxanne said. "What makes you think that?"

"You'd be surprised what those closest to us are capable of doing," Laura said. "Now, take me to Jeremy."

CHAPTER ELEVEN

LAURA

Laura went into the conservatory. Jeremy was sitting there, his eyes red. His cheeks flushed. He was speaking quietly to Catherine, who was sitting opposite him, feeding him tissues, and filling in the sudden death paperwork. From where Laura was standing, there was something seriously wrong here.

"Why are you filling that out?" Laura said. "At this point, she's just missing, right?"

"Just preparing for the worst, Ma'am," Catherine said, barely looking up.

Jeremy's eyes shot to Laura. He looked like shit. As one would expect. The worst day of his life and the police were here to ask him questions. Laura thought it to be a funny old world, how the tables can flip in a day. Even if a cop gets pulled over in their car, something that every cop has done a hundred times or more, they still get that flare of anxiety in their hearts. Laura welcomed it. It meant that they weren't ever so far removed from the public that they thought they were invincible.

"Laura," Jeremy said. "Oh my God," he stood up, and moved to her. He wrapped his arms around her tight. "I don't know where she is," he said, sniffling into her shoulder. Laura put her hand on his back. He smelled rancid. She knows he had been sleeping in his car and that he wasn't home last night. That his car had been last seen on the A road near his home and hadn't moved since the night he went home. She had already checked that finer details. After her own experience, no one was above suspicion. No one.

He pulled away from Laura, still holding onto her shoulders as if he let go, he would vanish into nothingness.

"I know," Laura said. Laura looked at Catherine, who was taking notes. "What have we got so far?" She said. Catherine opened her notes.

"Well," she said, clearing her throat. "Mary was last contacted by Jeremy at two AM when he came home and found that she wasn't here."

"Two in the morning?" Laura said, eyeing Jeremy. "Where were you?"

"I left the nick the night before, like you said. I parked the car here on the driveway, but Mary wasn't home. I waited, and I waited. When she didn't come home last night, I called it in."

"Why did you wait so long?" Laura demanded.

"I know what you're going to say," Jeremy said, body stiffening. "Like most normal people, I don't call the police as soon as I find something amiss. I called her at two. She didn't answer. It went straight to voicemail. Then I waited up for a bit before going to bed. I didn't sleep much. I kept flinching if I heard a car go by. Eventually, I swallowed my fear, and I called it in." Jeremy felt his eyes begin to burn with tears again. "I didn't want to think anything was wrong."

"Her car is parked outside," Laura said. "Why were you expecting a car to drive by?"

"She could have gotten a taxi?" Catherine jumped in. Her tone was bitter. "What's your point?" Laura ignored the comment. Catherine had a bee up her arse over something. Jason, maybe? Had he told her? Had she found out and this bullshit passive aggressiveness was her way of telling Laura? Fuck it. Who cares? She needed to know if her sergeant was telling the truth or not. Fucking someone else's boyfriend isn't illegal. Murdering your wife is.

"But things have been wrong for a while, haven't they?" Laura blurted. Everyone in the room felt as if the air had been sucked out of it. After a moment of silence, Laura looked for an answer. "Well, you might as well tell us?" She said, crossing her arms. "It will help us understand why Mary has gone missing, and why she was drinking at the table."

"What do you mean?" Jeremy said.

"Oh, didn't you know?" Laura said. After getting no response, she spoke freely. "Mary was drinking wine in the kitchen. I imagine it was late evening. But here's the rub. No one drinks wine alone at the table."

"You drink it alone in the living room watching TV or in the bath," the voice behind them interjected. Roxanne was standing there, notebook in hand. Jeremy's face turned from pain to rage in a blink.

"Sorry," Jeremy said, "just exactly who the fuck are you?"

"Never mind who she is," Laura stabbed.

"You're seriously trying to fuck someone at my home when my wife is missing?" Jeremy said, his voice rattling with rage.

"Jeremy," Laura said. "Start talking. Did you and Mary have an argument before she went missing?" Jeremy's eye lingered on Roxanne. Laura turned to her. "Leave us to it," she said. "I'll be checking the bedroom next."

"Why do you need to check the bedroom?" Jeremy said. "I told you; she isn't here." Laura nodded.

"You'd be surprised how many people have said that to me in the past," she said. Jeremy had to fight the urge to punch Laura square in the mouth. "Now start talking. Did you and Mary have an argument before she left?"

"No," he said, swallowing his resentment. He knew this was standard questioning by the police. To establish the circumstances of someone going missing. But why was Laura being such a bitch about it?

"Thank you," she said. "Is this time of year significant at all?" He shook his head *no*. Laura turned to Catherine, who was sitting there in stunned silence. Her jaw parted. Laura clicked her fingers and pointed to her notepad. "You're supposed to be writing this down." Catherine, like a flick of a switch, began to write down Jeremy's responses. Laura looked at her, vexed. "Have you been writing any of this down at all? Have you been doing your job?" The scratching on the paper stopped.

"I was getting to that," Catherine said. "I was just checking that he was okay."

"He's breathing, isn't he?" Laura said, gesturing to

Jeremy's heaving chest. "But Mary might not be. So, we can give him the *I hope you're okay let's light a candle for her* bullshit later on. I have the superintendent breathing down my neck. I still have the dirt and grime from a woman I dug out the ground on me from last night. The media is having a frenzy because someone decided to get the CSI here. I have a woman in her sixties vanishing in the middle of the night. No call, and no medication, coat, or transport when there's a damn psychopath on the loose playing games with us. So no, of course he isn't okay, so let's stop playing around and focus on finding her, and we can do the feely, feely, lovey shit later." Laura turned on her heel. "I'm going to the bedroom."

She took a step and Francis appeared, dithering from the cold, with a coffee in his hand. Laura took it, a smile on her face.

"Thank you," she said. "Now come with me. I need your keen eye and your cold heart." Francis followed her step, and then moved with her, feeling the shocked eyes of Catherine, and the fury of Jeremy's gaze stabbing into his back.

"What was that all about?" Francis said, moving with her as they moved past CSI officers and headed to the foot of the stairs.

"Don't worry about it," she said. "Tough love to get the job done."

"Is he okay?"

"I don't know," she said, as she ascended the stairs to the bedroom. "But I know one thing," Laura said. "Jeremy's tears quickly dried up when I put some heat on him."

CHAPTER TWELVE

LAURA

Roxanne passed Laura and Francis a fresh pair of gloves as they got to the foot of the bedroom, before she resumed photographing. The bed was made. Not a single mark or blemish on any surface. No clothes left on the floor. It looked, in essence, like a show home. Sterile. *Staged*.

"Why are they doing all of this?" Francis said. "She's only missing." Laura felt a wave of cold run over her. She turned to Francis, her tone low. Grave.

"Francis, how long have you been a cop?" The question took him back. He looked her in the eyes, his guard up.

"Over twenty years. I retire soon. Assuming I don't get sacked before then." Laura held his gaze. He knew what she was getting at, regardless of whether or not she said it.

"Then you know that something is going on here, don't you?" He studied Laura, then looked down the staircase where they had come from. Francis sucked in a breath.

"You don't think…" He said, his eyes widening. Laura raised her hand.

"All I'm saying is that with everything that has been happening, the superintendent wants a proper job doing from the outset. And," she leaned in. "I agree with him.

We aren't talking about some kid that lives in a care home and goes missing every ten minutes. We're not talking about someone that went out at the weekend and met up with some guy and spent her weekend getting pounded in between vodka and cocaine. We're talking about Jeremy Marriott's wife, who is currently missing. Her coat is still hung up by the door. Her car hasn't moved, and her and her husband have been having issues." Laura ran her gloved hand across her fringe, pinning a wisp of hair behind her ear. "Downstairs, there's a wine stain on the dining room table. Here," she gestured to the bedroom. "Well, I don't know about you, but my bedroom has *never* been this clean." She was whispering now, leaning in close. "No note. No motive. Nothing. Just disappeared. And you heard how upset Jeremy got at just the routine questions. So, we have to assume that there is more going on than meets the eye right now. We might be wrong, and my God, I hope to holy fuck we are, but…" she looked in the room again. "If experience has told me anything, is to not believe a word that comes out of anyone's mouth. Especially those closest to you."

The CSI officers were standing on small platforms about a foot wide by a foot long, placed around the room and the bed, so not to disturb the integrity of the scene. The plastic coverings on their feet rustled as they moved. Roxanne approached the two detectives.

"Want to take a look?" She said, holding out a pair of overalls. Laura and Francis took one each and donned them. Then, they put on hair nets and face masks, and stepped onto the platforms around the bed.

They moved around the room, careful to not step off the platforms. They watched in awe as the CSI operatives swabbed, bagged, and peeked under every nook and cranny. Places they wouldn't even think of looking. Under the bedsheets. Behind the headboard. They even pulled out a blue light torch and cast it over the bedding. Nothing.

"Has anyone checked the bathroom?" Laura said, pointing to the en-suite. The faces of those in the room turned to her like a group of meerkats hearing the rustling of a crisp packet.

"Yes," Roxanne said. "All clean." Laura pondered this. She held out her hand for the UV torch.

"You mind if I take a look?" Francis took her arm.

"Ma'am," he said. He shook his head. His eyes wide. "You're serious?" Laura shrugged his arm off.

"The torch, please," she said. Roxanne gingerly passed it to her, and Laura moved into the bathroom. It was surprisingly large. A shower. Bath. Nice stone-grey scale tiles. A sink and a medicine cabinet and, of course, a large shitter with handles on the sides. She regarded the shit box. "Did Mary have mobility issues?"

"I have no idea," Francis said, following closely behind her.

If she was missing, then how did she leave in the night, with no car, in the freezing cold, intoxicated and mobility issues? We'd have found her crumpled up on the pavement by now, dying of hypothermia.

Laura moved to the shower and shone the torch inside. Nothing. Then the floor. The toilet, and finally the bath and surrounding walls. No blood. No bodily fluids. It was clean. Even the sink was clean. It was like no one had ever set foot in this room.

"Anything?" Francis said, watching Laura work. Laura continued to look under the bath, touching her gloved hands. Moving old shampoo bottles, soaps, and razors out the way. All clean. "Ma'am, have you found anything? Or can we let the CSI take over now?" Laura let out a long breath. She straightened and moved back into the bedroom.

"What do we know of Jeremy's movements over the last forty – eight hours?" Again, Francis was taken aback.

"Ma'am…"

"Answer the question?"

"Response The Sergeant put him at the station around midnight. He said he saw him before he left. CCTV at a local garage shows him buying flowers around two in the morning. His car hit the ANPR camera shortly after en route here. Since then, there has been no movement on ANPR."

"Neighbours CCTV?"

"Seriously?"

"Detective…"

"No neighbour CCTV picked him up after the ANPR hit. Any neighbours that *do* have CCTV either don't cover the road or don't work."

"And Mary?"

"Same deal there. No CCTV hits."

"And what about buses?" Laura said.

"I don't get you?" Francis said.

"Buses. Big things with wheels that people ride on." Francis scoffed.

"I know what a bus is, Ma'am."

"So, you know they have cameras. I want you and Catherine to look into the bus CCTV cameras that travel this route. I also want a press appeal to anyone who might have dash cameras who travelled along this route." Francis rolled his eyes.

"She's only missing right –"

"I don't remember it being a question, Francis." Her scorn was like hellfire. Francis felt his skin peeling off under her gaze. He forced a smile.

"Of course, ma'am." Laura nodded. It was a start. People don't just *vanish*. Everything leaves a trace. Something else was niggling in Laura's mind.

"Do you ever cut yourself shaving?" Laura said.

"I don't see what that has –" Laura shot him a look so fierce Francis felt his testicles disappear into his stomach. "Sometimes," he rebuked.

"And Jeremy is clean shaven, right?" Francis nodded.

"He looks a little rough right now, a bit of stubble, but yeah. He's clean." It wasn't adding up. Not a single fleck of blood in the bathroom or on the razors. Blood stays on surfaces for months, even years, if it hasn't been cleaned thoroughly.

"There is not a fleck of blood anywhere in that bathroom. Not a single smudge."

"Maybe they keep it clean?" His cynicism was grating on Laura's sleep deprived nerves.

"I keep my bathroom as clean as the next person. But

think about it. Not a single fleck of blood *anywhere* in the room?"

"Okay?" He said, his voice high. "What are you suggesting?"

"He definitely didn't see Mary returning home until he called it in?" Laura said, the tension in her face growing. The mask clinging to her face from perspiration. Her heartbeat picking up.

"I mean, we could ask him to clarify his movements?" Laura nodded.

"Great idea, detective," she said, moving out of the bedroom. "Follow me."

CHAPTER THIRTEEN

LAURA

Jeremy was sitting again, this time with a cup of coffee in his hand, which filled the room with its welcoming aroma. His hands were shaking. His eyes staring into the distance like a man who had come back from war. Catherine was writing out the missing person's report. Something that should have been done as soon as they arrived. She understood why he didn't call the police as soon as he realised Mary wasn't home. As a police officer, you grew to expect the worst in every scenario, but to think like that all the time would drive you insane. Unfortunately for Jeremy, the one time where overthinking and insanity would have been helpful, he opted for the safer option of burying his head in the sand and hoping that everything would be okay. That Mary would walk through the doors with a bag of shopping or smelling of another man's aftershave. Anything would have been better than the mystery, torture, and grief that was etched all over his face as he gripped his coffee, answering the questions that were being fired at him from Catherine in short, stifled intervals.

Laura stepped back into the conservatory. She was about to further rampage through his misery with her next question.

"Can you verify where you were last night?" She barked. Catherine stopped mid-sentence and looked up at Laura.

"Ma'am," she said, "you can't be –"

"I wasn't speaking to you," Laura bit. Catherine's eyes widened, her mouth still open, slack jaw and hanging open. Laura regarded Jeremy. "It would really help us." She said. Jeremy looked at Catherine with a look of utter disbelief in his eyes. "She won't answer for you," Laura said, pointing to Catherine. "Unless you two were together and there's something you aren't telling me?" Both queried each other, and Jeremy mouth agape, searching for the right words.

"You aren't seriously thinking—"

"Humour me," Laura said. "We have two possible scenarios here. The first, Mary is getting her arse blasted by someone right now and she will return home when she is good and filled up."

"Laura!" Catherine barked.

"Believe it or not," Laura said, "that's the *best-case* scenario. The second is that she's dead, and if she is dead, either *you* know more than you are letting on, or she's another victim of the Butcher." The colour drained from Jeremy's face.

"Wha…" He began. Laura folded her arms.

"After last night, pulling **Rebecca** Shaw out of the ground, and a script for her to read with my name all over it, I'm not taking any chances. So, Jeremy, stop with the tears, and answer the damn question." A silence filled the room so thick it could grab a man around the throat and choke him. "Well?" Laura stabbed. Jeremy shifted in his seat.

Does that make you uncomfortable, Jeremy? Your body language is giving you away.

"I was at the police station until late evening. I said goodbye to the response Sergeant, Marcus Lake, and I went to the garage to buy Mary some flowers. I came home, she wasn't here, and I waited. I didn't move until I called it in this morning." He waited for Laura's response, but she gave none. "You can check the ANPR cameras!" He shouted. "They'll show I'm not lying. I called Mary a few times, and the last being around two this morning. I called the police around six." Laura held his gaze. He wasn't telling her something. She could taste it. But there was only so much she could do right now without pushing him right over the edge. She turned to Francis.

"Verify it." He stood in place, like his feet were nailed to the ground.

"Ma'am…"

"Just do it, Francis." She put her hand to her head. "Jesus, can anyone actually see I'm actually trying to eliminate a suspect right here?" Francis' face looked like he was chewing on a wasp. He thought about arguing back. He thought about screaming that Laura needed to take her foot off the gas for a moment and have a little compassion. But he didn't. Instead, he turned and moved out of the conservatory to another part of the house and was speaking into his radio, asking for telecoms to be checked. "Have we searched the house?" Laura said, addressing Catherine.

"Obviously?" Catherine said, her voice filled with

petulance. Laura wanted to dive over to her and drive her hand so far down her throat she could rip her arsehole out of her mouth. Laura threw her gaze outside and into the back garden. A small shed sat at the back with the padlock hanging open.

"Have we checked in there?" She said, and before she got an answer, she moved to the back door and stepped outside.

The grass was wet, and she felt the mud clinging to her pants as she moved over. Adding to her dishevelled state.

Laura took out some fresh gloves, stuffing the spent ones in her trench coat pocket. Carefully, she took away the padlock and opened the door. She could feel the others watching her, like a pair of vultures on a branch of a dead tree, waiting for Laura to stumble and fall to the ground, ready to move in when she stopped twitching. Digging their beaks and talons into her body, like a butcher carving open cold cuts to serve to the world.

Jeremy was hiding something. Her gut was telling her he was lying, and she always trusted her gut. Even when those around her didn't believe her, she was always right.

The Butcher was forensically aware. No fingerprints. No hair. No bodily fluids left at the scene. The Butcher was good. Disturbingly good. Laura hoped Mary was just missing, and that Jeremy or the Butcher hadn't done something terrible to her, because that would be her fault. It was her face all over the news, and now it was her that was the target of the killer. And like a true force of malevolence, the Butcher was going to isolate her, and then come for her, and by the feeling of knives digging into her back from the glaring of Catherine and Jeremy, he was doing a good job of it. She just hoped that out of the possibilities of Mary's murder, that it was Jeremy. The Butcher enjoyed drawing out the agony for as long as possible. She couldn't think of Mary being subjected to that. It turned her stomach. Eyes blowtorched out, solidified on the victim's pale face like a dried runny egg. Tongue removed. Fingers crushed. Genitals mutilated. Stomach filled with battery acid that ate its way through the flesh of the victim. The worst part? They were often bound in place with barbed wire wrapped around them. Alive, and able to feel everything. CSI showed through bloodwork that the victims had high doses of adrenaline in their systems, meaning that the killer made sure that they couldn't pass out, and their eyelids were removed so they would have to watch every part of what was being done to them.

The memory of those scenes would keep Laura's nightmare supply well and truly filled for the rest of her life. She doubted she could ever sleep again.

Laura pulled the shed door open, which creaked as it moved. The inside was small. There were tools. A lawn mower. Large red toolboxes that looked neat and well attended to. There were saws and hammers resting on nails that had been hammered into the wood. Underneath some shelving, she saw gloves, aprons and even plastic sheeting. There appeared to be some rolls missing. She took notes of the inventory. The bottom shelf of the workbench housed an array of chemicals. Most Laura didn't recognise. She took notes of their labels and how full they were.

She closed the door and moved back to the house. Her phone rang. Laura stared at it. Her heartbeat bouncing.

"Not now…" She hissed. It was Jason.

Catherine was looking at her through the window. She couldn't answer the call in front of her. There was being deceptive, and then there was taking the piss. She hung up the call and took a deep breath before moving back into the house.

She shook off the cold and damp that clung to her, wiping her grass covered heels on the mat. Moving back inside the house, she shook off the cold and let the warmth of the room sooth her skin.

"Well?" Jeremy said, his tone vicious. "Did you find what you were looking for?"

Don't punch him. Laura thought. *As much as you want to, don't do it.*

She looked up at Francis, who had since joined them again.

"Well?" She said.

"Checks out. Jeremy made calls to Mary. All straight to voicemail. I also checked with a neighbour, and they verified he came home in the early hours, and he didn't see his car move throughout the next day." Francis pulled a face of disdain. "Maybe *he* killed her? The neighbour?" Francis said sarcastically. Laura clenched her eyes shut.

Don't punch him either, she thought, *not where there are witnesses, anyway.*

"Well," Laura said. "I think we're all done here. Let me know if there are any developments," she said to no one in particular. Her phone was buzzing in her pocket again. The vibrating filling the air.

"Are you going to get that?" Catherine said, her tone flat. "It could be the superintendent wondering why he is the one getting questioned by a spotty journalist and not his star detective." The sarcasm lit something in Laura. She felt her body fill with rage.

Fuck it. She thought. *Break the bitch's jaw.*

"You think you're fucking funny!" Laura raged, lunging for Catherine, ready to rip out her blonde hair and stuff it down her throat. Francis dived in front of her, grabbing Laura by the shoulders. Laura screamed, pointing at Catherine, trying to push past Francis. Her coat lashed in each direction like a hungry whip, searching for flesh to score.

"Calm down!" Francis yelled, hauling her away. Laura stepped back, her hands held out.

"You've come a long way from doing crosswords and Sudoku, Catherine. Remember that. Remember who gave you the kick up the arse that you needed." Laura's breath was ragged.

"Take a walk!" Francis screamed. "Go have a smoke. Calm your fucking head."

"Watch your mouth –"

"No Laura, you watch yours," Francis said, his chest heaving, teeth clenched. Jeremy looked at her, fighting back the tears and anguish. Catherine looked at her with solid eyes of hatred. Francis swallowed hard. "Whatever shit you have got going on, don't go taking it out on the team. We have a woman to find. A case to solve, and a public image to protect. You're the one messing it up with your outbursts."

"How dare you?"

"I don't give a shit anymore, Laura," Francis said. "I'm sick of tiptoeing around you and your moods. Speak to your councillor. Sponsor. Whatever you need to do. We helped you through your breakdown. All of them. I'm not doing it anymore. Go sort yourself out and take a walk before you fuck everything up." Laura looked at the three of them, all eyeing her with venom and disgust. She had fucked it. She knew it. There were only so many times you could smash a mirror before the reflection you see can't be fixed. She was a wrecking ball, and she was doing what she always did. Destroy everything closest to her. Francis. The one person who never questioned her and was always there to fight her corner. She had pushed him to the brink, too.

"I'm sorry," she said. "I —" Francis batted her hand away.

"Just go," he snapped. "We'll finish up here."

Outside, Laura smoked two cigarettes before stopping to think that she was probably on camera outside of a crime scene. She wanted to care, but frankly, she had had enough. Had enough of everything. She fought and overcame one battle, only to find herself facing the next. It never ended, and she was beyond tired of it all. Self-destruction was her drug, and gosh, didn't she enjoy getting her fix of it?

A police car pulled up to the cordon. A dog unit.

"Well, it's about time," Laura said, throwing the spent cigarette onto the floor. She had made the call whilst en route to Jeremy's home. Bennett wanted a proper job doing, and she was pulling out all the stops.

The handler stepped out. He was clad in black. He had a police baseball cap on, and his hair was salt and pepper. His hands were tattooed, and his chin fuzzy with short prickles.

"Ma'am," he said, gesturing to Laura. Laura smiled. She looked back at the rabble of photographers and cameras.

"How did you get through?" She said. The officer's face warmed with a broad smile, and his eyes were a silver grey.

"The trick is to blast your horn and not slow down. People move out of the way then." Both laughed. A little unorthodox, but he was right.

Laura eyed his name tag stitched onto his black body armour above his X2 Taser. *McCarrick*. She recognised him from the Straw Man killings. He had found the picture of her in the woods, with a candle burning atop a dead heart. She never stopped to think about the poetic symbolism of that. That Ron's sick and twisted love would continue even after his heart had stopped beating. She could call him many things, but one thing was certain. He was true to his word.

McCarrick opened up the boot and pulled open the cage and the biggest land shark she had ever seen came bounding out.

"Big dog you have there," she said, eyeing the hound.

"Cerberus," his name, he said. Quite a name for a German Sheppard. His fur was a dark caramel, with patches of black intertwined in brown, like a field of hay trampled in the mud.

"Is he friendly?"

"To me? Yes. To you? He'd take a couple of fingers." McCarrick pulled Cerberus' lead tight. He was panting. His long pink tongue falling out of his tooth filled maw.

"I have a cat," Laura said.

"Oh, really?" McCarrick said. "Name?"

"Bagpipe." McCarrick furrowed his brow.

"Why Bagpipe?" He said. Laura rolled her eyes.

"Everyone asks that," she said. "Because no matter what you call a cat, it won't come to you. So, I named him 'Bagpipe.'" McCarrick thought about this and pressed his lips together. "Why is he called Cerberus?" Laura said.

"Because he stops people getting away. Drags them back to me." Laura nodded.

"I see."

"And," McCarrick said, driving his hand into the dog's fur. "Because he's a good boy," he said, leaning down, and letting this animal that could rip someone's face off lavish him in kisses. McCarrick stood back up. "Where am I needed?" He said, wiping the slobber from his face. Laura fished out a small jacket from her pocket that she had taken from the hanger by the front door.

"This is the missing person's jacket. It's been a couple of days since it was last worn. But see what you can do."

"I'm sure we'll manage," McCarrick said, taking the

jacket and smothering it in Cerberus' face. Cerberus took a huge sniff of the garment. "Cerb," McCarrick said, unclipping the hound from his lead. Cerb looked up at him. "Find it!" In an instant, Cerberus was racing around the cordon, his nose glued to the floor, his tail wagging furiously. Laura watched in awe. She thought she was part dog. She was getting good at smelling people's bullshit from a mile away. "He's onto something." Laura felt a wave of excitement rush through her. There was something they had missed. They were going to get a breakthrough. A lead. Something to help them find Mary. Or what was left of her, anyway.

Then Laura's heart sank. Cerberus was moving to the outer cordon, where the reporters were. "Cerb!" McCarrick shouted.

The reporters saw teeth on legs bounding towards them, and they rushed out of the way. Cerberus bounded past them. McCarrick following closely behind, and Laura racing behind them.

"Fuck!" Laura shouted. "Get him under control!"

"Cerberus!" McCarrick yelled, trying to catch him. Cerberus was out in the open, and tonnes of cameras and bystanders all waiting for something to go wrong. But what happened next was something Laura could have never imagined. Something that turned her life upside down.

The dog was barking, spinning in circles, and pawing at the boot of a car. Laura slowed to walk, before stopping completely, her stomach filling with dread.

Cerberus was barking. Snarling. Trying to get into the

boot of the car. McCarrick grabbed a hold of his dog's collar and hooked him back on his lead. He looked up, searching the area.

"Whose car is this?" He said, pointing to Laura's Audi. Laura's Audi that Cerberus was very interested in. Swallowing hard, she could feel the cameras on her, and she dreaded to think what the next minute of her life would look like.

"It's mine," Laura said, meekly. McCarrick didn't hear her, again calling out, "Whose car is this?"

"It's mine!" Laura said, louder, clenching her eyes closed. The wind cutting through her, which seemed much colder than before. She heard footsteps appearing behind her.

"Laura?" A voice called. Laura opened her eyes and turned to see Catherine standing there, and Laura's face exploded in pain. "You fucking slut!" She screamed, diving to Laura, grabbing a fistful of her hair, slapping her face and head. Laura screaming. Blood pouring. The dog barking. Cameras clicking and flashing. Voices cheering. Some booing. Footsteps. Rapid on the ground. Catherine pulled away, cursing. Thrashing. "How long have you been fucking him?"

"That's enough!" A voice called. It was Francis, holding a flailing Catherine. She dropped to her feet. Catherine was red faced, breathing heavily, staring through Francis and at Laura, who was holding her nose, blood pouring through her fingers. "Take a walk!" Francis ordered Catherine. He looked out at the camera crews converging on them. Reporters chattering into their microphones.

"Brilliant," he said. "I'm gonna get sacked." He turned to Laura, placing his hands on her shoulders. Her eyes red and streaming with tears, blinking rapidly. Her hair was a mess. "Are you okay?" Francis said, eyeing Laura.

"What the…" She said. Then she saw it. Her phone was on the floor. The screen smashed. She picked it up. Her bloodied, shaking hands fumbling at the passcode.

Jason had called her over and over. The vibrating in her pocket in the conservatory. That was him. A voicemail. Two. Three voicemails. Her phone must have dropped out of her pocket earlier when she went for Catherine. She had seen it. She had listened to the calls. Seen the messages pop up. His saying he needs to see her. That he was angry last night. That he loved her until the end of the world. She slipped her phone in her pocket.

"I need to go," Laura said. "I need to go home." Francis watched as she took a step towards her car.

Then cutting through the rabble, the distinct sound of a car boot being pried open. Attention snapped to McCarrick, holding a crowbar. Cerberus went crazy, digging his snout into the small gap before the lock gave way. Cerberus dived into the boot and rose up with a bloodied blouse in his jaws. McCarrick took it from his hound's mouth, and he eyed Laura, his face draining of colour.

"Laura," Francis croaked, the sound of the press going haywire. Shutters clicking. Feet shuffling. He turned to Laura. "Laura," he said again. "What have you done?"

The cold settling in. The fear and horror of all that is, and all that will follow, crushing down on her like collapsing mountains. Through quivering lips, Laura whispered,

"I don't know where to begin."

CHAPTER FOURTEEN

LAURA

"It isn't what it looks like," said Laura, as eyes fell onto her, and the jaws of the wolves closed in. That's all she said, all she could say, like a spouse that was being screamed at for being unfaithful. They could only protest their innocence, but that just made the accuser angrier.

"Laura," Francis said, his voice filled with horror. "You're going to have to come in."

"Bullshit!" Laura screamed. "Someone planted that there! I haven't ever seen that before in my life!" Her words fell on deaf ears. Her protests of innocence did nothing to shake the look of shock, pain, and anger on the officer's faces that were eyeing her up. Laura looked around the street. She was on camera, too. Her downfall was being broadcast for the whole world to see.

McCarrick shook his head, unable to find the words, and simply placed the bloodied rag into an evidence bag. And just like that, Laura's fate was sealed. She was done. Worse than done. She was utterly and completely fucked without a prayer.

"Laura…" Francis whispered, the press moving closer. Clicks and shutters of cameras going haywire. Laura fought through the tears that were gathering on her eyelids. Francis held out his hand. "Come on. Let's not make this any worse than it already is." Laura shook her head. This couldn't be happening. How the hell did that get in her car? She tried to think, but all she could focus on was the pounding of her heart in her head.

McCarrick's radio came to life. The robotic voice cutting through Laura's horror.

"McCarrick," they said. "You're needed at Pennington Flash. A local PCSO has been flagged down by a member of the public. We think we've found something. It looks like a body."

A body, Laura thought. *They've found the body.*

"I need to go to that scene," Laura said, taking a step towards her car. Almost in a daze. In a dream world. No. A nightmare that she couldn't wake up from. "I have to help…" She took a step, and then another. Then another transmission broke through the radio channels. This time, from everyone's radio, including her own.

"Arrest her," the transmission said. Laura stopped in her tracks. An icy chill filled her, like someone had doused her in ice water. Her mind spiralling. The word moving further away as a void consumed her filled with terror and numbing helplessness. Laura recognised the voice, and like one last stab in the back, she turned, fighting through the tears that were gathering on her eyelids. Jeremy was standing by the cordon. A radio pressed to his mouth. His eyes were hard. And with one final twist of the knife, he gave the command. "Arrest her for the murder of my wife."

Hands grabbed her. She didn't know whose or where from. But they grabbed her, and they forced her arms behind her back.

"Let me go!" Laura screamed. All reservations. All reputation. All integrity. Dissipated in the face of self-preservation. Tears fell from her eyes so hot they could melt steel found her mouth. She felt like she was drowning. She couldn't breathe. Her breath stabbing in short, sharp expulsions.

"Get off her!" A voice called, pushing in between the bodies that had converged on her. Laura looked up. Francis was standing there, holding onto her shoulders. His eyes filled with pain. "Laura, look at me," he said. Laura focused on him. On him, and on nothing else. She saw him, and she saw a man who had a duty, but a duty to his friend too. No matter what she did. What she put him through. Her explosions. Her pain and trauma passing onto him. He was always there to fight her corner, and he had been there since the start. Always ready to save her from drowning. "You need to relax. Don't make them cuff you. Think about the long game here." His words cut through her pain. She nodded.

"You do it," she whispered. Francis' face slacked, like it had been melted.

"What?" Francis said, fighting through the lump in his throat.

"Lock her up!" Jeremy called from across the street. Francis locked on him, his gaze that of fire.

"Just give me a minute!" He returned to Laura. "I can't," he said. "I can't."

"I don't want anyone else to touch me," she croaked. Then sucked in a deep breath and composed herself. Her face set in stone.

Francis heard the words, but they didn't register. A battle waging in his mind. He turned his head, and saw Jeremy standing by Catherine, both looking like two wolves waiting to move in and have their fill. Francis swallowed hard, and then spoke.

"Laura Warburton," he said. "I am arresting you on suspicion of the murder of Mary Marriott." He cautioned her, each word that escaped his lips cutting him deeply, like he was pulling barbed wire out his throat. Laura nodded, then looked to the floor.

You murdered Celine.

Ron disappeared.

Everyone you get close to ends up dead.

Now it's your turn to face the music.

"I'm being set up, Francis," Laura croaked. "Someone else did this."

"We'll get to the bottom of it," Francis said softly, smoothing out her shoulders with his thumbs.

"You believe me, don't you?" Her eyes burned with pain. Francis pursed his lips, and then, after a moment, he nodded.

"I believe you." Those words cut Laura deep.

"Take my house key," Laura said, reaching into her pocket and pulling out her keys. "They're going to seize my car, anyway. Make sure Bagpipe is fed and looked after while I'm away."

"You aren't going anywhere," Francis said, taking hold of the keys. The sound of an engine. A prisoner van pulling up the road. Laura looked at it, the threat of breaking down completely scratching at the back of her throat, waiting to burst out in a flood of anguish. But she held it together, straightened herself out, and swallowed hard.

"He likes his food in the small dish that I keep by the door. Make sure he has plenty of blankets laid out to sleep on. He might not like you at first, but just make sure he is taken care of for me. He's all I have." An officer appeared by the side of them and took Laura by the arm.

"We have to go," they said. Laura leaned into Francis.

"Follow the blood," she whispered, as she was taken away.

CHAPTER FIFTEEN

LAURA

Laura sat with her fingers pressed to her lips during the entire journey to the custody suite, the stop off before prison for the worst forms of human: Murderers. Drug dealers. Sadists. Rapists and all other people were unable to leave their animalistic depravity behind and live in a civilised society. Now she would be walking through those big metal jaws and see the world close behind her.

For the second time in her life, she was a prisoner. First by Ron, who imprisoned her with control. This time, a prisoner of the state, by those she had bled with in the pursuit of justice.

Her mind raced in that quiet cage.

Catherine knew about her and Jason. There was evidence of Mary's murder in the back of her car. How the hell did that get there? The only person she had been near was...

Jason. That was it. It was the only explanation. Jason knew where Jeremy and Mary lived. He had been there before with Catherine. Knew Jeremy's car and work schedule. He was a big guy, so moving the body wouldn't have been a problem. He had been in Laura's company the night before. In her car. Maybe he killed Mary and put the rag in her boot? Dread filled her.

If Jason was responsible, then Catherine would be next. She had to help her before she ended up on a cold slab too.

"You need to let me out!" Laura shouted. The officers didn't hear her. She banged on the thick glass wall that separated them. "Hey!" She screamed. "You need to let me out, now!" The passenger – a woman in her mid-forties who was wearing way too much makeup, turned around.

"Just be quiet," she said. "We'll be there soon." Laura felt the wave of panic grip her tighter.

"No!" Laura protested. "You don't understand. He's going to kill her!"

"Yeah, yeah," the officer dismissed.

Catherine was in danger, and the only person who knew was currently locked in the back of a police van. Laura kicked the cage wall in frustration.

"Calm it down!" The passenger ordered.

"It's Ma'am!" Laura screamed. The officer laughed and shook her head.

"Not for long, it isn't." Laura pressed her face to the barrier between them. She squinted her eyes, straining to see the arsehole officer's collar number.

"How much service do you have?" Laura shouted through the glass. Her voice was muffled.

"Five years," she said, almost cockily. Laura scowled.

"Not for long."

The van stopped, and the officers ejected from the cab of the vehicle. The back door opened, and Laura squinted at the overhead lighting in the custody holding area. The officer with the attitude held out her arm and regarded Laura.

"Come on," she said, like beckoning a child. Laura shrugged the hand away and stepped out of the van.

"I know what to do," she said. "I'm not a kid."

It's going to be okay, Laura thought, as they walked into the cell holding area. *Speak to the sergeant. Put everything straight, and I'll be out in no time.*

The floor was a linoleum white, with the reflection from the lights that were fitted into the walls making Laura's eyes burn. She couldn't believe it. She was here. In this place. Her mind screaming at her to go crazy. Start fighting. Throw shit at the walls. Claim she has swallowed loads of drugs to get out of custody and escape. She hadn't been handcuffed. It would be easy.

"Sit down," the officer barked, pointing to the small holding cell with a white bench behind a heavy door with thick glass.

"I can't believe you've been locked up," the officer said. "Bet you're regretting all that shit you did last year. Driving through the gates of that house." She shook her head, a sarcastic smile slapped across her face. "It's about time this caught up with you. You should have been sacked ages ago."

Don't react, Laura thought, clenching her jaw. *They're just trying to get a rise out of you. Over inflated ego as soon as they are handed a warrant card.*

"Collar number?" Laura said as she sat down in the cell.

"I'm not giving you that," the officer scoffed, sitting opposite her. Laura smirked.

"That's fine. When I get let out of here, I'll check the custody log. It won't be hard." The officer stood up and moved to the cell doorway.

"You think you're funny, don't you?"

"I'm bloody hilarious," Laura cackled. "Now get away from me and stop talking to me. I'm under caution, remember?" The officer's face turned like she had just bitten into her tongue and shit had poured out. She retreated to the bench and sat down.

Seconds dragged by. Then minutes. Before they knew it, they had been sitting there for over an hour. After what seemed like an endless time of staring into space and being tortured by her own thoughts, she heard the intercom go and she was led inside the custody suite to the Sergeant's desk.

The desk towered over her, and the sergeant looked down on her like he was a God about to pass judgement on all that ventured through hell to stand before him. The sergeant was a large man with black hair. Laura put him around mid-fifties. He had no wedding ring, but saw he had a faint tan line around his ring finger, but nowhere else. She presumed he had been away on holiday married, and then it quickly led to a separation. A make or break? Maybe. Laura knew what that felt like. The sound of the waves of South Africa still crashing in her mind. She doubted she will ever be able to forget that storm for as long as she lived.

The sergeant typed away, staring at his computer.

"Name," he said.

"Laura Warburton," Laura said. The Sergeant's fingers

stopped rattling on the keyboard, and his eyes started from his screen to Laura. His mouth dropped.

"Oh shit," he said, standing up and coming down from behind the custody desk to stand next to Laura. He was big, and his stature dwarfed the other officers standing with her. He ushered the officers away, like he was a drop of penicillin in a vat of bacteria. "Shit, Laura, I had no idea it was you out there. I would have brought you in here much faster if I would have known." He glared at the two younger officers and scowled at them. "Why didn't you tell me you were bringing in one of our own?" He bolstered. The cops eyed each other nervously.

"We didn't think..." the female officer stammered. Her frame shrinking. The sergeant cut the officer's drivel dead.

"You have a police officer in the holding cell, and you didn't *think* to let me know that detail *might* be a little important?" The gaze of the Sergeant was like a hot sun beam from a magnifying glass on a scurrying ant on tarmac. "Why is she here?"

"She's been arrested for murder," the officers said quickly. Laura knew what she had been arrested for, but hearing it said out loud in this environment made it all seem much more real, like the walls were closing in on her. The tightness in her chest was growing. But she remained calm. Composed. There was a time to break down, and a time to be strong.

The sergeant shook his head.

"Disgusting," he said, and moved back behind the desk. "Leave us," he said. The officers scurried out of the suite quickly, like rats escaping a burning building.

After she was booked in, Laura's clothing was seized. Everything down to her underwear. She was handed a set of grey jogging bottoms and a grey jumper and led to her cell by a detention officer. She walked in, and she stood in the empty room, looking at the markings of old prisoners that had been carved into the pus-coloured walls. The unblinking black eye of the CCTV camera watching her.

The detention officer stood at the foot of the cell with her hand on the door. Laura turned and met her eye. Her face filled with kindness. Her eyes were etched with remorse.

"Do you want the light left on or off?" The officer said. Laura fought through the lump that was growing in her throat.

"On, please," she said meekly. Her composure slowly slipping away, like peeling away layers from her body. The officer closed the door a little more. "Can I get a coffee?" Laura said, sitting down on the blue mattress in the corner.

"Of course." The officer went to close the door.

"Any chance you can leave the door open?" Laura said, desperately. "I don't like small spaces." The detention officer's face turned to pain.

"I'm sorry, Laura," she said. "But it has to be closed." Laura's lips went tight. She nodded, and Laura pulled the suicide blanket around her and curled up against the wall, pulling her legs into her chest.

The officer closed the door, and Laura Warburton of the Major Investigation Team, survivor of domestic violence, with an exterior as fierce as a winter wind, cried herself to sleep.

CHAPTER SIXTEEN

LAURA

She was walking through the void again. The lantern in her hand as she stared out into the stretching abyss.

Her foot caught something. She leaned down into the spiralling mist.

Celine was lying there. Lying with her eyes open.

"Baby," Celine said. Her lips were a hypothermic blue. Her hand reached out, and Laura took it. Her touch was like ice. "I'm so cold in the ground," Celine said. Laura crouched down, holding her hand tight, like clutching ice.

"I'm here," she said. "I'm here with you."

Laura knew this was a dream. Celine was dead. Buried in the Wigtown cemetery and being feasted upon by worms. Still, she welcomed this black void. A place to hide her fears. A place to disappear into the dark, just for a few moments, and hide away from the monsters. Laura lay down next to her.

The ground wasn't hard, but soft and coated with thick, luxurious blankets, and plump pillows.

Celine was naked under the covers. Laura could see her caramel skin and the top of her breasts peeking out. Celine ate her up with her dark eyes and ran her fingers through Laura's hair, twirling it in between her fingers.

"I miss you," Celine said. She leaned in, and Laura felt her lips and hot breath on hers. Lips as real as anything she had felt in her

life. "Don't leave me again," Celine whispered. "Stay here, with me."

"I can't stay," Laura said. She didn't want to leave. The darkness bled away. Lights above them. Golden. Welcoming. They were in her bed. Scented candles burning. Bagpipe sleeping at their feet. It felt so good. So real. So intoxicating. But Laura knew she couldn't stay as much as she wanted to. Despite what had happened. She and Celine had been in love. They had been happy at one time. This was all those emotions and feelings concentrated on a single point. No pain. No harrow. Just the two of them in a timeless space.

It was heartbreaking.

"I need to go," Laura whispered, tracing Celine's body with her fingertips. "I have to help people."

"Are you happy?" Celine said. The words stopped Laura like a punch to the gut.

"I haven't been happy in as long as I can remember," Laura whispered. "But that's life. We live. We die. We're forgotten. The cycle continues."

"I won't forget you," Celine said. "You will live in my mind forever."

"You're dead," Laura said, sitting up in the bed, trying to fight away the tears that were brimming on her eyelids. "You're gone. This isn't real. I'm going to wake up, and I'm going to be in that cell, and I will have to fight. To fight and fight and fight until I have nothing left, and then I will have to fight some more. Because that is what I signed up to do. It never. Fucking. Ends."

"You're a good person, Laura." Celine whispered behind her. Laura felt her hands on her shoulders. Laura held them tightly and turned back to face her. But Celine's face was no longer warm. Her smile was impossibly wide and twisted like a Halloween mask. The lights around them dimming. The bed fading away. Dirt under her. Cold. So much cold creeping into her bones. "But you have your flaws." Laura felt the warmth in her stomach strip away. Her breath slipping through her lips like ghosts. "You use people. You get people close to you, and drink them like a vampire, then toss them aside. You use people and use them until they're all dried up. You know it. Which is why you self-destruct. I knew it, which is why I lost my mind. Your colleagues know it, which is why they turned their backs on you. Your family knows it, which is why they never call you."

Teeth peeled away Laura's flesh, and salt found the open wound.

"I cut them out," Laura said. "They think I was responsible for Ron's death." Celine snapped her head to the side, neck bent like someone hanging.

"And were you not?" Celine's teeth turned black. "There's a reason you can't forget about him, Laura. It's not trauma. It's guilt, and it's eating you alive." The flesh at the tip of Celine's nose began to bubble and peel away, like paper being slowly devoured by a flame. The smell of mould. Grass. Rot. "I was perfectly happy in my life before I met you. Where am I now? Worm food." Celine's face turned pale, and black spread like mould devouring a wall, starting at the edges, until her face was consumed by decay. Her pupils died away like headlights slowly turning off, leaving a white void, like a pot of curdled milk. "Ron had a career. Was respected. And now where is he? At the bottom of the ocean being eaten by fish. Sheree. Probably in a back alley with a needle in her arm. Her lips blue and body growing cold. Jamie Green. Devout father to Oliver Green. Dead. Oliver was now an orphan, being passed through the system. Clara Weaver. Screaming herself to sleep in a *psych ward. All because of you. You don't help people, Laura. You ruin them." Celine's eyes ran down her face like melted jelly. Beetles and grubs erupting from the fleshy holes, scurrying around her face.*

Laura tried to scream, but all she could taste was dirt that matted on her tongue. She felt like she was choking. Something crawling from the back of her mouth. She hunched over, trying to breathe. To cough. The blockage released onto the ground in a detonation of black bugs coated in blood that wriggled and writhed, scurrying away into the darkness. Her eyes itched, and she poked her finger to the white which went right through the mushy meat. Unspeakable fear ravaged her, and she thrust her hand to the wound, half blinded.

"And now," Celine continued. Laura looked around her. The walls high. Worms wriggling inside them. She was in a grave. Her own grave. She looked up and saw Jeremy, Francis, and Catherine standing above her, each holding a shovel. Their faces ashen, wearing black. Laura tried to call out, but out of her mouth poured clumps of soil.

Hands made of bone gripped her face like a hungry crab, forcing Laura to face Celine. Her skin mostly gone. Black skin tags ravaging what little flesh she had left. Cheeks missing, her skull pushing through the gore in a sickening grin.

"You are damned." Celine pulled Laura into her embrace. Laura thrashed, trying to break free as dirt was shovelled on top of her. The hole filling. Consuming her. Filling her mouth. Her lungs. Drowning in dirt.

Laura got one last glimpse of the black spiralling sky above, with lightning so fierce it could split the heavens apart with booming trumpets of thunder. She saw another figure standing there. His face, although monstrous, was one that Laura recognised instantly.

Ron picked up the shovel and scooped up dirt.

"You did this," he said, before throwing soil onto her. "Because of what you did to me."

She gasped awake, choking on the scream that had been locked in her throat. Thrashing, kicking out, and pounding the walls. Shooting up, touching her hands and face and body, gasping for air. Looking around her desperately, Laura rubbed her hands over her face. Her body dripping with sweat. She let out a long breath.

Someone stood at the door of the cell. A face Laura was happy to see.

"It's time for your interview, ma'am." It was Francis. The relief she felt was short-lived, and dread set back in. A churning feeling, like the slopping of rotten eggs in Laura's stomach.

"Why are you here?" Laura said, panting. She pulled her hair from her face. "What time is it? How long was I asleep for?"

"It's early evening, ma'am," Francis said, his voice soft. Then, sensing her confusion, he followed with, "I'm not the one interviewing you. I asked, but I wasn't allowed to. However, I demanded that I see you before you're questioned." He paused. "Am I right in thinking that you don't want a solicitor?" Laura swallowed, still coming round from the nightmare.

"That's correct," Laura said. "I have nothing to hide." Francis' face turned sour.

"A solicitor doesn't mean you have —"

"I said I'm fine," Laura barked. Then reigned herself back in. "Sorry," she said, closing her eyes and rubbing the sweat from her face with the blanket. "Long day." Francis shook his head, pinching the bridge of his nose.

"If you aren't having a brief, then you better get your mind straight," he said. "Because you won't like who they brought in to talk to you." Laura felt like she had been slapped to the face. She knew who it would be. The only person it *could* be.

"Are you taking the piss?" She said, bursting out in laughter. This was happening. This was actually happening to her.

Francis didn't reply. The answer was written all over his face, and Laura knew it was going to take everything she had not to scream.

CHAPTER SEVENTEEN

JEREMY

After he watched Laura being dragged away in the back of the police van, Jeremy Marriot went inside his home and locked himself in the utility room in the kitchen, where they kept the washing machine and dryer. It was about the only place he could think to go to where he wouldn't be disturbed, and where no one would see him smiling.

"They took her," he whispered in the dark. Scheming. Daring to dream. Bringing his hand to his face. He let out a long breath, fighting between guilt, laughter, and hysteria. He was sending her down. They weren't friends. She had been a thorn in his side since the moment she had appeared, and now she was going to be thrown to the wolves. An endgame of his own making. It was going to happen, eventually; however, Laura would just keep causing more destruction. She was like a dog that needed to be put down.

He had staged it perfectly, but even he couldn't imagine it had gone down this well. The media. The audience. It was all falling into place. He would walk free, and the one person who could stop him was the woman that was going to be convicted. With Laura out of the way, he would be in charge of the MIU. He could manipulate reports. Tamper with evidence. Do everything he could to ensure Laura went down for this, and not him.

He would play the role as the mourning husband, and even if Laura was cleared, there was nothing that could tie the murder back to him. His alibi was tight. Laura knew he was having marital issues, which, of course, put him as suspect number one, but in the absence of evidence, it meant nothing. He had covered his tracks which had taken the eye of the law off him and put it on another. He had destroyed evidence, and there was, of course, the *Butcher*. The work he had done with Mary would mean that even *if* Laura was cleared, all eyes would point to *him*.

The work.

The phrase knocked him sick, and he buckled over onto the washing machine, jamming his fist in his mouth. The memory of him cutting into her. Snapping her bones. Bleeding her, then cleaning up afterwards.

Jeremy shook the thoughts from his mind. He was so close to freedom that he could practically taste it. He couldn't lose his head now, so he had to keep his mouth shut and do what needed to be done.

He thought about his mobile phone. Cell site data. Location services. He was clear on that front. He took out his SIM card before he disposed of the body and left the handset at home, connected to the Wi-Fi all night. As far as the police were concerned, he went to his car, and he drove home in the early hours of the morning and found his wife to be missing. He waited. Made the call, and that was that.

Laura, however, was out in the middle of the night, and

they could track her car to where he had hidden the murder weapon. Not to mention she frequents where he had hidden Mary. Even Laura couldn't talk her way out of this one.

Plus, now that she had been caught sleeping with Catherine's partner, her colleagues wouldn't fight to get her neck on the chopping block. They would just fight over who got to swing the axe.

He could hardly contain it. His smile stretching from ear to ear. His blood pumping hot around his body. He was going to get away with murder.

A knock at the door startled him. He composed himself, wiping the smile from his face, donning the mask of a grieving husband who just needed a minute alone. He took a deep breath and gingerly opened the door. Catherine was standing there, her face etched with concern.

"You okay, sergeant?" She said, her gloved hand lingering on the door handle. Jeremy sucked in a short breath through tight teeth. He nodded.

"Yeah," he said. "But just call me Jeremy. I don't need any of that *sergeant* bullshit right now."

"I understand," Catherine said, nodding. She looked in the washroom. "What are you doing in here?"

"I'm just having a minute," he said, which was true. *A minute to mourn sweet death, and to savour the freedom it would bring. His career would take off. His pension would triple. His social standing elevated, and the knowledge that he had put a bad apple away that was turning all around her rotten.* "I just needed a second to digest everything, you know?" Catherine did indeed know. She had just found out her boyfriend was screwing her boss.

"I know exactly what you mean." The two shared a silence, listening to the sounds of the forensics officers working away in the house around them. "What now?"

"They've found her, haven't they?" Jeremy croaked. Catherine's lips went tight. Her eyes widening.

"Yes," she said, nodding, careful to be as compassionate and as delicate as possible. "I believe so, but… Jeremy…" She tightened her grip on the handle. "You stay here. I've got this. Me and Francis. We can go and see." Jeremy considered this. But he needed to see her. A part of him needed to see what he had done.

He straightened himself, smoothing out his clothes. He stepped out from the utility room and closed the door with a slight *click*.

"Come on," he said. "I want to see what that bitch has done to my wife."

CHAPTER EIGHTEEN

LAURA

Laura sat on the chair that was bolted to the floor, staring at the Styrofoam cup of water that she wished was vodka. Fuck, she needed a drink. That old itch getting harder to ignore by the day. The first thing she was going to do when she got released was find Catherine and warn her about Jason. She wouldn't listen, of course. But then Laura could leave her, knowing she had done what she could. She could do more, but right now, she didn't care. She wanted to get drunk. Get utterly shit faced and dance around in her underwear to heavy rock music. Maybe smash some furniture and pretend she was a rock star. Drink herself into oblivion. Anything to stop the voices in her head from telling her what a waste of space she was.

That this was a setup. Jason had put the rag in the back of her car, and then they would arrest him, and they would forensic the shit out of all his clothing, his home, his car. Fuck, even his cock. If there was DNA of Mary on him, she would find it, come hell or high water. And when he was behind bars, she was going to quit this job, spit on the floor as she left the station for the last time, sell her house and move away to somewhere with a nice beach and tall glasses of wine. Fuck the nightmares. Fuck sobriety. She had been a drunk and shit was bad, and now she was sober, shit was still bad. So, fuck it. She decided right then and there that if she was going to play by her own rules, it would be with a bottle of Malbec in her hand. Sensible, *'trying to hold it together'* Laura had failed. *'Bitch, I'll do what I like, when I like'* Laura was making a stellar coming back, and there was nothing anyone could do to stop her.

The door to the interview room went. Laura looked at her. Her pencil skirt was without a crease, and her blue shirt was buttoned up to her neck. Her glasses seemed thicker than the last time she saw her, and her smile twice as wretched.

"Shall we begin?" DCI Amy Burnell said. Her voice was laced with glee. How long had she been waiting for this moment to put Laura away? Laura could practically see the damp patch on her skirt at the idea.

Laura gazed upon her with so much disdain, she hoped her cunt would rot. Burnell. Amy mother fucking Burnell was here to interview her about the case, and Laura bet she practically came in her underwear when she got the call.

"Why the fuck are you here?" Laura bit, her arms folded like a petulant child who was being scalded by her headmistress.

"I see you haven't changed," Burnell mocked. She pointed to the recorder. It was still off. Her name in hazy green writing with a tape reference number underneath it. "Do you want me to turn this on?" She said smugly, taking a seat.

"Answer my question," Laura bit. "Why the hell are you here? You don't work at the MIU. After that bullshit apology you gave me when I last saw you? Did you *personally request this case* too?" Laura said in a mocking voice. Burnell sat there and took it. "You tried to bring me down last time and you were proven to be utterly and completely full of shit. So, what? You thought you would try again a second time?" Laura glared at her so fiercely she hoped Burnell would start smouldering. "If you turn that recorder on," Laura said, jabbing her finger to the console, "I will fuck you so hard you won't know which hole is for pissing and which is for eating."

"Is that a threat?" Burnell said, lacing her hands together.

"It's a goddamn promise," Laura said. "I'm not speaking to you," she said. "I want someone else here. This is a conflict of interest." Burnell waited for Laura's tirade to finish. Without breaking eye contact, Burnell defiantly reached out to press the RECORD button. Laura bolted to her feet, slamming her palms onto the table. "Touch that record button and I'll break your God damn fingers." Burnell hesitated, and her lips curled into a wry grin. Laura's breath was ragged. Her face flushed. She bared her teeth, like a wild animal about to be dragged off to the abattoir.

Do it, Laura thought. *I dare you.*

Burnell pressed the button. Three beeps succeeded it, and the interview began.

"This interview is being digitally and *visually* recorded." Laura felt a wave of cold run through her. She looked up at the ceiling. The stupid CCTV camera was there. She had been being watched this entire time. She felt stupidity ravage her.

Think of the long game, Francis' voice whispered in her head. Burnell continued to talk.

"Can you state your name and your date of birth for the tape?" Laura dropped her head, closed her eyes, and shook it. She returned to her seat. Burnell's smile grew. She wasn't even trying to hide it anymore.

I thought so. Now, it's my time to call the shots.

"Laura Warburton," she said, and then her date of birth. Burnell continued the introduction, and then asked if she wanted a solicitor. "Fuck you and the cunt you rode in on," Laura responded. Frankly, she didn't care how she came across. This tape would never be heard in a court, because Laura was innocent. Didn't mean she had to be nice, though. She just needed to get this over with, get bailed, and speak to Catherine, and then hit the off license. Once she told her, then as far as Laura was concerned, she was in the clear.

Burnell cautioned Laura, and then said in a condescending tone, "Do you need me to explain the caution to you?" Laura didn't give a response. She only continued to glare. Burnell sat back and continued to scribble down on a piece of paper. "Very well." She leant forward, taking in a large breath. "You have been accused of the murder, torture, and prevention of the lawful burial of Mary Marriot. Tell me about your alleged involvement in this offence."

"Torture?" Laura said, somewhat stunned. "I don't

know anything about torture. Are you sure you have the right suspect? There's a serial killer disembowelling people and feeding them their own eyes. Maybe you should go find them and ask that?" Burnell didn't bite. The silence between them dragging out. Laura rolled her eyes. "I don't know anything about any of that. Mary was missing when I was involved. But I know someone else you could speak to about it…" Burnell's ears pricked up, like a bat searching for a moth in the night.

"Who?" Burnell said, her eyebrows rising. Laura thought she heard her skin crack at the movement.

"Jason."

"Jason, who?"

"I don't know his last name. Catherine's boyfriend."

"Why would he know about it?"

"Because he is the only person who could have put that into my car," Laura said, trying to compose herself. "I was with him last night, and we were together. He is the only person who could have done it."

"When you say you were with him?"

"He was bending me over my car bonnet and fucking my brains out," Laura blurted. "Is that enough, or do you need more details?" Burnell raised her hand. Probably the first time she had heard someone describe it as 'fucking,' and not just 'intercourse,' or 'touching pee pees.'

"I don't think that's necessary," she said. Laura slapped her hand on the desk.

"Then good. Now go arrest him, and we can put that bastard behind bars." Burnell shook her head.

"Not just yet," she said. "So, you were sleeping with

171

Catherine's partner? A woman you work with?"

"Is that illegal?" Laura bit.

"It's immoral," Burnell countered. Laura pressed her tongue to the roof of her mouth.

"I didn't know this was a morality interview. What about when you ignored evidence and suspended me for doing my job? Nearly let an innocent woman go down for murder?" Laura let out a laugh. "You haven't learned, clearly. And they made *you* a DCI? Who did you get on your knees for that promotion?"

"This isn't about me and you," Burnell said.

"This is about nothing other than me and you," Laura said. Burnell didn't respond. Laura could feel her body shaking. She needed to compose herself. "Look," Laura said, leaning forward. "I am not proud of it, and frankly, professional standards can lick my arse. I am done with this job, and with this career. Yes, I was having sex with a colleague's partner. Yes, I enjoyed it. Yes, if I wasn't here, I would probably be home, biting the pillow while he used my thighs as earmuffs. So, less of the bullshit questions." She sat back, looking away. Her eyes growing red.

"You're upset."

"No shit."

"Why?" Laura scoffed, smiling, biting down on her tongue.

"Because I didn't kill anyone."

"You killed your ex-partner, Celine?" Laura felt like she had been sucker punched.

You really want me to break your nose, don't you? Push my

buttons? Settle the score for your own professional embarrassment?

"Yes," Laura choked. "And I was cleared of that. I have Jeremy and Francis, who both corroborated my story."

"So, they kept you out of prison?" Burnell said. Laura nodded. "So then, why did you kill Jeremy's wife?"

"I didn't kill anyone." Burnell let out a slight laugh. She was enjoying this. She was actually having a good time, like a mean kid who focuses a magnifying glass on an anthill, watching them burn and frazzle in the sun. Burnell pulled out a photo from the folder that was on the desk and slid it to Laura. It was of a bloodied rag laid out on a table. A pyjama top, soaked in blood.

"Then tell me why this was found in the boot of your car? Tell me why the blood on that garment matches the blood of Mary Marriot." Laura picked the photo up in her hands, and held it between her fingers, like if she was too rough with it, then it would eat her alive. After a minute, she threw it back to Burnell.

"I haven't seen that before in my life."

"You're going to have to do better than that," Burnell said. "Where were you last night?"

"I told you. I was biting my lip whilst getting pounded by Catherine's boyfriend, Jason. He is the only one who had access to my car. We were down by the industrial estate near Robin Park on the outskirts of town. We went there because it was quiet. We couldn't go to a hotel. It was too boring, and at my place? Well, we have fucked in every room going, so I thought we could go somewhere new. Somewhere exciting. Be like horny teenagers again, ready to get our rocks off anywhere we could."

"Were you not afraid of getting caught?"

"That was part of the fun. But no. It's so vacant. So far away from anything that we weren't afraid of that."

"And did you see anyone else there?"

"No."

"So how do you think Jason planted this in your boot?" Laura searched her mind.

"I don't know," she said. "He could have slipped it in at any point."

"Then what happened?" Burnell said. Laura dared to think she was taking her seriously.

"We had an argument. He said he didn't want to do this anymore. I told him to fuck off, and then he told me he loved me." Burnell's eyes widened.

"You take him to the middle of nowhere, treat him like a piece of meat, toss him to the side and he tells you he loves you?" Burnell almost couldn't believe what she was hearing. Laura knew it all too well. She had experienced enough of *love* to know it was anything but simple. Laura leant forward.

"Trust me," she said. "People are weird, which is why I prefer cats."

The two continued talking a little longer. Burnell produced more exhibits regarding Laura's movements of her car. Then she pulled out another stack of photos, her face grim.

"Whilst you have been here," she said, "we have done checks on ANPR cameras on the night Mary went missing. They showed you on the A road leading to Pennington Flash, where Mary's body had been discovered." She peeled out photos that were grainy and dark, taken from what looks like the CCTV from a storefront. "These," she said, laying them out, "are CCTV stills of your car, with you in the driver's seat, driving to the location on the same night that Mary went missing." Laura could feel the heat in the room rising. Her heart beating out of her chest. She had nothing to fear, but looking at this evidence, and sitting where she was, this didn't look good. Didn't look good at all.

"We have since attended the location," Burnell continued, "and searched the woodland." Burnell's voice turned grave. "A body was found. A body that was so mutilated and disfigured that I don't even think I can show you the photos." Laura snatched the folder from in front of Burnell and pulled out the photographs. As soon as she saw them, her mind fractured.

"What the…" Laura said, unable to speak; the images she was seeing was worse than any nightmare her mind could conjure.

It was Mary, or at least, what was left of her. She was laid out and crudely covered over by dead and rotting leaves. Dirt smeared along her naked, white and flabby body. She looked pasty, like an egg white left out in the rain. Her fingers were missing, just bony stubs like snapped twigs protruding from scored flesh. She had been burned. Part of her body was as black as coal. Dull muscle and tendons poking through the seared flesh, like a barbequed steak left out to rot. Her face was unrecognisable. Teeth shattered into shards jutting crudely out of black gums. Her stomach was torn open, and the insides were left out to be fed on by the birds.

Laura pushed the photos away, and looked away into the distance, staring at a spot on the wall.

"They're horrific," Laura said, tears brimming. "Is that Mary?"

"You tell me."

"I'm guessing the fact you're showing me her means that's Mary. Jesus fuck," Laura shook her head, trying to stop herself from vomiting. Laura felt like her world was going to implode, like the walls would cocoon her and sink into the earth into the blackness, where she would forever stay in a tomb of her own making. "I had nothing to do with this."

"What were you doing there at that time in the morning?"

"I was out running," Laura said.

"Can anyone verify that for you?" Laura searched her mind.

"No," she said meekly, the wind taken out of her sail. "No. I didn't see anyone else there." Laura took a deep breath and gestured the scenes of gore in front of her. "How would I have done that? How would I have abducted her from her home, mutilated her, and ditched her body like that?"

"That's why we're here," Burnell said. Laura slammed her fist against the table, making the pictures jump. Burnell didn't move an inch.

"Mary was with someone the night she died. She was drinking wine at her dinner table. There are stains that are the shape of a wine glass."

"Wine?" Burnell said, her eyes narrowing. "You enjoy wine." The insinuation cut through Laura.

"I'm sober," Laura hissed through clenched teeth.

"Laura," Burnell said, stacking the photos in a neat pile and then laying each one out, one by one, in a deliberate, delicate fashion. "We can put you at the scene of the crime on the night Mary went missing. The rag was in your car. You have a history of violence. You're under a lot of strain right now, and frankly, your alibi is not checking out." She sat back and looked at the tape recording. "Is there anything else you would like to say before we end the interview?" Laura searched her mind. How the hell was she going to prove that she didn't do what they were accusing her of? Not just murder, but torture. Mutilation? Hiding a dead body in the woods and leaving her there to rot?

"I didn't do this," she said. "You have the wrong person, and the longer I am here, the longer you aren't looking for the person responsible." Burnell met her gaze and held it for a few long, agonising seconds.

"We'll end it there... for now."

CHAPTER NINETEEN

JEREMY

Jeremy sat lurched over with his head in his hands. A plastic shopping bag clutched in between white-knuckled fingers, filled with contents of his stomach. Catherine was sitting by the passenger door and smoking a cigarette, listening to the sounds of the ducks and the birds flock around by the lake. There was even an ice cream truck. A fucking ice cream truck, and it was still serving to customers at the car park entrance not five hundred feet away from the police tape.

"I can't..." Jeremy said, his eyes bloodshot from vomiting. "I can't believe what I have just seen. Who the fuck would do something like that? Who the..." He hurled again, the bag rattling and shaking with the contents. Catherine looked out at the mob of onlookers. Members of the public recording with their phones. Journalists. News vans.

"Vultures," she said. She looked at Jeremy. His face devoid of colour. His lips swollen. His eyes red and puffy. Long strings of bile dangling from his lips. "You don't need to be here," she said to Jeremy. "I can take you home." Jeremy wiped his mouth on a piece of blue roll, gingerly took a sip of water, and turned to her.

"No," he said, swallowing hard. "Go back to that crime

scene?" He shook his head. "I doubt I'll step foot in that place again."

"I could take you back to the station?" Catherine said, trying to come up with a solution.

"I'll be fine," Jeremy said. "I need to be here. I needed to see her again." Catherine knew she was fighting a losing battle. Grief did strange things to people.

Stepping out of the car, Catherine moved under the police tape and walked through the thicket. A blue roll of tarpaulin had been laid out for the forensics officers to walk on to get to and from their vans, that were guarded by officers that were half frozen to death.

Catherine moved along the tarpaulin and saw Francis standing there, speaking to the forensic officers on the scene. He nodded and had a grave look in his eyes when he turned to meet Catherine.

"They found Mary's clothing in Laura's car boot," he said. His tone was dark, like he didn't want to believe it himself. Their own leader. A killer. Not just a killer, but a sadistic one at that. Francis had seen Mary's corpse. What was left of it, anyway? She appeared as though a butcher had ruthlessly hacked away at her, leaving her resembling a mangled piece of meat.

"Fuck her," Catherine said. Her eyes burning with a silent rage. Her stare hard, looking through the thicket and shrubbery. A stare only someone develops that has been wronged in every way imaginable. "I hope she rots." Francis clenched his teeth. He wanted to defend his superior. They had gone through so much together, but he couldn't find the words, nor the resolve to. It was clear cut. The evidence didn't lie. At this point, interviewing Laura was just a formality. Jeremy had specifically requested that Burnell be tasked with the privilege because of her experience. Francis thought otherwise. Ever since the Clara Weaver case, and the shit show he had caused and the fact that Laura had not only knocked him down from his position upon high charity, but that she had publicly humiliated him in showing his ineptitude to everyone that would listen. He couldn't help thinking that bringing in Burnell into this investigation was nothing short of personal.

"There has to be an explanation," Francis said. He could feel Catherine's stare, like someone holding a cigarette lighter to his skin.

"You can't be serious?" Catherine barked. Her face warped with both fury and pain. "Oh my God, you actually *are* serious?" She scoffed. "You think she didn't do it, don't you?" Francis' lips went tight.

"I'm not saying that she didn't do it," he rebuked.

"Then what are you saying, Francis? What are you trying to say? Think exactly about who Laura is. Since she arrived on the team, things have gone from bad to worse. That is not a good leader."

"No," Francis said. "I was late to the team, granted, but she is good at what she does. Her methods ... arguable, but her results speak for themselves. I don't know why she would risk throwing this all away for this. I mean, Mary? Of all people?" Catherine shrugged.

"The evidence shows it, Francis. It's time to stop looking at how you want things to be and start looking at how things actually are." Catherine flicked her cigarette into a shrubbery. "Trust me. You'll feel much better that way."

The hours ticked by, and Catherine had blown up Jason's phone enough times to get her locked up for stalking with fear of violence. Her voicemails went from being calm and controlled to catatonic. She was going to rip his dick off when she got hold of him. See how much of a 'Big Man' he was when she removed his testicles.

The sun was setting, and Francis and Catherine had done all they could for the time being. It was time to leave the scene, let CSI continue doing their work throughout the night, and then pick it back up in the morning. Catherine stood smoking a cigarette by the side of the car, where Jeremy was sitting with his head in his hands.

"You should go home, Sergeant," Catherine said, taking in a deep inhale of the toxic smoke, before blowing it out in a satisfied sigh.

"What home do I have?" He said, and Catherine didn't offer a rebuttal. He was right. If the same thing had happened to her, she doubted she could ever step foot inside that house again. Jeremy straightened. "I'll go back and grab some things. Some clothes, toothbrush. I'll head to a hotel for the night, and then see where we're at in the morning." Catherine nodded.

"Good idea," she said. She reached over and touched Jeremy's hands. He was as cold as a corpse. "I'll give you a ride back to the nick. I think we're done here. Just wait for Francis to get back and then we will head back to the station and call it a night." Jeremy smiled.

"Thank you, *sergeant*," he said, mockingly. Catherine laughed. A gallows laughter. A laughter laced in misery. She held a smile and looked at Jeremy. He looked like warmed-up shit. His hair was ruffled. His tie was loose. His shirt and pants were unclean. He had hardly stepped foot out of the car whilst they had been at the scene, just giving directions here and there of what he wanted the officers to do. He had been asked many, many times to leave the scene, as it wasn't good for him. But he demanded that he stay put. Catherine thought it was a kind of grieving process. The same way how people go to the chapel of rest to say farewell to a loved one. Although by that point, their loved one has had their eyes and mouth sewn shut, their organs removed and pumped with formaldehyde and preservatives. By the time the mortician finished with them, they were just an echo of who they once were. An empty shell.

"I got us three coffees," Francis said, appearing by the car door. The coffee cups pressed between his hands. Catherine regarded him.

"Where did you get those from?" She said. Francis gestured across the car park.

"The Salvation Army turned up an hour ago. They do it with a lot of the major crime scenes. They turn up completely for free and give out food and coffee to officers that are on scene. They even brought a Portaloo." Catherine had to fight to hide the shock and surprise on her face. Even though she was standing not one hundred metres from her colleague's mutilated wife, and she had found out that her boss had been sleeping with her new boyfriend behind her back whilst she was working on the case of a sadistic serial killer, there was still some good in the world.

People often ask police officers why they have such a bleak outlook on the world, and why they don't see the best in people. The simple answer is, because they so often see monsters, they forget there are normal, hardworking, and decent people out there who do things out of the goodness of their hearts and don't want anything in return. It was refreshing.

"Thank you, Francis," Catherine said, taking hold of the coffees. She offered one to Jeremy, but he sat there, staring out of the window, like a broken toy in the corner. Catherine placed his drink in the car cup holder. "Right," Catherine said with finality. "C'mon," she looked out into the distance. The sun had passed the horizon, and the sky had turned the colour of a melted flamingo. It was late winter, with spring kissing the skyline, meaning their darkest days were nearly behind them. Or so she hoped.

"I'm going to head to custody," Francis said. "See what needs doing." Catherine was going to object, but she didn't have the energy. She just wanted to go home and turn the light off on this miserable day. She checked her phone. Jason hasn't called her back.

"Do what you want," she said. I'm giving the Sergeant a lift home to grab some things." Without another word, Catherine closed the door, put the car keys in the ignition, and fired up the engine. She flashed at one of the officers on the scene and gestured to them to lift the police tape so they could go through.

Jeremy had fallen to sleep. The stress wiping him out. His face slumped against the window. Catherine drove on, heading towards Jeremy's home. It was only a few miles away.

She felt hot tears running down her cheeks. Memories of her and Jason together. She tried to call him again. It went straight to voicemail. Like a swimmer lost in a black sea filled with sharks, Catherine's mind fell into those dark places filled with teeth. The state of Mary's body. It would take someone seriously strong to do that to someone and then drag her body into those woods.

Jason wasn't answering his phone. Come to think of it, Catherine hadn't spoken to him since the day before all this happened.

What if Laura was innocent?

What if she was in love with a killer?

SIN

I will make you cry.

I will make you bleed.

I will make you suffer.

And my God will enjoy every part of it.

I have a song ready for you. My symphony to the Devil himself. It will be my masterpiece.

CHAPTER TWENTY

LAURA

ONE DAY BEFORE THE OFFERING

How did I end up in this place? Not just the inside of a cell, staring down the barrel of a gun, but in this position? When I joined the police all those years ago, I thought I would help people and saving lives. But, I have just seen a world of misery. Of blood. Of pain. Ron. Abuse. Alcohol. Celine. Sex. Jason. Betrayal.

Am I the problem? Or is it this sordid, awful world that chews you up and spits you out? They promise you everything. They tell you that you can be whatever you want to be growing up, and then, in the next breath, they tell you to be careful what you wish for. I know what they mean by that now. This is all I ever wanted.

I moved up here to get a clean start. Something fresh. But all I have found is misery and pain. Nothing but agony at every turn. And the worst part is? I'm wilfully destroying my life. It's like I can't help it. I have had counselling. I am still having counselling. I have an AA sponsor. But here I am, still sitting in a cell after being interrogated by a woman who would love nothing but to put me away. My friends have left me. My family wants nothing to do with me. As the saying goes, 'if the character of a man is unclear, then look at his friends.' Well, I have none of those left, and were they even friends to begin with? From the moment I walked into the police station, it was like the universe tipped an egg timer and told me that when it reached zero, my time would be up, and I would walk into the supernova of annihilation.

But before I roll over and die, I will get the fucker who is trying to frame me. I will make them pay and make them rue the day they ever thought that they could fuck with me. I have come too far. Worked too hard and been through too much shit to roll onto my back and let the wolves feast on my insides. Not me. Nope. Fuck them all. I will do this alone. I'll dig myself out of here if I have to.

Francis. I need to speak to Francis. He will know how to help me. Jeremy is a fool, and Catherine is too upset with me to help. Francis is my only hope. I just have to hope that he sees this for what it is and doesn't become corrupted by the misery that is prevailing in the unit.

Laura rested her head against the cell wall. Her thoughts running riot. She could do some meditation, as the councillor and the rehab clinic prescribed when she was feeling too overwhelmed. But right now, the idea of sitting with her thoughts was nothing short of torture. She couldn't overthink her way out of overthinking. She needed to move. Needed to do something other than sit here and wait for the axe to drop.

She got up and walked. Paced around the cell like a wild animal. She had requested a book from the detention officer. A hard back. Not one she had seen before, nor one she intended on reading. She threw the book into the air and let it land on a page, and that was how many paces around the cell she did. Two hundred and forty-two. Eighty-one. Nine. Three hundred and four. Pacing. One step in front of the other, whilst she let her mind work.

Jason. It had to be Jason. But how did the rag get in the back of the car? It had to be from someone she knew. Someone who had access to her, which led her back to Jason. Suspect number one.

But Mary? What was the motive? It was the one piece of the puzzle that didn't make sense. Jason had the means, but what was the motivation?

He didn't love Catherine, despite what he said. He was a user. He treated women like shit. Catherine had only been seeing him for a few months, and she had already come to work on more than one occasion with bloodshot eyes after they had had an argument. Laura kept quiet. She didn't need mothering; she was a grown woman. But Laura had taken it upon herself to do some digging on him.

She had run him through PNC. He wasn't known. On the face of it, he was just like any other ordinary human being walking around on any day. Which was why she didn't trust him. He was too clean, and from Laura's experience, it was often those who acted with such altruism and morality that were the dangerous ones. The types that do nothing but smile their way through life and post nothing but flowers and animals on their social media. They were often the ones that were the ugliest on the inside.

But if Jason *did* kill Mary, then why was there not a single trace of his DNA on any of the clothing or evidence that Burnell had shown her?

Burnell. The thought of her made Laura pace faster. She

was a snake. She had been sitting, waiting for Laura to fuck up so that she could swoop in and make a fool out of her and to scream that she was the superior detective. The better leader for the MIU and her team. She hoped that if they put it to a vote, that Laura would come out on top. However, right now, the odds were stacked heavily against her. There was a mutiny afoot, and she was one step away from walking off the plank into the deep blue sea.

She focused her mind on the case, pushing away the thoughts of Burnell. She was a distraction.

A distraction. Someone to rile her up. Make her incriminate herself.

But who had made the call to bring her in? Someone who has links to her. A past with her.

Jeremy. His name was a hot coal in her brain. It could only have been him. He knew how much Laura hated Burnell, and he knew Laura wouldn't be able to contain herself if she was in the same room as her. Is that why he called her? Perhaps. The possibilities right now were endless.

Laura stood at the edge of the wall of the cell. She placed her hands on the wall. She dared entertain the ideas in her head for a moment. Say it *wasn't* Jason? He could confirm her alibi. They were together on both nights. She parked him as a suspect for the time being and thought about other possibilities.

In nearly all cases of domestic murder, the prime suspect was the partner, and most of them were guilty. But Jeremy was at home. There was no movement of his vehicle. Unless he had tricked the ANPR cameras? The cops hadn't checked the CCTV of the surrounding shops on any other night because his car didn't flag up, only Laura's. Was he framing her for something *he* did? But why?

The answer was simple, and it steam rolled into Laura's mind.

He knew Laura would figure it out, and this was his way of not only getting away with murder, but getting Laura out of the picture for good. By the time it was figured out that she was innocent, any CCTV of his travels would have been erased.

Laura thought back to the house and the bathroom of Jeremy's home. It was spotless. Francis said to himself that he occasionally cut himself shaving. Not to mention them both being men and not being able to piss in a straight line if their lives depended on it. The place was *wiped clean*, to where even the forensics department couldn't even pick up a single shred of blood, piss, or bodily fluids. Jeremy had an arsenal of chemicals in his shed, and no one else found this slightly strange? As soon as she thought she had it, another factor entered the picture.

The wine stain on the table. Mary *was* with someone that night. Had Mary been having an affair, and Jeremy came home and found out? Lost his mind and killed her? Who would believe that hypothesis?

Her mind raced, but she had another fact on her side. She wouldn't be able to drag a body into the woods without help. Mary wasn't a small woman. Like Jeremy, she had overindulged in her time. Laura wasn't one for fat shaming, but standing at five foot nine and weighing around sixty kilos, she would struggle to drag Mary, who was almost twice her weight, into the woods unseen. Plus, there was the act of dismembering her and mutilating her. Jeremy was a large man. Strong. And flooded with adrenaline, anger, and fear, he would have been able to make such butchery happen.

Butchery. The word made her pause in her mental monologue. Beads of sweat dripping from her brow that fell by her feet. Her breath was heavy from all the walking. She must have done over a thousand paces while time seemed to crawl along broken glass whilst she waited to see if they were going to charge and remand her, or she was going to go home and do some serious police work. The Butcher.

No forensic evidence.

The mutilation fit the M.O.

Targeting Laura and those around her.

Was this the work of the Butcher? Was not only Catherine in danger, but *everyone* she knew?

Laura was pulled from her thoughts when the cell door was pulled open, and the light above her flicked on, like someone pulling her out of her bed and shining a torch in her eye. She shielded her eyes and let out a sharp hiss of breath. Gingerly, she pried her eyes open. It was Francis. He didn't look good.

"Ma'am," he said, quickly. His chest rising. His face flushed with red.

"You have to get me out here," Laura said, breathlessly.

"It's not Jason. It's the Butcher." Francis held her gaze. His face filled with dread. "What is it?" She said, the sinking feeling of harrow in her stomach. "Am I getting remanded? Are they charging me with this bullshit?" Laura slapped her hand against the wall. Her breath was ragged. She moved to the back of the cell, resting her head in her hands and her elbows dug into the windowsill. "Just get it over with," she said, sniffling. This was it. The end of the road. She couldn't help anyone anymore. She had been defeated. Finished. Her cat would need to be taken away from her. Her home would stand as an empty shell for years. Laura felt her mind spiral, like a ship swallowed in a violent whirlpool and dragged to the bottom of the abyss. She turned with fire in her eyes. "Well?" She said. "Are you just going to stand there, or are you going to put me out of my misery? Fuck, I can already taste the inside of the prison cell now." Then she righted. Straightened herself. Body becoming taut. "No," she hissed. "I'm not giving up that easily. If the CPS want to charge me with some bullshit, then I will rip the courtroom apart, and then the MIU, and the Wigtown Constabulary can answer to the public why there are still bodies piling up in the streets from this sick fuck, and why their lead detective, their *best* detective..." spittle flew across the room, and Laura's legs gave way, her anger tipping her over the edge, hammering its fist against the dam of despair, until it broke loose and drowned her.

She crumbled to the ground, her back against the wall, her head between her legs and fingers digging into her red hair. Laura watched Francis standing there, unmoving, and taking the onslaught of abuse. "... I haven't done anything..." She choked on the last word. Still Francis didn't move. Only then did Laura notice the phone in his hand. Laura regarded it. "What's that?" Francis didn't know where to look. His eyes darting around the room. Laura wondered who the hell could be on that phone.

"It's…" Francis uttered, trying to cough the words out of his throat.

"Spit it out!" Laura screamed, forgoing all reservation. Now, her fortress lay in ruins, its walls destroyed and trampled. As the dust cloud rose high, the sun was blocked, leaving her feeling cold. Nothing but cold. Francis raised his hand, gesturing her to take the phone. Laura saw her standing behind him. Burnell. The sight of her made her blood boil. Why the hell was she here? Did she want a front-row seat to Laura's demolition? But even Burnell's face looked worried. Laura again regarded the phone. Who was on the other end…

Laura got to her feet, slowly unfolding herself like a beaten dog that was being offered a treat and a hot bath. She closed the distance and took the phone. She held her breath and put it to her ear. Laura swallowed hard. She could hear heavy breathing that chilled her to the bone, like she was on the phone with Death himself.

"It's a pleasure to speak to you, Laura Warburton," His voice was gravelly and laced with filth. Laura felt her skin crawl. "Are you the Devil who has been tasked to bring me down?"

It was the Butcher. The Butcher had come to claim her. Laura eyed Francis and Burnell, who looked back at her like she was about to unveil a magic trick. Their hearts in their throats. Burnell gestured to her.

Keep him on the call, she mouthed.

This was bigger than her and Burnell now. Laura cleared her throat.

He was reaching out. Showing himself to them. This faceless killer who they had been hunting. He was speaking to them, and Laura needed to reactivate her game face quickly. She glimpsed Francis' face. His eyes scrunched up when he heard what she said. She had to be more careful. She could be smart. Be coy. This wasn't someone smack head or drug pusher. This was a monster, and Laura knew from her time in the police that you can't reason with monsters. You had to play them at their own game.

"You should be flattered," Laura said, quickly composing herself.

"Laura Warburton. Sagittarius. Owner of a cat named Bagpipe. Paid for her home from the bereavement money following the untimely demise of her ex-partner, Ron Harper, two years ago. Death by misadventure, the coroner concluded." He was taunting her. She knew it. She knew how manipulative people worked, and he was begging her to bite. "You were a proud detective when you first started. Yet, your fall from grace is nothing short of poetic. I admire your dysfunction. Your destruction. Who better than the Devil to send someone like you to stop me?" Laura bit down, willing herself not to rise to the bait. This was a game. He was playing with her. "I enjoyed cutting them open," he said. "I prefer it when they scream. When they beg." He continued. "Are you sure you can stop me? How are you going to do that in your cage?" Laura furrowed her brow. How did he know she was in custody? He was taunting her. She could hear it in his voice. That slight inflection at the end. She could almost see his grin in her mind's eye. Her eyes went to Francis.

"What's he saying?" He whispered. Laura focused on the call.

"Why are you doing this?" Laura whispered, fighting through the pain in her heart and the lump in her throat. "What do you want?" It was a simple question, but one that was so complicated to answer.

"When a man is born, he is made in the depiction of the Lord. His first breath is one of pain. A cry. A scream. He has been brought into this world and the first thing he feels is the air on his skin, which seers him like a burn. He feels the rough hands on his supple body, and he is dripping in his mother's blood. Now why do you think that is?" Laura thought of the answer.

"What does that have to do with anything?" Laura said.

"Humour me," the Butcher said.

"Not until I know who I am talking to." Laura said, daring to establish some kind of dominance in a game in which she didn't know the rules. "You know so much about me. I know nothing about you. So, tell me. Who am I speaking to? What should I call you? It's only polite, and you strike me as someone who values morality."

"The Devil shalt employ many tricks when trying to turn the believers away from their God. And you, detective Laura Warburton, are better than that." He let out a breath. "However, I will give you a name." Laura gestured to Francis, clicking her fingers with urgency. Francis took out some paper and a pen. She needed to be careful. Everything that came out of his mouth could be a lie. This was a man who would happily eat his dinner next to her disembowelled corpse. However, they could still work with that. It was when they remained silent that things got tricky. But he wanted to talk, which is why he had called the custody suite and asked to speak to her. To bridge the gap. To play this game. "Gabriel," he said. "You can call me Gabriel." Laura mouthed the words to Francis, who quickly took out another piece of paper and wrote them down. Burnell snatched the paper out of his hand and scribbled violently, as if she was writing for help on burning parchment. She gestured to Laura with the paper.

Keep him talking. almost got a trace.

"Okay, Gabriel." Laura said. "In answer to your question. It's childbirth. It's the natural cycle of things."

"It is indeed," Gabriel said. "But say the mother dies, and the child is left abandoned in the street to be feasted on by a stray, starving dog. What kind of world is that?"

"A shitty one. But the one we have."

"Indeed," he reiterated. "My Lord the Devine. He creates pain and death. He wills it. From the moment we are born into this miserable life, we are to suffer. We are to bleed. We are to cry. And this world is now fractured. People eating themselves to death. The whore in the tree. The liar you dug from the ground who hailed herself as a false God. A God of altruism. Of love and happiness, who was nothing more than a fraud. There is one God, and He is that of pain. Only in a world filled with such comfort are people so miserable. It makes no sense. The demons that invade their minds — depression. Anxiety. Mental illness. All symptoms of the Lambs losing their way. Running from pain has led them straight to it. Mankind has sleepwalked into the very hell they wished to avoid. And I bestow that gift back to the world." Laura sucked a breath through her teeth.

"And what gift is that?" She said. A pause, and then a deep rumble passed through the receiver.

"Agony." Gabriel said. "Only through pain. Only through agony do we truly feel alive. Sex. Love. Drugs. It all pales in comparison to *pain*." Gabriel pronounced the '*p*,' with a distinct *pop*. "Pain is the gift which the Lord has given to the earth. Yet his children commit blasphemy, cursing the Lord when something tragic happens. Cursing His name, that we dare to understand the actions of the Devine. I have been given the holy task of completing the Lord's work. To give his gift of pain to mankind. Those I have offered to the Lord are not worthy of breathing the air he provides into the lungs that he crafted. He is our Lord, and I am his servant."

"You suffocated Rebecca Shaw and had her broadcast it to the world," Laura said. "That isn't anything sanctimonious. Isn't anything righteous. It's sick."

"A vehement whore who lied and cheated her way to infamy. She was a virus. A sickness. A plague. The man. The Lawyer, who built his empire on allowing the most deprived and monstrous human beings walk free. The disease spreading whore. So ungrateful to be alive. So unfulfilled with the life she was given, that she squandered it and, like a rat on the ships of the Europeans, to spread her disease around the world. Injecting her body, the temple of God, into her veins so that she might numb herself from her own self-loathing."

"And what about Kacy?" Laura said. "Kacy Milton. The young girl."

"The corrupted youth," he hissed.

"They were people," Laura said.

"They were vermin!" Gabriel screamed. Laura licked her lips. Her next question was risky.

"And what about Mary?" She said. "Mary Marriott."

"Who?" *Who?* Laura thought, her mind cracking.

"Mary Marriott," she said. "The woman you left in the woods." A low growl of laughter crackled through the receiver.

"Come now, detective," Gabriel said. "Don't insult me. My work is curated. Not amateur." Laura felt like she was standing in quicksand, the world falling away. "And now," he continued. "I will offer you a chance to redeem another soul." Laura's heart picked up. She gestured for the paper and pen. She was passed it by someone, she didn't look who, her attention too focused on the next lot of details. "Old hooks call for cold cuts, for all they see around them is dust." Laura furrowed her brow.

"What does that mean?"

"You, and you alone, must go," Gabriel said. "You have two hours."

"Wait!" Laura urged. Burnell gestured to her to keep him on the line. "I need more information. What do you mean? Cold cuts? It makes little sense. Let's talk about this –" Laura's voice was cut off as she heard the sound in her ear. The sound of someone crying. A woman.

"Please," her voice said meekly, fighting through the tears. "Please come quick. He's got a knife." The call went dead.

CHAPTER TWENTY – ONE

LAURA

Laura regarded the phone, then threw it on the blue mattress. She aimed for the cell door and raced for the exit.

"I need to leave," Laura yelled. Burnell moved in front of her like an immovable obelisk. "You aren't going anywhere," Burnell said.

"Amy!" Laura shouted. "He has someone else. I heard them on the phone. If I don't go to where he wants me to be in the next two hours, someone will die!" Her eyes were burning. Frustration gripped her. She was ready to explode, staring through Francis and Burnell at the space behind them, like there was a lion standing in the way of her and her crying child. "Move out of the way now." Burnell shook her head.

"You aren't free to leave," she said nonchalantly. "You're still under investigation and you haven't been granted bail." Laura's mind felt like a hall of glass that had had a cannon ball fired through it.

"You're serious…"

"Deadly," Burnell said. "Why would I let a murderer go free to run around and look for the clues left by another murderer? That wouldn't look good on the front of the tabloids now, would it?" Laura shot a look of desperation at Francis, who was standing next to her.

"Francis," Laura said. "Go speak to the custody sergeant. He'll listen to me."

"What exactly did he say?" Francis said, trapped between a rock and a hard place. Burnell's burning gaze melting the side of his cheek off.

"He said 'I must go alone.'" Laura begged. "He said that I could save someone."

"Go where?"

"He didn't tell me. He gave me a riddle." He said, "Old hooks call for cold cuts, for all they see around them is dust." Burnell and Francis regarded her. Laura thrust the scribbled piece of paper into Burnell's.

"That's what he said?" Laura nodded.

"But there's more." She said with urgency. "At the end of the call. A woman, I think. Crying. She told me to come quick, and that he has a knife." Francis' face drained of colour.

"This is stupid," Burnell interrupted, stuffing the paper into her pocket.

"Amy!" Laura screamed.

"It's DCI Burnell to you, *criminal*," she barked, "and you aren't going anywhere." She turned and marched down the hallway towards the custody desk. Her heels clicking on the ground as she moved, like she had a firework jammed up her arse. "I'm going to track him down and bring this to an end."

"Ma'am!" Francis shouted, following her in her step, leaving Laura lingering at the cell door. Burnell spun round with a face of war.

"You can't seriously believe Laura?" Burnell said. "We found evidence, *hard evidence*, that she has murdered and mutilated another officer's wife! She is banged to rights! There is no way on earth that she can be allowed to leave the suite." Francis stood frozen in place, his mind torn. He had been at the crime scene. He had seen what had happened to Mary. But something inside him scratched at that last bit of hope that they had missed something. That something was seriously wrong with this whole thing.

Laura's heart caught in her throat. She watched him from afar. He would not fight it. He would say nothing. She couldn't just stand by and do nothing. She raced out of the custody cell and met Burnell, her face an inch from hers.

"You're making a mistake!"

"Why did he want to speak to you?" Burnell bit, fury in her eyes. "Why, of all the people he could have chosen to speak to, did he want to speak to you?"

"Look," Laura barked. "We don't have time for this! I have no idea why he wanted to speak to me? Maybe it's because this whole thing has been made public? Maybe he's a sick bastard who enjoys playing games with people? I don't know. But what I know is that if you don't let me walk out that door and we don't play his game, then more people will die. Look what happened to Rebecca! He knows what we're going to do! He wants us to fight each other. He is counting on it!" Burnell looked Laura up and down like she was a cockroach that had just crawled onto her Christmas dinner.

"Death follows you everywhere you go," she hissed.

"Why is that?" Laura was taken aback by the comment. It expelled all the air out of her burning lungs.

"Ma'am," Francis said, finding his bravery. "He said he wants Laura to go. We don't even know where he is." Burnell straightened, and her eyes glared at Francis behind her glasses. He could feel them boring into his brain.

"Thank you, detective," she said firmly. "You are dismissed." Burnell turned to walk away. Francis' jaw went tight. He curled his fingers into fists.

"You can't be serious." Francis hissed. Laura placed a hand on his shoulder.

"Let it go," Laura said. Francis couldn't think of anything even close to *letting it go*. He watched Burnell take a few more steps. The anger building inside of him, like a pressure cooker.

And then it blew.

"You bitch!" He screamed. The blast of his rage bellowing through the suite. The custody sergeants stopped typing and looked up from their desks. The detention officers stopped their checks and turned to him. Even prisoners and officers that were walking around the suite stopped, like their feet had been nailed to the floor. And Burnell. Her face crumpled like paper, and she turned to meet Francis' eye.

"What did you say to me?"

"I said you're a bitch, Chief Inspector!" Francis continued. He closed the space between them. Francis stabbed a finger towards Burnell so fiercely it could smash through steel. "After what happened last time?

After what happened with Clara Weaver and Alex Weaver. You still have a bone to pick? A score to settle!"

"I think you need to be reminded of who it is you're speaking to…" Burnell said calmly. Her voice was slippery, like a serpent.

"Fuck you!" Francis blasted. "We have a maniac on the loose and he is playing games with us. The clock is ticking, and we have no idea where he is, and he specifically asked for Laura, the lead investigator on the case, to go to where he said he was. He asked for her. A girl in danger spoke to her, and you can't see past your own revenge."

"Laura Warburton, as of right now, is being held in a custody suite for the suspected murder of Mary Marriott. She is no longer the lead investigator. I am. And I say that she stays here, and that she is to be kept here because of overwhelming evidence." She smiled at Francis. A smile he desperately wanted to rip off her face. "I think it's a little more than professional interest you have in Miss Warburton," she said. "I think you are seeing this more than a professional endeavour." Francis' breathing slowed.

"Are you insinuating what I think you are?" He said. "Because if it is, then you are way out of line."

"You have walked through hell for this woman. Been assaulted. Stabbed. You have disobeyed my orders since the day I walked into that office because of her." She shook her head *no*, followed by a gasp of laughter. "Is she really worth your career?" A beat of silence. Next, "I have checked the number that called us." She peered past

Francis' shoulder. "I don't need Laura and come to think of it…" she said, letting the words hang in the air, like a noose begging for a neck to hug. "I don't need you, either. You're dismissed, detective." A rush of cold ravaged Francis.

"What do you mean, *dismissed*?" Burnell's lips curled into a sneer.

"What is it you always said? *You're going to get me sacked?* Well, detective Francis Cline. It looks like she finally has. Head back to the station. Pack your things. Leave your warrant card on my desk. I'll arrange a formal meeting with your HR representative in a few days. Until then, let me do my job, and you can keep thinking about how you let your feelings for a murderer destroy your career."

CHAPTER TWENTY – TWO

CATHERINE

Catherine tried to call Jason for the fiftieth time. It had stopped ringing and was just going straight to voicemail. She was in the right mind to drive to his house and have it out with him there. But why give him the satisfaction? He was a snake. A coward. He wasn't worth losing her career over.

Still, she sat there in the station's *Quiet Room*, staring at the photos they took together. The two of them were in Spain for their first holiday together. They had only been serious for a few months, but after a long stint of being single and terrible first dates, Catherine was eager to jump at the chance of being important to someone. Being special to someone. Meaning something to someone. She had offers around the station, but cops shouldn't date other cops. She had heard of so many times when things had gone bad. Cops having affairs with other officers. Cops being caught having sex on duty. Cops getting together and then it all falling to pieces, and they still had to work and be in the same room as each other while others gossiped and whispered about them. To hell with that. She would rather jam a toothpick down her toenail and kick a wall as hard as she could.

Another photo flicked by, and the tears flowed more

freely. Them in a hotel bar. Them out having food. She was in love with him. Like, *really* in love with him, and he had betrayed her with her own boss. Someone she called a friend. Someone she had bled for. Gone through the worst situations human beings can do to each other with her by her side. And here she was, staring at the photos of the man she loved, knowing that the whole time, he was betraying her. Jamming a knife in her back and twisting, and then Laura comes and rubs salt in the wound. She was broken. In pain, and now that Laura was locked up in a cell, how well did she really know her? Laura always portrayed that she was the victim. That she was the one being thrown into the fire and her ex was the venomous one in her life. Well, from where Catherine was sitting, it certainly seemed that Laura was the rotten apple in a healthy bunch.

Since she had come to the station and took over the MIU, things had gone from bad to worse. She was poison. And what do you do with poison? You flush it out of your system before it can infect and kill everything it touches.

Catherine tried Jason again. The phone rang. Two. Three. Catherine stared at the grey-coloured walls and felt her nails digging into the plump cushions on the couch she was sitting on. The décor of the room, cheap and cheerful from a budget store. Posters with 'Dance like no one is watching,' and 'Live. Laugh. Love.' She hated those kinds of pictures. She found them tacky. It used to be a game to her when she would go out on a job and find herself standing in a front room with no carpets. Dog shit on the floor. Piles of clothes stacked up in the corner of the rooms, whilst someone cried at her that their ex's new girlfriend was calling them a slag on Facebook. The game was, 'How long is it before we see one of those posters?' And as God as her witness, Catherine saw a 'Live Laugh Love' poster on the walls, or on the fireplace, amid ashtrays, and empty beer bottles, every single time.

She jumped up from her seat and snatched the offending poster off the wall, screwed it up and stamped on it. She eyed the phone in her hand. It was still ringing. She went to put the phone down when she saw the timer count up. Her mouth went dry, and a fire ignited in her stomach. She put the phone to her ear.

"You have some explaining to do." She said. But it wasn't Jason's voice that answered. It was another voice. Deeper. Graver. Sinister.

"Catherine," he said. "DC Catherine Morris. I have been expecting your call."

CHAPTER TWENTY – THREE

LAURA

Laura watched Francis turn from a solid mountain to a crumbling building. As Burnell walked away, her heels clicking on the ground and turned the corner away from their line of sight, Francis almost disintegrated into the ground.

"Francis…" Laura said, grabbing a hold of his shoulder. He shrugged her off like her hands were made of acid. He turned to her. His eyes blazing with fury.

"Thanks," he said. "Thank you, Laura. After all I have done. After everything I have done for you. Sticking my neck out for you once again, and where has it gotten me? Hmm? Fucking fired. My life is over. I have had twenty-three years in this job. Twenty-one of them spent on the front line. I come to your unit and look what happens?" His breath was heavy. His voice strained, trying his best to not explode. Laura had to tread carefully, like a bomb disposal expert trying to keep their cool while figuring out which wire to cut. One wrong move, and it was game over.

"It's not like that," Laura said, quickly. "He called me. I need to go. You know how it is. I'm so sorry," she continued, her mouth running faster than the beating of her heart. "I am so sorry. I can fix this. If I just go where he needs me to go, then we can put all of this right."

"No!" He blasted. Laura had cut the wrong wire, and the bomb had detonated. "No Laura. There isn't a *we* anymore! You have done enough. I have bled for you. Been stabbed for you. Been beaten. Fought. Risked my career for you. And where did it get me? Standing right here, face to face with a murderer." The last word scraped out of his throat.

"You don't mean that," Laura said, her throat knitting shut. "Please don't leave me. You have to believe me; I didn't do this. Believe me Francis. You're all I've got in the whole world." Her trembling hand went out to Francis, but he pawed it away and sucked in air through his bared teeth.

"You've done enough. *I have done enough.*" He took a step back. "Go back to your cell. This is over. I'm not bailing you out of your mess anymore." Francis turned and walked to the custody desk and moved out of sight. Laura crumpled to the ground, screaming into her hands.

She was placed back in her cell, and the door was closed, leaving her alone to sob herself into a nightmarish sleep where the demons of her past were waiting.

CHAPTER TWENTY – FOUR

CATHERINE

"If you go for help," Gabriel said, "I will kill him." Catherine sat nailed to the spot. She placed a hand to her mouth and swallowed dryly.

"Please don't hurt him … Please don't hurt my boyfriend." Catherine whispered.

"And what if I do?" Gabriel laughed. "You'll kill me? For this worm?"

"You're lying," Catherine said, fighting through tears that were spilling into her mouth. As soon as she said it, she knew it was a trap. That she shouldn't have waved the red rag to the bull, because no sooner did the words leave her mouth, did she hear the unmistakable sound of Jason's voice in the distance let out a long, bloodied scream. It seemed to go on for hours, and the sound was a rusted nail dragging down Catherine's nerve. "Leave him alone!" She begged, standing to her feet, pressing her hand to her face. She felt helpless. At the mercy of a faceless killer who had the man she loved more than anything in the world. "Please…." She whispered. "Leave him alone…" The screaming stopped. Cut dead in an instant. Catherine checked the call. They were still connected. Her heart was in her throat. Daring not to breathe too loudly. Soft whimpering came from the speaker. "Hello?" Catherine uttered, as loud as a terrified door mouse. "Jason? Answer me. Baby? Are you there?"

The phone buzzed. Catherine looked at it, shaking out of her skin. It was a picture message. Catherine hesitated. She didn't want to see it. She didn't want to see what that picture was.

"Open it," the voice on the phone said. "Open it and tell me what you see." Catherine had no choice. She clicked on the notification, and the picture opened. She held back the scream that came blasting through.

Jason was tied to a chair. His face bloodied. His mouth bleeding. His hands wrapped in barbed wire to a steel chair. The picture was grainy, like it was taken in the dark. The walls concrete and cast in shadow.

"Funny," Gabriel said. "This man. This worm. Has been unfaithful. You should hate him. Hell, I'm sure that you do. Very much. Does the thought of him here, with me not fill you with glee? Instead, it is not joy which fills your heart at the thought of his blood being spilled, but agony. Now why is that?"

"You're a monster," Catherine hissed.

"There are no monsters between Gods and Men. There is but the divinity of His holy light, and those that hide in the shadows."

"Holy light?" Catherine barked. "You think what you're doing is right?"

"Is he not a sinner?" He said. "Has he not caused the pain in your heart? Betrayed your trust and bedded those closest to you?"

"You need help," Catherine said. She began pacing on

the spot. "I can help you; you know. I know things may seem bad now. But you can redeem yourself. You're a man of God? Is that right? We can help you. Maybe you're just lost. Lost in this crazy world we're in."

"I have a question for you, Catherine." Gabriel said.

"We can get you help. Support. You can talk to us. We can support you through—"

"Catherine…"

"The CPS will listen. I know they will. Just don't do this. Just don't –" An ear-piercing scream capable of destroying windows, one so high, so shrilling that it could rock bones, prevailed through the receiver.

"Jason!" Catherine screamed, crumbling to her knees. Her tears like heavy rain on the ground. Her nose running. Her breath was ragged. The screaming stopped.

"Do not bargain with me, you petulant heretic," Gabriel spat down the phone. "You do not get to understand me. I am no man, but a God. I have been sent by Him to do his holy work, and you hold the deepest arrogance of man, believing that you can reason, rationalise, and even understand a power that you cannot possibly fathom."

"I'm sorry," Catherine said, quickly. "I'm sorry. Please. Please, I'll do whatever you want."

"Then answer me this," Gabriel said, his voice like hell fire. "If you lie, I will cut this worm's throat and send you the video." Catherine felt a rush of cold. Silence stretched across eons. "Do you love him?" The question wrapped around Catherine's throat so tight it was choking her.

"Please…" she said.

"Do you love him?" Gabriel repeated, enunciating each

word like the metallic *thwack* of a hammer nailing a coffin shut. She dug deep into her mind. She hated him. But by God, as much as she hated to admit it. Yes. Yes, she still loved him. She wouldn't get back to him, but as with the nature of love and hate, you couldn't just flip a switch and it was gone.

"I do." Catherine whispered.

"Louder."

"I said I love him."

"Louder! Louder Catherine! Convince me I shouldn't cut his throat right here and now!"

"Yes! Yes, okay, I love him." She said, her breath rapid. Harsh bellows of hot breath blasting out of her lungs. "Just let him go. Please. Let him go." The only thing she heard was her own heartbeat, and the sound of her nerves being pulled so tight they would snap like tort violin strings. Dead space filled the air. Catherine checked the call. They were still connected. She dared not speak. Jason's life in her hands.

"If you love a man like this," Gabriel said. "Then you are so truly, truly lost." The hissing of the last syllable nearly made Catherine scream. What did that mean? What was he going to do to him? "However," he said, saving Catherine from drowning in her own misery. "Unlike our friend here, I am not a liar. I will not hurt him, providing you do something for me." Catherine was faced with an impossible choice. Help a killer or become a killer. The decision was hers.

"What do you want?" Catherine whispered.

"Your inspector. Laura. I want her. Tell me, is she

coming to see me?" Catherine knew Laura was in the cells. She knew she wouldn't be able to go free.

"I don't know…"

"Then find out," he said. "Speak to someone. Put the phone in your pocket. Let me listen. Do not end the call, or I will end their lives."

End their lives? Who was he talking about?

"You have one minute to get my answer."

There was no time to think. Just do. Do as he says.

"Now go."

Catherine looked around her like she was on a sinking ship without a lifeboat. She pushed the phone into her pocket and stumbled as she moved out of the room, quickly rubbing her eyes and composing herself as she stumbled into the main office.

With legs like jelly, Catherine moved past the officers going about their business and moved to the Sergeant's desk.

"Sergeant," she said, trying to sound calm. The sergeant waved her away. He was on a video call with DCI Burnell. She checked the call timer. She had only forty seconds left before Gabriel killed Jason. "Sergeant," Catherine urged. He shot her a look, with Burnell talking in his ear.

"I'm busy," he said. Catherine looked at the screen. It was a live link to armed officers moving in on a location. The POV of a body camera. Armed officers, holding HK 416 assault rifles, storming through an old building with double doors that were chained shut. An old butcher shop. Catherine knew something was wrong. Something unspeakable was going to happen.

"Sergeant!" Catherine blasted. The Sergeant looked at her with fire in his eyes.

"Permission to breach, ma'am," the officer said.

"Breach," Burnell said. The firearm officers exploded the chains from the door, blasting them free. A large cloud of smoke billowed out as the doors blasted open and officers rushed in.

"He wants Laura!" Catherine cried out. She checked the call. Fifteen seconds left. "You have to get them out of there!"

"Laura is tied up," the Sergeant said. "Now shut the fuck up and let me do my job, detective!" Catherine checked the time. Five seconds left.

The officers breached a second door, and Catherine saw the firearms officer's torch find the walls of a grey room with grey concrete flooring. A body sitting in a chair. The call ticked down.

Three … Two…One…

"There's a girl here, tied up. Tied to a chair," the officer said over the intercom. PC Simon Foster. A wife. Two kids. A dog named George. "She's…" he began.

The speaker from Catherine's phone. Gabriel again.

"You failed me, Catherine." Catherine tore the intercom from the sergeant's head and screamed into the intercom.

"Get them out, now!"

"She's attached to something…"

The console under the girl's chair lit up, flashing wildly. The body camera flashed a bright white light, and all communication was lost.

CHAPTER TWENTY – FIVE

JEREMY

Jeremy returned home after Catherine had dropped him off. She had bid him goodbye and said that she was there should he need anything. He smiled and stepped out into the cold, before moving through the police tape surrounding his home and disappeared inside. He wouldn't need anything from her. He had done enough to ensure it was just plain sailing from here.

Jeremy moved past the CSI officers who regarded him. Swabbing. Collecting pieces of evidence that might be useful later down the line. He paid no heed, wandering through his home like a mourning husband. His face was still. His eyes were absent.

He collected a few belongings he had requested to be laid out. After the CSI took photos and swabs of the garments – a navy blue jumper, a pair of black shoes and a pair of jeans – he put them in a duffel bag, along with a toothbrush and other belongings for a few nights. He had been booked a night at the luxurious Premier Inn just outside the centre of town, all paid for by the Wigtown Constabulary. A forty-minute drive away from the station. Close enough to go in when required, but far enough away to not cause suspicion.

Jeremy packed up the belongings and went to his car.

He looked over his shoulder, seeing the coast was clear, and checked that there wasn't any residue of black insulation tape he had used to disguise his registration plate. Satisfied, he threw his bag on the back seat. He would have used the boot, but the thought of staring into that mouth, knowing what he had held there, was too much for him right now. He was a killer. A liar. A fraud, and he didn't need to be reminded of it. His internal monologue and adrenaline spiked every time he heard a siren.

As he drove to the hotel, he checked his mirrors incessantly. Checking if he was being followed by a marked car, or more likely, an undercover officer. He had seen the work that the undercover team did. Suspects of serious crimes had not a single clue that the police were on to them, until they were breaking down their door in the early hours of the morning and they were being hauled into custody, with detectives there waiting with a file full of evidence.

He waited at the traffic lights. A light pattering of rain falling onto the windscreen. White smoke from his exhaust pooling around him, like a magician, before they disappeared. Something he wished he could do right now.

He let himself think about what had happened for just a moment. Alone in his car. Unspeaking. Just him and his thoughts. Knowing there was nothing that could betray him, with the red glow of the traffic light casting his face in malevolence, he dared to let out a long, toothy grin.

Her past had done all the heavy lifting for him. Laura had made enemies in the police. The past she had been running from. Her self-destruction. Mental instability. Her addictions. It had all been for this moment. Her downward spiral into nothingness, and when this was all over and she was rotting away in a cell, screaming herself to sleep, she will be the furthest thing from anyone's mind. Just the way Jeremy wanted it.

His sick smile grew. He pulled away from the green light.

He was going to get away with murder, and he felt so happy he could cry.

Jeremy wasn't out of the woods yet. It was important for him to keep up the facade of a mourning husband as he made the funeral preparations. He would jump through the hoops that the police wanted him to go through and speak to the family liaison officers when they came knocking. As requested, he would appear at the press conferences. Over time, he would build his way back to where he wanted to be. He could climb the career ladder even faster this way, leaning on the empathy of others. He wouldn't stop as the head of the MIU, either. No. He had his eye on the very top. Jeremy had laid favours in his career. Said yes to the right people when it was required. Pushed narratives and political agendas. He was in favour with those he needed, and they were in his pocket. He could smell the pay rises, promotions, and power right now. Then there was the house. With Mary out of the way, he could sell it for pure profit with the way the markets were going. And no one would question it either. Why would he want to live in that place? Too many bad memories. Then, when done, he would disappear. He would move to the other side of the world and spend his retirement years on the beach with a glass of brandy in his hand, knowing that everything had fallen into place, and all it took was Laura Warburton repeatedly messing up her life and Jeremy to capitalise on the opportunity.

There was nothing the police could do to pin this on him.

But little did Jeremy know, it wasn't just the police that were watching him.

He pulled up to the Premier Inn hotel and took out his overnight bag and the small bottle of brandy he had purchased on the way. He was eager for a drink, and he did eye up the larger bottles. But a loose mind means a loose mouth, and he needed to be very careful from here on out. He remembered interviewing a killer a few years back. Some gangland hit man who had played too much Grand Theft Auto. He said on interview, looking Jeremy dead in the eyes, that 'If you ever kill someone, you can never, ever tell a single soul. Not one. Ever.' Jeremy thought it to be an odd piece of advice, and yet here he was, running that same phrase around his mind like a song he couldn't get out of his head.

He walked through the front doors of the hotel. The receptionist, brunette, around twenty-two, with glasses and fair skin, looked up from the desk as he walked in.

"Welcome to the Premier Inn," she said. Her voice was soft, yet the cadence went higher at the end, almost as if asking him why the hell he was here when he could stay anywhere else in the world.

"I have a reservation," Jeremy said. "Jeremy Marriott." The receptionist typed away on the computer that looked older than her.

"I have you here," she said. She stood and looked through a filing cabinet that had the keys filed away, fingering through them. Jeremy looked at her arse in her tight pants. He imagined what she looked like naked, and blood flooded to his cock, and he could feel his old pecker awakening at the thought of young, fresh meat. In his marriage with Mary, the first thing to die was sex. She didn't seem interested, and Jeremy was always working. Their marriage had died a long time before Jeremy crushed her windpipe.

The receptionist turned and handed him the key to his room. Jeremy eyed her breasts poking through the gaps in her shirt between her buttons. She was wearing a white bra, but she didn't strike Jeremy as a virgin. No. This girl *loved* to fuck. He could practically feel her lips caressing his dick as she smiled at him.

"No problem," he said. He took the key and eyed her a moment longer, savouring the sight of her. "Do you do room service?" He said. The receptionist smiled at him.

"Yes," she said. Jeremy nodded.

"Good," he said, his flabby unshaved face rising into a grin. "I might call you up to my room later."

The hallways were quiet, like driving down an empty road. Old and chipped tables that looked like they have been painted repeatedly, to keep them looking new, lined the hallways.

Jeremy took the lift and headed up to the second floor.

He moved through the heavy fire doors and down the hallway.

He could hear the sweet sounds of fucking coming from one of the rooms. He hovered his ear an inch away from the door. Moaning and grunting. It sounded like a real party in there. Jeremy smiled. His room was right next door. He had his own private viewing to the show.

He swiped his card and slipped inside, closing the door behind him. His body buzzed, like someone had set his veins to vibrate.

The room was nothing special. Small, but enough. The iron's plug was bolted to the outlet and coat hangers hooked to the rail with round, theft proof aluminium heads. The bathroom was brightly lit, and he looked at himself in the mirror. He looked the part of the was grieving husband. Bags drooped under his sunken eyes. His skin dull. The whiskers on his chin were unruly and dishevelled. Although he was nearing fifty, he had never looked, or felt, older in his life.

He moved to the bed, threw his bag on the mattress, and lay on it. It smelt a little musty, and he didn't know if the sheets were just pulled tight, or they resulted from days of sweat and bodily fluids that had simply hardened on them. He never liked hotels. A little-known fact to the public was the number of suicides and human trafficking that occurred inside them. Jeremy could say, with almost absolute certainty, that every hotel room someone stayed in had either had a suicide or a rape inside its walls. That was why you couldn't ever get a goodnight sleep inside them. Because the ghosts of the dead were watching you.

Jeremy lay back and listened to the muffled sounds of the people next door screwing. He unzipped his fly and took out his member, and began stroking it.

He finished quickly. Quicker than he would ever admit, and moved to the bathroom to clean himself off. When finished, he pulled out the bottle of brandy, cracked the cap and swigged right from the bottle. He grimaced then drank another finger's worth of the brown liquid. His gums went numb, and he felt the tightness in his muscles relax.

He turned on the news. The first thing that showed up was an aerial view of the Pennington Flash, where CSI tents were still working. Then, it flicked to his home, and reporters outside talking to cameras and reporting on what had happened. The face of Mary flashed up on the screen, and Jeremy felt his heart pause. A photo of her looking done up and lovely. It was then; he felt his eyes beginning to burn.

"What have I done?" He whispered, like a dark cloud closing in on him. The photo reel continued to move, showcasing pictures of the woman he had shared a bed with for the last twenty years, and who he had murdered in that same bed.

It flicked to a press conference that was being held. Superintendent Bill Bennett was standing there, dressed in his black tunic and hat. Shirt and pants freshly pressed. The crowns on his shoulders were prominent, like bulging cysts.

"We are deeply saddened by the loss of Mary Marriott," he said. The sounds of camera shutters going off and flashes of light striking him. "We have someone in custody, and they are being questioned at this time." He looked up at the crowd of reporters. "We are not yet saying that the latest homicide is connected with the other deaths we have had. We do not know at this time if these are connected, or if this is a copycat."

Copycat.

The word slammed into Jeremy's mind. They were onto him. He knew it. He took another mouthful from his bottle.

"At this time, I must urge anyone with any information to come forward. If you have seen something that appeared strange, or you know something and you don't know if you should come forward, then please, you must help us. No matter how insignificant. No matter how trivial. We want to know what you have to say."

Jeremy stared at the screen. Could he be assured that he had covered all his tracks perfectly? That not a single person had spotted him driving near the Flash or seen him in the compound? Could he be certain, beyond a shadow of a doubt, that no one would place him somewhere he said he wasn't?

No. The answer was no.

Jeremy sat up, watching the screen intently as Bennett began taking questions.

"Is DI Laura Warburton still working on the case?" One reporter asked.

"I cannot comment on that," Bennett said, batting the questions off with the same dignity as a politician. "Next?" He gestured to another reporter.

"Is this the work of the Butcher?" One piped up, followed by more rumbles of cynicism.

"We are not yet saying that these are connected," Bennett said.

"How long is this going to go on for?" The reporter blurted out. "Why haven't the police got someone in custody for these crimes?"

"We are pursuing all possible leads. Our detectives are working around the clock on every possible lead that presents itself. In the meantime, we must remain vigilant, and keep ourselves safe. We have increased our patrols to ensure public safety and be a very visible presence in the community."

More questions were fired at Bennett, and Jeremy didn't think he saw a flicker of doubt or a drop of sweat grace his brow. The man was composed and collected. Something Jeremy could only envy.

He darted up from his bed and stuffed his clothing into his bag. He needed to relocate. The cops knew he would stay here. They could have bugged the room for all he knew. A copycat killer. They knew something was up. He looked at his reflection in the bedside mirror. Was there a camera in there? Had he said something to himself that could implicate him? They had watched him pleasuring himself, and then watched him drinking and watching the news. He felt a wave of paranoia rush through him. He moved to the mirror, trying to look behind it. Adrenaline filled him, and he hurled the brandy bottle at his reflection, smashing the glass. In a frenzy, Jeremy began pulling away the shards, hoping desperately to find a camera or a listening device. But nothing showed. He checked his hands. He was bleeding.

"Fuck!" He hissed, and ran to the bathroom, picking out tiny diamonds of glass from his fingers. He put a tea towel in his mouth and tore at it, creating a thick, makeshift bandage.

He turned his attention to the bed, pulling away from the headboard and flipping the mattress. Still, there was nothing. He was losing it. Losing his mind. He knew it. He had to keep a lid on it.

Still, he couldn't stay here. Even if they weren't on to him right now, they soon would be. He was a sitting duck.

He stopped in his frenzy like a squirrel caught in headlights. He listened as he heard the lift doors open and then close. Footsteps, slow and deliberate, moved down the corridor, through the heavy fire door that slammed shut, and then towards his room.

Jeremy picked up a shard of jagged glass from the broken mirror and stood waiting, staring at his hotel room door.

He breathed long and slow, his nerves taut. He waited for the door to blast open, and the laser sights of rifles to dance around his body like fireflies.

The footsteps drew closer, and his grip on the shard grew tighter. The blood from the gash in his hand seeping down his arm and dripping onto the floor. He couldn't go to prison. He wouldn't last a day. He would take his own life if they came for him. Drive the shard so deep into his jugular and then snap it off and dive out the window.

The footsteps moved past his room and continued down the hall. He felt relief unlike anything else. He was being stupid. Being ridiculous. The police may have thought someone else was involved, but that didn't mean they were pointing the finger at him.

He sat back down on the bed and reassessed his situation. He had to stay put. To suddenly move location would be a bad move. It would raise further suspicion.

Innocent people don't run, he thought. *Stay here. Jump through the hoops. Answer their questions.* He looked around the room. The glass. The blood on the floor. He needed to clean this mess up and quickly.

The sound of sex from next door had stopped.

He got up, composed himself, and began cleaning up the shards, picking them up one by one, and putting them in the waste bin by the desk that jutted out of the wall.

He stopped dead. Something was wrong. He could hear it. Coming from the room next door. The sound of screaming. Calling for help.

Like instinct from his twenty-plus years in the job, Jeremy raced out of the hotel room to where the screaming was coming from. The same room he had heard screwing.

He hammer-fisted the door, painting the wood in droplets of blood from the gash in his hand.

"Police!" He shouted. "Open the door!" The booming of the wood and his shouts echoing through the corridor.

At the end of the hallway, someone appeared. A figure, broad and tall, with a cleaning trolley.

"Hey!" He screamed. They didn't hear him. Jeremy saw

the headphones on the figure's head. "Hey!" He shouted again, the screaming still coming from the bedroom. The cleaner didn't respond, moving in and out of another room with fresh bedding. They had no idea what was happening just a few yards away. Jeremy could run and get their attention, explain what was happening, tell them to call for help, but that would take too long. He needed to get inside that room right now.

Jeremy weighed up the door, and seeing no alternative, took a step back and drove his boot into the door just below the handle as hard as he could. He saw it come away slightly, and then, with another strong boot, it came away completely, bouncing off the wall. He raced in.

"Hello!" He screamed. He stood in an empty room. The bed was freshly made. Cleaning utensils were on the floor.

No bags. No belongings. No signs of life. The television on the wall was loud, the screaming coming from a woman in some horror movie. No. Jeremy saw. His heart stopping. It wasn't a horror movie. It was camera footage. Camera footage of someone having their eyes blowtorched out.

"What the hell?" Jeremy began, before the sound of the door being closed, and the plastic bag was shoved over his head. He struggled, kicking out, breathing heavily. His breath slowing. Straining. The plastic filling his mouth. Body becoming heavy and limp as he clawed at this assailant. Then the world fell away, and all went black.

CHAPTER TWENTY – SIX

LAURA

Laura chewed on her nails until she drew blood, spitting out the fragments onto the cell floor. They had been gone for God knows how long. The words Francis said racing around her mind, like someone was rampaging through an antique store with a baseball bat and a bad attitude.

Face to face with a murderer. Francis was the last real friend she had. Jeremy. Catherine. They had burned their bridges with her. Now Francis had turned his back on her. Whoever was setting her up was making sure that she was completely and utterly alone.

Laura picked up the book that was open on the floor and threw it against the wall. It landed open on a page, and she did that many laps around the cell. She was going crazy, sitting there waiting. Endless waiting in a timeless void. Even the sounds of the outside world had gone mute. The lights of her cell dimmed to resemble a strange kind of twilight. It was as if she was in a locked box that was floating through space. Never to be seen again. Never to be heard. Just locked in her own mind, where the only company was her screams. How long were they going to leave her sitting there waiting? Were they hoping she would crack up and confess? Were they going to catch Gabriel and hope that he confesses to everything that happened and clear Laura's name? She had the world against her, and not a single person she could turn to. Maybe she needed to speak to Jason? Maybe he was innocent in all of this? Maybe Laura had got it wrong, and he was actually her only friend left in the whole world that could help her and clear her name? But was she just using him again? She didn't love him. There was nothing between them other than flesh and sweat.

Had she lost him, too? Had her emotions, or lack thereof, caused her only lifeline to sink into the sea?

Sink into the sea.

He fell overboard.

Did he?

The memory of her nightmare coming back. Laura stopped pacing. It wasn't working anymore. She needed something harder. She dropped to the ground and placed her fists on the floor. The hard ground pressed against the knuckles and the pain made her wince. She lifted her legs onto the bed, and she did push-ups instead. Counting through gritted teeth and a burning chest. The fire in her muscles igniting her anger.

She was the one trapped in a cell for something she didn't do. She was the victim of a psychopath who had tried to destroy her life and made her move to the other end of the country. She was the one who's ex tried to poison her. She was the one who had fought every step of the way to make sure that Clara Weaver didn't go to prison after years of abuse at the hands of her partner. She was the one who Jeremy had tried to screw over to help his own career. She was the shit. She was the flame.

She was the mother fucking detective inspector of the MIU that had walked through the fire and enjoyed the damn heat.

She did more push-ups, moving past the number on the page and kept going. Her arms shaking, her triceps burning like someone was pressing a hot iron into her flesh. She pressed on, gritting her teeth. Pushing. Heaving. Forcing through shaking arms and burning lungs to the top of the final rep. She was the woman they should be afraid of, and she was going to make sure they all knew it.

She stood up, wiping the sweat from her forehead, and moved to the intercom on the wall. She pressed it, not taking her finger off it, until finally someone came to the door.

"What?" The detention officer said.

"I want my solicitor," Laura barked.

"You said you didn't –"

"I changed my mind," Laura blasted in the dark. Red faced and panting. "Now get my solicitor. I want one right now." The detention officer rolled her eyes and shut the cell door, muting the light.

She turned, facing the wall, and considered her next option. Gabriel wanted her, and he didn't get her. Meaning there were a few things that would have happened.

The first, they caught him where they thought he was. But he wasn't stupid, and he didn't want to be caught. So that was dead in the water.

The second possibility was that Gabriel was never where

they thought he was going to be, and that this was all a wild goose chase.

The third, and most likely option, was that they went there to find him, and he saw Laura wasn't there with him, and he set a trap.

Set a trap.

Like a shattering of glass, Laura found clarity. She rushed to the intercom and pressed it again. She pressed and pressed like it was giving out free fifties at the cashpoint. This time, the flap went down in the cell door.

"Your solicitor is on her way," the detention officer said.

"I need to speak to DCI Burnell," Laura barked. The detention officer laughed in her face.

"You have no chance," she said. "She's on a call. Dealing the with a case that *you* were supposed to be sorting. Thanks for nothing, by the way. To think, I trusted you. Even looked up to you, and here you are in this damn place, rotting like the –" Laura raced to the door and slammed her hands against the cell.

"It's a trap!" She screamed. "Gabriel. It's a trap and he'll see that I am not there. It's a game! It's all a game. Whatever Burnell is planning, tell her to stop right now!" The detention officer's face turned from smirking to horror in the blink of an eye.

"How do you –"

"Just trust me," Laura said. "The longer you keep me in here, the more things will go wrong, and more people will die. Tell Burnell to pull whatever cops she has out of wherever they're going and to…" Laura shook her head.

"Just fucking get her here, now!"

CHAPTER TWENTY – SEVEN

CATHERINE

Catherine stood in horror, slack jawed and mouth open wide, staring at the body camera footage on the sergeant's screen. The blast, or whatever it was, had knocked out the microphone, meaning that she was watching a terrifying, silent movie. She snatched the radio from the table and pressed it to her mouth. The response sergeant was frozen. Burnell's face had turned to white snow.

"Can anyone hear me?" Catherine shouted down the radio. The office's eyes were on her. She looked at the officers standing there, slack jawed. "Go!" she screamed. Go now!" Like a fire alarm had just been raised, the entire station emptied, and a flurry of sirens and revving engines filled the air.

"Dispatch," a gravelly voice cut through the radio silence. Catherine's nerves shot.

"We're here," she said. "What can you see?"

The line went open again. The sound of screaming. Wails of agony. Coughing and spluttering.

The camera, once black, came back into focus as it pulled up from the ground. PC Simon Foster crawled back to his feet. His camera taking in the sights through the dust and smoke.

Devastation. Blood. Arms ripped from sockets. Faces of

the fallen. Mouths wide and fixed in silent screams. Simon moved quickly, the torch from his helmet bouncing around the grey and black like a lighthouse cutting through thick fog.

"I've got multiple casualties," he said breathlessly. "Several officers down," he was straining. Trying to sound calm while the world around him was on fire. "I need more patrols. I need medical support. Fuck..." He said. "Fuck, I ... I need everything."

An officer lying on the ground came into focus. His face bloodied. Shoulder nothing more than a gored stump. The bone sticking out like a jagged, bloodied tooth, and the flesh around the wound was black like charcoaled pork. His face covered in claret. He let out a long, silent scream. His teeth were missing, like shattered tombstones.

PC Simon Foster's hands patted him down, tearing open clotting agents and pouring them into the open wound. The gloves on his hands torn open, pawing at the officer on the ground, stuffing fingers into holes that were bursting with blood like small guizers, soaking his black body armour. He slipped off his belt quickly and tied it around the officer's bloodied stump, trying to quell the bleeding.

Catherine and the response sergeant could only imagine what he was saying. What lies he was telling. That he would be okay, and help would be there soon. Catherine swallowed hard as she saw the camera pan to the where the officer's leg used to be, and as he wrapped another tourniquet above the knee and twisted it until it resembled a crumpled aluminium can.

Catherine called up to the control room.

"We need ambulances," she said, her voice not sounding like her own.

"How many?" The operator said. Catherine swallowed hard, forgetting what it felt like to have moisture in her mouth.

"All of them…"

PC Simon Foster moved from the screaming officer to another body. The camera moving past the chair where the bomb had gone off. Only the woman's hands were visible. The rest resembling a gore filled sight of charred meat and bone. Simon found another officer.

"Simon," Catherine called down the radio. "Is there anyone else with you?" There was no response, and that silence was the worst sound she could have possibly imagined.

They watched the screen as Simon began CPR on an officer. Each compression expelling a fountain of blood from their mouth. Simon stopped, looking around, and abandoned the officer. He was already dead. Most of his stomach had been blasted open. He raced to another, and then another, doing what he could. Anything he could.

"I need more officers," Simon cut through, sounding broken. "I need more support." he was barely holding it together, running on nothing but adrenaline.

"Help is on the way," Catherine said. "We've got everyone on their way to you."

The response sergeant finally snapped to his senses, pulling himself away from the precise of madness, and got to work, directing resources and officers to where they needed to be. Liaising with senior officers that were watching from the high tower of headquarters. Burnell's face was still awash with horror, and as Catherine could see, her eyes told a story of guilt and shame.

The phone rang in Catherine's pocket. She felt it, not wanting to answer it. Without looking, she knew it was *him* calling her. Calling to taunt her. She took out the phone and her heart dropped. The number showing private. Catherine peeled herself away. She had to answer. She had no choice. She didn't think the sergeant even noticed. He was already throwing on his stab vest and grabbing a set of keys. He was halfway out the door before Catherine reached the double doors leading to the Quiet Room.

Catherine answered the phone.

"You monster!" She screamed. "Do you know what you have done?" Tears streaming down her face. "Those officers had families!"

"I told you to get me Laura Warburton," Gabriel said. Voice devoid of emotion.

"What does she have to do with this?" Catherine stammered, the response nearly flooring her. "Are you in love with her? Is that what this is about? Or did she arrest you on some stupid charge years ago and you want to settle the score? Is that what this is all about?"

"I don't feel such basic emotions," Gabriel said. "Revenge. Love. Hate." He let out a long breath. "They're so … primitive." The way he spat that last word made Catherine's skin curl. Popping the *'p'* like he was stepping on a swollen maggot. "Those officers that are moving to help their dead," Catherine's lip began to tremble. "There will be more pain. More dead. More offerings of agony to my lord. If you do not get Laura Warburton, then I will detonate another bomb and I will kill them all." Catherine thought of all the officers that raced out of the building. All the officers with families that were racing to a death trap to help their comrades. She felt her mouth turn acrid and her eyes widened. Her hand coming to her mouth.

"Don't…" That's all she could manage. "Don't. Please…" She knew her words were just wasted air. You can't reason with monsters.

"The Lord is the arm," Gabriel said. "And I am his sword. If you call up on your radio, I will know that you have warned them, and I will bring *everything* crashing down. You have been warned. Get me DI Warburton. I will call again, and if she does not answer, more offerings will be made." A sucking of breath through teeth, and Catherine knew he was smiling. "You have thirty minutes." The call went dead, and Catherine raced out of the office to her car like the Devil himself was on her back.

CHAPTER TWENTY – EIGHT

LAURA

The cell door pulled open, and Burnell stood there. Laura turned to her, pulling the nail out of her mouth that she had been chewing on. The end of her finger was raw and bleeding. She welcomed the pain. It's how she knew she was alive, not just breathing.

"You have to let me out of here!" Laura said, moving to Burnell. "It's a trap! I have to go!" Laura rampaged, but she stopped dead when she saw the look on Burnell's face. Her hair was messed up, like she tried to pull it out by the fistful. Her eyes were red, raw. Her face was ashen. Once proud and formidable, her stance now resembled that of a broken, defeated person. When her eyes met Laura's, she started talking.

"They're dead," she said. The words were like a punch to Laura's temple, knocking her off balance. "I should have listened to you. He detonated a bomb. It killed three officers and another civilian that was being held there." Laura's legs turned into rubber, and she leaned against the wall, only to collapse onto the floor like a broken doll. In a burst of agony, her heart exploded, causing her to cry out in prolonged anguish. Clutching her knees to her chest, she cried in quick, painful gasps.

They were dead. They were dead, and she tried to stop

it. But no one listened to her. She should have fought harder. Reasoned. Bargained. Anything. They were dead, and it was her fault.

"You sent those officers to that place," she croaked. "You knew he wanted me. He was playing us. He was playing us every step of the way. He knew I wouldn't go, and because of that, he killed those officers." Laura grabbed a fistful of her hair and clenched her eyes shut. "This blood is on your hands, Burnell. Not mine," she hissed. "You knew what he was going to do. And still you sent them without me."

"I'm sorry…" Burnell said. Words as mute as a bird's cry in a hurricane. "He knew we were tracing the call. He knew we would come, and you wouldn't be there." Then, a thought crashed into Laura's mind.

"He said, *'Old hooks call for cold cuts, for all they see around them is dust,'*" Laura gasped. The rage returned, and Laura got to her feet and marched to Burnell, stabbing her finger at her like a spear hungry for blood. "Cold cuts. Cold cuts of meat. Dead bodies. Death, death, and fucking death. All they see around them is dust. *A bomb.* He told us from the very beginning what would happen if we went there. We thought he was being cryptic about his location. But he knew we would trace the call. He knew we wouldn't solve the riddle and would jump the gun and that I wouldn't be there. He told us right from the start, and you were too arrogant to listen."

"I didn't know…" Burnell croaked, her voice like a scream in a violent wind. Lost. Lost to the void, barely audible.

"He's toying with us until we give in and play by his rules," Laura said, shocked by her own words. "We have to do what he says." Laura let out a long, deflated breath. All she did was fight. Fight her friends. Her colleagues. Her demons. Now, fighting was making it worse. She had to concede. "He's in control," she said, defeated. "Not us. We need to stop fighting and just play his game. It's the only way to stop him." Burnell took a deep breath.

"Why does he want you so *badly?*" Burnell said, almost sounding envious. "Why are you so special?" Laura shook her head.

"I don't know. Maybe because the media has plastered my face in every newspaper, on every single channel. Maybe he wants to see if I can catch him, or if he will win. He's some kind of religious nutcase, right? Calls himself *Gabriel.* He must see this as a fight between gods and monsters. But to him, we are the monsters. The Devils. The heretics, and he is the messenger from God, or whatever the fuck he worships. It's like in his mind, this is some kind of reckoning. The last fight against hell on earth." They both fell silent then. Laura composed herself. "So, what now?"

Burnell rested her back on the cell wall. Her bloodshot eyes were filled with tears that streamed down her face. She stared at her hands, knowing she could never wash the blood off them. Her gaze met Laura's, and whispered -

"I need you to tell me what we need to do."

Footsteps boomed loudly as someone ran down the hallway, catching the attention of the two women.

Catherine stood there, her face flushed red, thrusting a phone at Laura.

CHAPTER TWENTY – NINE

FRANCIS

Francis arrived back home and threw his coat on the chair. He turned on the light of his kitchen and sat down, staring at the wall. He checked the time. He wasn't due off duty for another few hours. But fuck it. He might as well just call it a day now. His career was over. Everything he had worked for, gone up in smoke. He was in his forties. Worked the frontline of policing for the best part of twenty years and was on the last stretch before retirement. Paid into his pension every month, even though it took up a giant chunk of his wage. All for the promise of retiring early, with a good amount of money coming into his bank account for the rest of his life.

That was what had kept him in the police force for so long. The pension. The golden egg of policing. That when you're done, you're set for the rest of your life.

He decided he couldn't be doing nights anymore, and he needed a change. After completing his detective exam, his colleagues on the team were shocked when he left. He traded the adrenaline-filled fast car chases and the battered, bloodied body armour that had witnessed the darkest aspects of humanity, and was going to swap it for comfortable clothing and desk work. He had chewed on the idea for many months before signing up for the exam.

He studied hard, but he wasn't the most academic of officers. Francis joined the police force due to his excellent communication skills and street smarts. Although he didn't perform well on the initial tests, they recognized his potential. His work on the front line, assisting victims, combined with his ability to tutor and train new officers, made him an incredibly effective officer to have on hand during emergencies. But the real reason he took the leap into the world of complex investigations wasn't the slower pace, the case files, the fighting with the CPS or the higher level of detail he must learn to pay attention to. It was that when he was sitting there at his desk, staring into his cold cup of coffee, sleep deprived and barely able to construct a thought, he had seen her walk into the office, and he felt his heart stop.

Laura Warburton. The mysterious, yet infamous DI from the Metropolitan police. Whispers of her arrival had been spreading around the office, and even a few headlines that were shown to Francis before she landed. He thought her to be some kind of biblical deity. Foretold by the masses that she would come and save them all from their damnation.

Her eyes pierced through him as she was cut through the office on her first day at the MIU. Exotic was the perfect word to describe her. An exotic animal with hair like fire and eyes of ice.

When the vacancy came up on the MIU, Francis leapt at the chance to work under her and get to know her.

To fall in love with her.

He shook his head. Pulling himself from his thoughts.

Her hair was like fire, and as he had found out, if you play with fire, you get burned. He had let his feelings for her cloud his judgement. He had never told her how he felt. Nor would he ever. He was single, earned less than her, over ten years older and he lived on his own in a two up, two down terrace house and drove a fifteen-year-old Vauxhall Corsa which hadn't been cleaned since the conservative government last got in. And thanks to her allure, his career was over. He had nothing, and the woman he had risked it all for had burned him beyond recognition.

But now, as he sat alone in that dark space of solitude and despair, his thoughts turned bleak.

He stood up and walked to his fridge and grabbed a can of lager that was chilling on the middle shelf. The shelf was sandwiched between meat that had turned grey from working late nights and vegetables that had browned and leaked their rotting juices. The bottom of the fridge held a puddle of stringy and repugnant liquid. Francis cracked open the can, the hiss breaking the surrounding silence, and took a long drink. The booze burned his throat, and he let out a long, satisfied sigh.

He sat back down at his kitchen table. The thoughts in his mind growing teeth. He was single. Childless. Loveless. *Hopeless*. He had given his life to the police, and he had been hung out to dry. He had been suspended, and if Burnell had her way, she would ensure that she burned every memory of Laura Warburton from the Wigtown constabulary. Laura was done, and he was next. His pension vanishing before him. The last twenty years of dedication up in smoke, because he was trying to win the heart of an unlovable woman.

Francis finished the can and took out another, sinking it twice as fast. He cried. He cried, and he drank until he could feel only numb.

The more he drank, the more vicious the thoughts in his mind grew. He sucked in a sharp breath and wandered to the bathroom. His face was unrecognisable in the mirror. His skin was washed out. His eyes were red and swollen. Wrinkles were etched deep into his face, like crevasses, making him look like a man ten years his senior.

He pulled open his bathroom cabinet and pulled out the straight razor. He studied it in his hand. Its handle was made of rosewood. Smooth. Well crafted. The sharp blade's one long tooth glinted in the bathroom light.

He held it to his throat. Just one quick cut is all it would take. Not much pressure was needed. It took less than fifteen seconds to bleed out from a severed jugular.

His knuckles grew white as he gripped the handle. There were five litres of blood in the human body, and he would paint his bathroom with every drop. His eyes stared back at him, filled with pain, loss, and desperation.

He swallowed hard. His Adam's apple bobbed against the blade of the straight razor, cutting his skin. He winced at the sharp pain as it nicked him and pulled the razor away. Through weary eyes, he observed the drop of blood falling into his bathroom sink and began to spread around the porcelain, growing small streams that spread like translucent blood worms, and vanished down the drain.

The realisation sobered him.

He dropped the razor onto the floor where it rattled. The sound faded, enveloping him in silence and stillness.

"She was right," he said, his tongue like sandpaper. He clutched the sides of the sink basin.

Follow the blood.

"Jeremy," he whispered, like the utterance of the next syllables out of his mouth would be an act of treachery, and he would be condemned to hell. "Jeremy. It's all Jeremy."

CHAPTER THIRTY

LAURA

Catherine thrust the phone at Laura.

"Answer it!" Catherine urged. Laura looked at Catherine like she had been handed a screaming infant.

"Who is it?" She said in disbelief.

"It's him!" Laura filled with horror.

"What does he want?"

"Just fucking answer it!" Catherine urged. "Before more people die!" Like grabbing a life ring on a sinking ship, Laura snatched the phone out of Catherine's hand and hit ANSWER.

"Gabriel!" Laura blurted. "Gabriel. It's me. Laura. I'm here." At first there was nothing, and then the sound of heavy breathing filtered through the receiver. Laura waited for him to speak, trying to keep her own breathing under control. She watched Burnell and Catherine stare at her, like they were watching an execution, waiting for the trapdoor to open. Still, Laura held her nerve.

"You didn't come." He said, his voice was like a growl in the night. Laura noticed it then. Laura's skin came alive, her body ravaged by an icy chill that made its bed in her bones.

"I was occupied," Laura said. "Why did you kill those officers?"

"I would have killed many more if you didn't answer this call. Well done. You saved their lives."

"Why are you doing this?" Laura said, tightening her jaw.

"Because I can," he said. "Because you can't stop me." Laura clenched her fist.

"Why me, Gabriel?" She said. "What do you want from me?"

"Your armour, as shiny as it is portrayed, is littered with cracks."

"What does that mean?" She said.

"All will become clear soon." Shuffling of movement. Then he whispered, "I am Death, and I have found my home." Laura swallowed. "Are you tracing this call?"

"No," she said with finality. The sound of wind. The distant caw of a bird on the call. Laura focused on it.

"More offerings were made to the Lord," Gabriel said. "You could have saved them. But you refused." Laura's body was shaking, trying to contain her emotions. The urge to scream. To smash the phone against the walls of the custody cell. But she held her nerve. Right now, she had to play *his* game, or more would die. She had to do what she never wanted to do. Do nothing. Do nothing, and just listen.

"I didn't refuse to come," Laura said, snaking an eye to Burnell. "I was unable to."

"Locked in a cell," Gabriel said. Laura felt the air suck out of her lungs.

"How did you know?"

"I watched," Gabriel said. "From afar. I watched as you

were taken. I want you out here, with me. I need you."
Laura pinched the bridge of her nose.

"You knew I couldn't come, and you asked anyway."
She said, her mouth turning dry. "You set us up."

"No," he said. "One thing I am not, Laura, is a liar. I
asked you to come. It was those around you that refused
to listen. The blood of those men is not on your hands,
but on theirs. If you were able to come, I would have
given you the girl. Freewill is an illusion," he said. "The
forces that control our lives give us the illusion that we
may come and go as we please, until we find ourselves
wrapped in chains, and our freedom is no more." The
sound of chains rattling. A door slamming shut. Wind
against the receiver. Laura focused on it all. "Tell me,"
Gabriel said. "Will your superiors make you stay and rot
further after they have seen a display of my power? Or
will they swallow their pride and allow you to walk free
and come to me?" Laura considered this. Given by the
look of death stitched onto Burnell's face, Laura could
ask her to hand over her home to her and she would be
ready with the keys.

"Tell me what I need to do." Laura said. A beat of
laughter.

"The next offering is ready. Ready for consumption of
the Lord. A man. A sack of meat filled with his own
delusions. A man so blinded by his own pride, he has
been consumed by it. Rage infects him, and that rage
destroyed all he is and all who will be. Rage that has bled
into the very essence of who he is, and all that touch him
are encumbered by it." Laura clenched her eyes. She was

quickly growing bored with the riddles and theatrics.

"Tell me where this *offering* is," she said. "Tell me, and I will do as you say."

"If you try to deceive me again, I will unleash hellfire." The words made Laura's stomach twist, like someone was grabbing her insides and trying to pull them out of her throat.

"How do I know you aren't lying?" Laura said and began pacing on the spot. Catherine and Burnell eyed her like she had just taken a shit on a war memorial. Laura raised her hand.

I know what I am doing, she said with her eyes. Catherine began chewing her nails. Burnell glared at Laura, like she was looking down the barrel of a gun.

"How do I know that this isn't another trap?"

"I do not lie, Laura," Gabriel said. "I have evolved beyond such mortal flaws."

"Cut the shit!" Laura barked. She couldn't hold it back anymore. "Enough of the riddles, the ploys, the games. I have a headache and I am going crazy listening to your voice." She was breathing quickly. "Let me speak to them. This *offering,* so I know that they're alive." The line went quiet. Laura focused on a point on the wall.

"Very well," Gabriel said. A moment passed. Laura's body tense. Ready to hear the voice of someone that was about to die.

"Laura…" The voice floored her. She put her hand to her mouth. Her lip trembling. *It was Jason.* "You need to help me," Jason whispered. "He has a gun."

"Jason," Laura said, her mouth quivering. Catherine's

eyes snapped open, and she steadied herself on the cell wall. Her face draining of colour. She moved to Laura. Moved to the phone and went to take it. Laura pulled it away, but Catherine couldn't control herself. She snatched the phone out of Laura's hand and pressed it to her ear.

"Jason!" Catherine barked. "Baby! Talk to me! Where are you?"

"Give the phone back to DI Warburton," Gabriel said.

"Give it here, Catherine!" Laura urged, lunging for the phone.

"Fuck you!" Catherine screamed to Laura. "Gabriel," Catherine wailed. "Let Jason go, now!" Laura moved in. Catherine pushed her away. Laura stumbled, falling onto her back on the cell bed. She rallied, racing to Catherine. But it was too late.

"Very well," Gabriel said. "Be free of your fleshy prison," he said. "And may you meet the Lord on the other side." Laura was an inch from her, her arm darting for the phone, when she heard the gunshot explode, and Catherine screamed.

CHAPTER THIRTY – ONE

LAURA

Catherine's scream tore through Laura like a hail of bullets, shredding her to her core. She caught Catherine as she crumpled to the ground, melting into herself like a plastic bag thrown to the flames.

Catherine felt Laura's touch, and in her despair, she thrashed, punched, hit and clawed at any part of Laura that she could find. But Laura took it, wrapping her arms around her tightly.

"I'm sorry…" Laura whispered quickly. "I'm so, so sorry," and she meant every syllable. What started as a simple affair of lust had now turned deadly. Like a stone thrown into still water, Laura's actions had first created ripples, then giant waves that devoured all around her. "It will be okay," she lied. But she knew the truth. Nothing would *ever* be okay again.

It was the only thing she could say when she knew that there was no hope, like the light had vanished from the sun.

She had said those words so many times in hopeless situations. When she was on scene to someone bleeding out on the hard pavement after getting stabbed, and the ambulance was miles away. When someone was turning pale, weary-eyed and barely holding on inside the mangled wreckage of a car after being totalled by an HGV. When she lay on the brow of that boat in South Africa. The heavens pouring onto her, Ron's screams dying away as the ocean swallowed him whole. *It will be okay, it will be okay*, she would say, knowing every syllable was a lie. Nothing would be okay. Never, ever again. There was no turning back this time, and from the look of anguish on Catherine's face, she knew that the same woman that crumbled to pieces on the floor in her arms would not be the same woman that stood back up.

"Amy," Laura said, turning to Burnell, who was staring into the distance. Her eyes two empty voids. Catherine's sobs turned into rabid stabs of air. "Amy!" Laura snapped. Amy Burnell came back to life like someone had flipped a switch. They shared a stare. They knew what needed to be done. Burnell nodded. She righted herself and sucked in her tears.

"Right," Burnell said. "I'll speak to the sergeant." She turned out the door, then, with one last glance to Laura, said, "you're free to go."

It had gone late evening, and the sun had retreated and darkness and befallen the earth. Laura sat in the office of the MIU. Her eyes tired and stinging. Catherine had been let go for the day. She was driven home by a uniformed officer. They said she didn't speak a single word during the car ride, like they were driving home a statue made of flesh. Hair. Breath. There was nothing behind the eyes, as if the person's essence had disappeared. Laura pulled out the photographs and evidence of the crime scenes. Kacy's burned body. Mary's mutilated corpse. Rebecca's suffocated scream. Keller's dismembered limbs. Mariette's entrails wrapped around her throat. It was all deeply disturbing, but the most disturbing part of it all was Laura felt nothing looking through them. She knew how to bury her emotions and how to get the job done. They were just pictures in a photo book now. Nothing more. Nothing less. She dehumanised them to protect herself, because if she let herself break, she would never put herself back together.

She had her phone next to her, waiting in cas*e he* called.

The lights of the MIU office buzzed above her head. The distant sounds of phones ringing. Laura sparked up a cigarette at her desk. This was going to be a busy shift. She looked up. Burnell hardly seemed to notice. She was half looking at the caseload, struggling to hold back tears.

Laura smoked quietly. Her throat and nose savouring the burn. Since returning to the office, she hadn't spoken a word to Burnell. The last person on earth she wanted to be near was the one person she couldn't get away from. Jeremy was away somewhere. Catherine was useless right now. Laura had tried to call Francis, but she thought against it. He wouldn't want to speak to her, even if she was back on the case.

Laura finished looking through the photos, then placed them down on the desk. She lay back. She couldn't find any kind of pattern. Nothing was jumping out at her. The deceased were all different sexes. Different heights. From all different backgrounds. Some had either no or minor criminal records. Others were much more extensive. Why was Gabriel picking these people? Was it random? Or was there something else behind it and Laura wasn't seeing it?

She loaded up the cell site data from the numbers Gabriel had called from. It was like trying to pin down a moving target. He was using something to reroute the calls from the other side of the world. He was a disturbing creature, but he wasn't stupid. The sim card the number was linked to had been topped up remotely using crypto currency. There was no DNA evidence at the scene. No pattern. No communications data. No CCTV. Nothing. Gabriel was like a shadow. Like Death himself. The only thing that linked the deaths to him was the method of execution, in which the victims were strangled and tortured whilst still alive.

Laura thought back to his phone call. He was male. Possibly around ages thirty to fifty. His throat gravelly, implying he either was a smoker, had been a smoker, or he had had some throat surgery. But if he was this sophisticated with covering his tracks, then he could be using a voice masking software, which lead her back to square one which was up shit creek without a paddle. Did he have a background in forensics? Policing? Or had he just done his research? She was shooting arrows in the dark, hoping to hit a fly. She had *nothing* to go off. Not a single lead, and she was quickly running out of time. Every question she answered sprouted several more, always leading her back to square one. The phone by her side, sitting there silently, waiting for his next call.

She wasn't out of the woods yet. There was still the fact

that Mary's bloodied clothing had been found in her car. She did have a background in policing. In forensics. She was the perfect suspect, and although the force and the media were counting on her to stop Gabriel, she knew she was one fuck up away from being charged with murder. The force needed a scapegoat to get the public off their backs, and if Laura couldn't deliver, then she would be thrown into the fire herself.

She leaned forward. Case documents littered around her, putting the cigarette in her mouth, then brushing off the ash that fell onto the table. Her head in her hands.

Think, she thought to herself. *There must be something to go off. Something I had missed. Think back to the phone call. Did I hear anything?*

Then it dawned on her.

Birds. The sound of a bird cawing in the call's background. Something so simple, yet it gave so much. He was outside when he was talking. He would want somewhere isolated where no one would hear him or his victims. Birds and isolation. What kind of bird was it? A pigeon? No. Pigeons don't *caw.* A crow? A raven? Everything he did was cryptic but intentional. If there were birds in the distance, he would have wanted Laura to hear them. This was his game, and he was feeding her information. He was giving her a chance. He wanted her to play.

"What did he say?" Laura whispered, the cigarette burning close to her fingers. "Are we tracing the call? No. He wants to be found, but not through conventional means." Then, like a light in the dark, it came to her.

I am Death, and I have found my home.

She knew where he was.

Laura looked up to Burnell, who hadn't moved an inch, like a marionette that had had its strings severed, sitting broken in the corner.

"Amy," Laura said. Like a necromancer recounting an abyssal spell, Burnell raised her head like the reanimated dead.

"Yes…" she said, voice barely louder than a whisper. Laura stamped out the cigarette on the table, got up, and moved to her. Excitement in her voice.

"Now, this is going to sound crazy," she said. "But I think I know where he is," she said. "I need a list of every single graveyard, mortuary, forest, whatever!" Burnell looked confused.

"Why?" She said. Laura threw her trench coat on.

"I heard a caw on the phone and wind on the receiver. Only certain birds make a sound like that. A crow or a raven. He is playing a game, right? We can't trace him on the phone because he locked us out. It would take weeks to unravel it, by which time he would have changed numbers and moved again." Laura ran her hands through her hair. "Gabriel means *'God is my strength'*." He then told me on the phone, *'I am Death, and I have found my home.'* He needs somewhere isolated to do his work. He wanted us to hear the birds and the wind on the call. Maybe I am being too literal here," she said, "but it's all we have to go off." Laura grabbed her phone off the desk and held it up for Burnell to see. "In case he calls." She expected Burnell to say something. To argue against Laura's reasoning. To fight her on every detail. But she didn't. Instead, she nodded and gave a tight smile.

"Where are you going?" Burnell said, a hint of fear in her voice. "You aren't going to find him alone, are you?" Laura shook her head.

"No," Laura said as she moved to the door. "I'm going to get my best detective back."

CHAPTER – THIRTY – TWO

CATHERINE

Catherine lay in her bed wishing she could die. She wanted to cut the thought of Jason out of her mind like a festering tumour. What was happening? She couldn't believe it. She felt so damn betrayed, and it was tearing her apart. The gunshot. She wondered if he had felt pain. If Jason, in his last moments, had thought of her or had thought of Laura.

The thought of her name made her cringe. Her cheeks burned with tears. There was a sadistic killer out there, and Catherine couldn't tell the monsters from friends.

Catherine clenched her eyes shut. Jason. He had become the voice in her head, like the scratching of an insect inside her skull.

Her heart was being torn apart. She hated him, but she loved him too.

How was it possible to be in so much pain and still be breathing?

Catherine turned over in her bed. She didn't want to see anyone. Didn't want to think. Didn't want to be close to anything. She just wished to lie here in the dark and be consumed by it. She needed to sleep, but whenever she closed her eyes, she imagined Jason sitting there, his jaw hanging slack. Face bloodied, and brain matter leaking out of the wound in his skull.

The doorbell echoed in the surrounding silence. She bolted up and checked the time. It had gone midnight. Reality grabbed hold of her and shook some sense into her. She was alone, and someone was at her door in the depths of the night. She tried to quell the fear rising in her chest and lay back down.

The doorbell went again, twice in quick succession. Whoever it was knew she was home, and they weren't going away. She moved to the edge of the mattress, sliding her hand between the bed and the frame, and pulled out the kitchen knife she kept there.

She silently moved down the stairs, staring at the stretching blackness of the staircase. She could see the frosted silhouette of someone pressing their hand and face against the glass. She couldn't make out who it was. Should she call out? Turn the lights on? Call the police? Or did she simply sit in the dark and hope the monster at the door didn't get in?

Hard knocks in quick succession rattled Catherine's nerves, causing her to jump. She clutched the knife tighter in her fist.

"Go away!" She yelled, unable to contain her fright. She put her hand to her mouth, stifling her scream. Why did she do that? Now they knew she was home. Home, and alone in the dark to be taken.

She should call the police. Call Laura. She shook the thought from her head. No. Even if she was being gutted alive, she wouldn't ever call that whore again.

The door handle went again. They were trying to get in.

Whoever was on the other side was trying to get in. Catherine moved. Where had she put her mobile? Why did she insist on leaving it *outside* the bedroom and opt for an alarm clock instead? She couldn't turn on the lights. She couldn't make a sound. Her heart was in her throat. Her hands turning numb as she stared at the front door. The blackness morphing her vision. Blurring it. Invading and violating her psyche.

Just open the door, she thought. A deep, menacing thought that growled in her mind. *Open the door, little pig. Let that big bad wolf in.*

Time seemed to stand still. She had no backup. No way to call for help. If she went downstairs to get her phone, they would see her. It was her against whoever was banging on her door. She wasn't brave. No. She was terrified. A terrified lamb ready to be offered to *the Butcher.*

"Catherine!" The voice called. Her senses were ignited, pulled from her frozen state of terror. She recognised the voice. "Catherine! Open the door!" Like someone had hit play, Catherine moved to the door quickly and pulled it open.

The cold air outside hit her sweating body and chilled her to the bone. Francis was standing there. She had never been so happy to see him in her life.

"Fuck me!" Francis said, rubbing his hands together, supporting a file of papers under his arm. "I need to talk to you," Francis said. Blowing into his cupped red hands like trying to light an ember. Catherine regarded him.

Why was he here? Why wasn't he at the office? Why is he at my home this time of night? She saw the bloodstain on his neck and his collar. She held the knife behind her back. She couldn't trust anyone.

"What's going on?" She said.

"I need to come in and talk to you," he said, his teeth chattering together.

"Why do you have blood on your neck?" Catherine snapped. Francis gave her a confused look, then regarded the crimson on his shirt.

"Oh," he said. "I cut myself shaving," he said. "I thought I had cleaned it." He looked past her into the dark. He slapped the top of the file under his arm. "Can I come in?"

"How do I know I can trust you?" The words rocked Francis.

"What?" He said. "Look, Catherine. It's me, Francis. I don't know what you're worried about. Can I come in so we can talk?"

"What about?" Catherine said, ready to slam the door in his face. She could smell alcohol on his breath. A man turning up in the middle of the night stinking of booze when everyone around her wanted to hurt her. *Fuck that noise.*

"I don't want to discuss it out here," Francis said. "Catherine," he said, his voice laced with pleading.

"How do I know you won't hurt me?" She said, quickly. Francis' eyes went wide.

"Hurt you?" He said, looking around, like he was searching for the right words. "Catherine, I haven't ever hurt you. I know we're all on edge right now, but we can't fall apart." He looked at the file and then touched his throat. "I think Laura is innocent," he said. Catherine's eyes narrowed.

"Goodbye, Francis," Catherine said, ready to slam the door. Francis lunged forward, stopping the door with his hand.

"Just give me a second to explain!" Catherine regarded him with malice.

"Go on." Francis shivered and looked around him. He leant in, holding Catherine's gaze.

"I can't say anymore out here," he said hushed tone. Catherine rolled her eyes. Fingers going numb from holding onto the door.

"After all we have seen, you still think Laura—"

"I tried to kill myself," Francis blurted. Now, Catherine's eyes went wide, and that feeling of empty cold was washed away with warm empathy.

"What?" She stammered.

"Burnell fired me. I went home, drank a lot of beer, and was going to cut my throat with a straight razor. I realised something when the blade was by my neck. That's why I am bleeding. That's why I smell of booze. That's why I am standing here in the freezing cold with this file at your door in the middle of the night." Catherine eyed him. Her face turning numb from the cold. "So, please, can I come in? I'll catch my death out here." Catherine fought this over in her mind. Francis looked dishevelled. He had so much to say, and she knew him. He wouldn't be here if he wasn't desperate.

Catherine nodded and moved out of the way, and

Francis moved in, leaving hypothermia at the door and shook off the cold. Catherine locked the front door and turned the lights on in the house. Francis noticed the knife in her hand.

"You weren't kidding, were you?" He said, regarding the blade. Catherine paused and looked at the weapon.

"Let me make you a brew," she said, "then tell me everything."

SIN

From the moment we are born, the Lord watches us. Guides us. Gifts us life, and judges us with the choices we make. Some wander through the earth sleepwalking, crying over their wasted lives as they watch the ferryman come to take them away. Others squander their lives and they blame the world for their own choices. Others make the world a better place. They find God. They embrace pain and suffering. Others wish to see the world and the Lord's name burn. But you, Laura Warburton. You're the worst kind. You have fallen. You are a liar, and you hold that lie deep in your heart, trying to drown it with alcohol. But you can reclaim your wings. You can reclaim your grace.

I offer you this. This one chance to redeem your soul before it is too late. All the pain you have felt. All the suffering. The drinking. The spiralling. The trauma. It can all be undone if you simply confess. If you confess to what you have done.

You wanted blood. I will give you a massacre.

CHAPTER THIRTY – THREE

LAURA

TWELVE HOURS BEFORE THE OFFERING

Laura arrived outside of Francis' home. It was in complete darkness. She tried to call him, but his phone rang out.

He's dead, the voice in her said, as she pounded on his front door. *He believed in you, and now look what has happened? Why does everything you touch die? Why should he be any different?* Laura ignored the incessant whispering in her mind. But the longer she thrummed on the door, and the longer there was no signs of life inside that dark cocoon, the louder that voice got and the harder it was to ignore.

"Francis!" Laura shouted through the letter box. "Francis, it's Laura! I need you to come to the door." She took out her phone again and called Catherine. The phone rang out again. She cursed, then put the phone in her pocket.

This is all your fault, you know.

She froze. She turned her head. Celine was standing there. Her eyes were bowls of milk. Her face stretched into a long grin. Skin dull. Body covered in dirt and worms writhing on her muddied skin. *He's lying dead inside that cold, dark home, because of you.* The world spun, and Laura placed her hand on the door to stop her legs from giving out. She breathed heavily, closing her eyes.

"Keep it together," she whispered. "Just keep it together. You're losing your mind, but that's okay because I know it isn't real. It isn't real." She felt breath on her neck. Her body turned rigid, and those tightly clenched eyes flicked alive like blinds being snapped open.

Kiss, kiss.

Laura recoiled, spinning around, and looked at the silent street. The streetlights were bright. Casting shadows that were long and stretched along the ground. She was alone. The moon above her was bright. Its face etched in an eternal scream. She turned to the door again.

"Fuck this," she said, and she drove her foot into the door, rattling it against the frame. She did it again, and again, until the door came loose and bounced off the wall before rattling still.

The hallway was black, and Laura took a deep breath before stepping into the maw.

She moved through the dark and looked for the light switch. She found it, fingering aimlessly through the blackness, and flicked it.

Nothing. Just thick, all-consuming black. The streetlights were on, and some homes elicited a golden glow through their closed curtains. There was no power cut, which made Laura more apprehensive.

I am Death, and I have found my home.

Gingerly, Laura stepped further into the house, ensuring that the front door stayed open, giving her a glimpse of light. Her footsteps were muffled by the thin carpet. She took out her phone and turned on the torch.

She found the living room. Francis' house was spacious. Empty. He had few possessions. A two-seater couch made of grey fabric. A television hung on the wall. A few photo frames and an acoustic guitar in the corner that looked like it hadn't been played in years, given by the amount of dust that had gathered on the fretboard.

She moved into the kitchen and found several empty cans of lager on a small wooden table that was tucked into the wall. One of them had tipped over, spilling the amber fluid onto the tabletop. Laura looked around for any clues. Someone's home environment was a good indication of their state of mind. The sink was clear of dishes. She opened the fridge. A plethora of old vegetables that stank to high heaven. She thought he was trying to eat healthier, but from looking in his kitchen bin, she found that there were remnants of old pizza and chicken nuggets. Probably bought the fruit and vegetables in a *new year, new me* cleanse, and then reverted to old habits of fast food. Laura closed the fridge door, welcoming back the darkness.

"Marco!" The voice cut through her like an icy wind. Laura felt dread bubbling in her stomach, and then rise to her trembling lips. Laura turned on a dime and faced the blackness. Nothing was there. No teeth. No figures. Nothing. Was she losing it? She rubbed her eyes.

Something was happening to her. She shook the chills away.

Another few steps and she was back in the living room. She froze.

The guitar was now on the couch.

Laura stepped away from the instrument. Her back finding the wall. She swallowed hard, her torch raised in front of her, scanning the room.

I need to get out of here. I need to get out of here right now.

"Marco!" The voice came again, followed by the sounds of footsteps coming from above her. Laura placed a hand over her mouth, silencing her breath. She could run. She could call for backup, but she dared not move. Terror had gripped her, holding her in place. Knowing that at any moment, the dark could take shape, and something come walking out of it. She listened to the night. The silence. It made her ears ring out in between the heavy thumping of her heart.

She willed her legs to move, and after some convincing, they obeyed. She stepped slowly, the torch raised, cutting through the darkness.

She heard a door slam.

Laura rushed out to the hallway. The front door was closed. She ran to it.

No, no, no, no!

Desperately, she grabbed a hold of the handle and tried to force it open. She turned, pressing her back against the door. The blackness greeted her.

Come out, come out, wherever you are … It seemed to snarl.

She had no escape, and something was in here with her.

Watching and waiting in the dark.

With everything screaming at her to move, she had to press on. Francis could be in here and he could be hurt. Laura eyed the stairs. The rungs of the banister looked like dried bones.

Her foot found the bottom step, and against all preservation, she ascended.

Laura shone the torch at the closed doors on the landing. Each one could lead to an unveiling of horrors. But what choice did she have? She had to find Francis to make sure he wasn't lying on the cold floor with flies laying their eggs in his eyes. This was *her* fault, and if she didn't finish this, then she wouldn't ever forgive herself.

She stepped along the landing, and she pushed the first door open. It was a bedroom. Laura shone the light through. Her mind begging her not to go inside, but Laura moved anyway. Focused. Fighting back the fear that bubbled in her stomach. Her breath heavy. Strained. This was her redemption. Everyone thought her a killer. Everyone had turned their backs on her, and she needed to clear her name.

She looked in the wardrobe. Clear. Under the bed. Clear. Mentally checking off each place someone could hide a body.

"Marco!" The voice cut through again. Laura moved more determined, fuelled by adrenaline. No more being a frightened little girl in the dark. Either the voice was in her head, and she was having a psychotic breakdown, or the voice *was* real. Both possibilities were equally terrifying. She stood on the landing. Closed doors meeting her eye. She stood in the silent dark, waiting for the voice to call her.

"Marco!" Dead in front of her. She swallowed hard, and without giving herself time to run down the stairs and out into the street, she charged to where the voice was coming from.

Blood. Blood on the floor. On the sink basin. The shower curtain drawn. Blood on the edge of the bathtub. Tissues on the floor, like roses that had been drained of colour. A bloodied straight razor on the ground. Laura swallowed hard. No phantoms met her vision. No monstrous sights. No decaying lovers or whispers from the dead. The voice had come from this room.

Which left one possibility…

Laura shone her light onto the shower curtain. She worked her lips. Body tight. Hesitantly, she gripped hold of the shower curtain which felt like thin cold flesh in her hand. A million horrors running around her mind.

Laura thrust the curtain open. The rattling of the rail, sharp, and metallic.

Empty. Drops of blood on the bathtub base. Laura let out a long breath of relief. She felt like she could cry. She composed herself. Holding her breath for a moment. She took out her phone, and tried Francis' number again.

Then she heard the breathing. She turned. The bathroom door slowly closing. A figure drenched in black emerged from the shadows.

"Polo!"

Laura let out a scream before hands found her throat.

CHAPTER THIRTY – FOUR

FRANCIS

The hot cup warmed Francis' hands as he dropped the bombshell on Catherine, who sat there, slack jawed.

"What?" Catherine said, her breath stopped like there was no air left in the room. "How could you suggest such a thing? Francis? Had Laura really gotten into your head? She's gotten into everyone's head!"

"Don't patronise me," Francis said, pulling himself out of his frozen state. "I came to the conclusion on my own. Jeremy killed his wife, and he is framing Laura for it." Catherine stood up, putting her hands to her face. The man she had worked with every day for the past few years. A man who she had gotten drunk with. Confided in. Who she had introduced to Jason. *Jason.* The thought of his name again made her heart break.

"I can't do this right now," Catherine said, moving for the door.

"Laura asked me to do some work on the Voyer's computer a few days ago," Francis said, getting to his feet. "Before we ended up in this utter shit storm. Well, I looked at the tapes to see what else he had been up to. This sick fucker had been watching women's restrooms for years! Hundreds of women on those tapes. Hundreds!"

"I don't care," Catherine dismissed. "What this has to do with Jeremy?" Francis continued quickly, afraid that if he didn't say what he needed to say right away, then he would be thrown out into the cold, and all hope would be lost.

"I loaded up the footage on my work computer earlier on this evening. I figured this is where all this started. I wanted to see if I could find anything else of Kacy. To see if there was something we missed."

"And what did you find?" Catherine said. Francis paused. "Francis," She said impatiently. "What did you find?"

"I saw Mary. Jeremy's wife is in one of the clips. She was with someone. I don't know who. But she kisses them and is *doing* other things with them in the cubical." Catherine felt bile rise in her stomach.

"So, she was having an affair?" Catherine said matter-of-factly. Her skin prickled. "Everyone has affairs Francis." She put her hand on the door handle. "I think you should go." She went to open it, and Francis dived at the door, closing it. His face in inch from Catherine's.

"She was there in the early hours of the morning, and she left with this guy. I checked the CCTV cameras. They left together, and she drunk drove her car home. Jeremy went home that evening, and then she was reported missing. What if he caught them? What if he found evidence of them cheating and he lost his head?" Catherine chewed on his words, then shook her head.

"You're being ridiculous," she said. "I need you to leave." Francis slammed his hand on the door again.

"I will go. I will go right now, but I need you to hear me out, okay?" His breath was putrid. The stench of stale alcohol turning Catherine's toes up. They shared a stare, and then Catherine retreated to the sitting area.

"Five minutes, and then you go." She said. Francis let out a satisfied sigh. He moved back to his chair and took out the bundle of papers from the file and laid them out on the floor.

"Mary left in the early hours of the morning with this guy." He pointed to the still image of them in the cubical. "They left in her car," another image. A grainy CCTV still of the car park. Mary's car in situ. "They left…" he pulled out an ANPR record. "and she arrived home a half hour later. No more movement on the vehicle." He studied the photos, awaiting Catherine's response.

"I don't know," Catherine said, studying the photos, pinning her hair behind her ears. "How do we know that this other guy didn't kill her?"

"And drag her body, unseen, all the way to Pennington Flash, several miles away, bloodied and dismembered?" He pulled a face of disdain. "Come on, Cath," he said. "You saw the state of her. That wasn't done in a heartbeat. It would have taken time to do that to someone."

"It could have been the Butcher?"

"Which is more likely?" Francis said, growing frustrated. "A killer who hides in the shadows, going to a nightclub filled with people and cameras, picking up a woman he has been having an affair with, getting in her car, leaving DNA evidence and then mutilating her and disappearing," he licked his lips. This wasn't just the part where the bombshell dropped, this was the part the world exploded. "Or the detective sergeant comes home and finds his wife to be having an affair, who is forensically aware, loses his mind, kills her, then stages her death to look like a mutilated victim of an existing serial killer? A sergeant who has it in for Laura. A sergeant who, for the past few weeks, we know has been having problems with his marriage. Has been coming to work in the same clothes, unshaven and unclean?"

Catherine processed the information. Francis could see her putting the pieces together. She hated Laura. Fuck, they both did with what she had done to them. But maybe their hatred was misplaced? Maybe Laura had been right all along, and she was being set up.

"You saw how defensive Jeremy got when Laura put some heat on him in the house," Francis said. "You saw how he couldn't *really* account for his movements. You saw how clean his house was. The chemicals in his shed?"

"He was insistent on coming to see the body of Mary," Catherine said, the penny slowly dropping. It slowly dawning on her, the realisation painting her face. "I just thought it was some kind of weird grieving process," she said. Francis leaned in.

"How often do we see perpetrators of crimes return to the crime scene?" He said, nodding his head. "You know this is true. You know something isn't adding up." Catherine stood up and moved to the door.

"Are you seriously still kicking me out?" Francis said, flabbergasted. Catherine grabbed her coat from the hook and threw it on her.

"It's freezing outside," she said. "And you can't drive." Francis felt a smirk creeping along his face. "So, we need to find Laura, and then we need to find Jeremy."

"She was telling the truth this whole time," Francis said, getting to his feet and collecting his papers. "And as much as it pains us to admit it, we were wrong, and we owe her an apology." Catherine shot him a look that blasted the cold from his bones.

"I owe her nothing," she hissed, fire in her eyes. "But I can't see someone innocent go to prison." Francis took that. That was fair enough. One step at a time. Laura had some grovelling to do to him herself.

Francis' phone rang. It was Laura. Catherine regarded the handset.

"Speak of the Devil."

"A poor choice of words," Francis said, and put the phone to his ear. "Ma'am..." he began, then his face turned to horror.

Screaming. Screaming and thrashing. Bodies slamming against something. Heavy breath. His heart picked up.

"What is it?" Catherine urged, seeing the panic in Francis' eyes. He put the phone down, looking at his location apps. He found Laura.

"Oh fuck..."

"What?"

"She's at my house," he said quickly, racing to the door. "She's at my house and she's screaming for help."

CHAPTER THIRTY – FIVE

LAURA

Laura was slammed against the bathroom wall. Her back thudded so hard that the impact made her vision flash white and her head rattle. The figure devoured her. Gloved hands finding her face. Harsh breathing. Laura screamed. Thrashing. Her phone ejected from her hands and fell onto the floor behind them, eclipsing away what little light she had. She was blind. Blind, alone, and overpowered.

Laura grabbed the hands that wrapped around her throat. She felt them squeezing. Thumbs pressing into her windpipe. The blood rushing to her head, making it swell like a balloon that was about to burst. She kicked and struck at the figure, but it was like hammering a brick wall. No matter how much she struck out, she couldn't seem to make a dent. She felt her breath close off. The pipeline of life clenched shut.

Gabriel had found her. She didn't know how, but he had found her. He was done playing games. He was choking the life out of her, and she would be left on the cold floor, alone in the dark, until the sun came up and someone came to find her. By then he would be gone like the wind, no trace as always.

Laura grabbed a hold of Gabriel's hand. His face was in

shadow. Features mute. Her eyes watering. Blurry. She felt something burst in her eardrums. Her strangled breath straining through his clenched hands, fighting to stay alive. Her heartbeat pounding loudly in her head. She saw the eyes in front of her glowing in the darkness. Hate filled eyes. Cruel and cold. She felt her strength beginning to leave her. The world falling away.

This is where it was going to end.

This is where she would die.

CHAPTER THIRTY – SIX

FRANCIS

The seat belt alarm blared louder than the rev counter as the car careened around the corner to Francis' house. Francis had his ear glued to his phone, desperately trying to get through to Laura.

"Come on, come on!" He urged. "Answer the phone!" He stabbed at the road with his hand. "Turn left here!" He ordered as Catherine drove through red lights. Cars slammed on their brakes and blasted their horns.

Catherine banked hard on the wheel, revving the car right through the red light. The engine screamed at her to yield. Her lips were tight. Her knuckles were white as her hands gripped the wheel for dear life.

"Take a right here," Francis barked, pointing to a NO ENTRY sign. Catherine went to protest, only a flicker, but Francis stomped the ember out before it smoked. "Just do it!" More horns blared. Their vision was filled with bright white headlights that flew towards them. Sharply cutting out of the way of oncoming traffic. She slipped into another gear, snapping the gear stick into third, barely letting go of the accelerator. The engine sounded like it was going to collapse from exhaustion at any moment.

They picked up speed, then cut through a small alley, pressing on the horn so pedestrians darted out of the way, cutting through them like a hot knife through butter.

"Left!" Francis screamed. He tried Laura again, but it still went to voicemail. He killed the call, then dialled 999. The call operator answered. Francis screamed that he needed police and armed units at his home address and then put down the phone. They could figure out the details later. He just needed them there, and he needed them there ten minutes ago.

He pointed to another turn, and Catherine did as instructed, then the flashing of a speed camera lit them up. Catherine felt a pang of pain in her gut. Her perfect licence. Ruined.

"Don't worry about that!" Francis barked, lunging over, and pushed Catherine's leg down harder on the accelerator. The engines cries piqued. The exhaust popping. They didn't have long. He could tell. He knew Laura was in serious trouble. She was screaming, and Laura *never* screamed. A scream that told him she wasn't just in trouble, but she was fighting for her life.

Laura rattled out a dying breath as she felt the hands squeeze tighter around her neck. Her vision rendered to black. Everything she had done in her life flashing before her eyes. All the good, all the bad, and everything in between. Her life as a child. Her teens. Joining the police. Becoming a detective. Her lovers and haters. Her friends, past and gone. Her dreams, old and new.

Surrendering to the blackness that was consuming her, her hands fell away, and her body relaxed. Inch by inch, until all that was left was a suffocating black. And death…

His hands relaxed a little. Just enough for her to heave a large breath, and her engine of survival fired up again.

Laura's eyes snapped open. From somewhere, she found the strength. Every fibre of her being willing her to fight. To stay alive. She would not go out this way.

Laura gasped for more air. The pressure around her throat returning. She could smell him. His hot breath on her face. A mixture of cigarettes and coffee laced with dog shit.

She kicked out with everything she had. Her body was still suspended inches from the ground. She struck him in the gut, but it was like a child hitting a giant. His grip around her neck grew tighter, like a snake wrapping its body around its prey, which struggled to escape. As the serpent coiled tighter, the prey's ribs cracked like dry branches.

Laura pried her fingers in between the attacker's death grip, bringing millimetres of space, allowing her to suck in a breath. Just one more breath.

And that's all she needed.

Laura swung her fist, catching something soft. A scream of pain, enough for Gabriel to drop her down just an inch, and her heel to catch the bathroom floor. She pushed herself off the back wall, propelling her and Gabriel along the bathroom. They stumbled backwards in the dark, colliding hard with the closed bathroom door. He was caught off guard by Laura's sudden drive of power, enough to loosen his grip, and for Laura to break free.

She coughed and folded in two, clutching her throat. Her voice strained; her throat felt like it was on fire. Each forced breath felt like razor wire, catching on her windpipe. The taste of blood in her mouth was metallic and potent. Gabriel lunged for her. Laura had no strength left to fight. That last ditch effort was all she had and it hadn't been enough. Her Adrenaline vanished, and her legs turned to jelly as death drew closer.

The punch collided with her temple, and like a rag doll thrown aside by a Rottweiler, she slammed her head against the wall. She slumped in the corner. Her vision swaying.

He converged on her. A fist full of her hair in his gloved hands. Laura tried to scream, but her voice had been crushed. All that escaped was a strained whisper. He slammed her head into the wall again and again like he was using it to knock in a nail. Each time, a blast of white erupting in her vision. How much more could she take? How much more could she fight through before she had to let go? How many times could a flame be stamped on before it went out?

Her hand found the cold floor as he slammed her into the wall again. Her skin split and blood poured down her face. Her legs went limp, and her fingers slid across the blood slicked floor. Pain sliced through her index finger. Laura's hands grabbed the straight razor on the ground. She brought it up with all she had and slashed in the dark.

The hand released her with a scream of anguish. The sound of clumsy and erratic footsteps stumbled away into. The shower curtain snapped, falling to the ground. Rings pulled off the pole and rattled onto the tiles. His blood hit the ground like heavy rain.

A door bursting open. Footsteps rushing up the stairs.

Familiar voices called out in the darkness. "Laura!"

The bathroom door opened, allowing the light from the street to flood through the landing window. She watched as Gabriel's silhouette flitted along the landing and into another room. The white eyes of torches flickered around the stairs and hallway. Keys rattled. Footsteps approached, heavy and echoing. The torchlight illuminated her face. She gasped and let out a scream. Laura raised her hand, pointing in the direction the attacker had disappeared in, but they didn't see, and Gabriel slipped away into the night.

Laura's hand fell away, and the last thing she heard was the bloodied straight razor clattering on the ground.

CHAPTER THIRTY – SEVEN

LAURA

Laura felt the bruises forming around her throat as she sat in the waiting room in A&E. She stayed conscious, somehow. The CT scan of her head showed that although she had taken a beating, she didn't have a concussion.

"You're made of strong stuff," the doctor had said.

You don't know the half of it.

"You need to take some time off," Francis said, who had been with her since the moment he found her half-dead on the ground. He still couldn't believe she was breathing. The state of her. Covered in blood. A sight he will remember for the rest of his life.

He and Catherine had stayed with her until the ambulance came. Laura croaked out that the Butcher had found her, and he raced away when she cut him.

"CSI," Laura said, barely louder than a whisper, pointing to the blood on the ground and the bloodied straight razor. "Area search. Dogs. Helicopter."

The cavalry arrived a few minutes later, and Francis' house was now a crime scene. He was just happy that he dropped the straight razor. Laura hadn't asked why it was on the floor. But the pain in his eyes told her more than enough. Maybe they would talk about it one day. Maybe not. Some things were best left unsaid.

"Are you listening to me?" Francis said again, leaning into Laura, who was staring into space. Behind her eyes, the nightmare was playing out repeatedly. She had been hurt before. But this was the closest he had ever seen her to death. This had really rocked her, which made him even more determined to catch this mother fucker even if it was the last thing he did.

Laura turned to him. Her eyes were bloodshot, and her cheeks with burst blood vessels. Her head was glued back together, and dried blood remained on her hair and scalp. "What?" Laura said, croaking the word, then rubbing her throat in pain.

"I said you can't carry on." Francis' face was wrapped with concern. "You need to leave this to us now."

"He tried to kill me," Laura croaked. Her eyes leaked blood. Face like stone, like a bloodied, weeping angel. "He can't win."

They sat in the quiet for a few more minutes before Laura's discharge papers came.

Back in the car, Catherine took to the wheel, and they drove in silence. Laura noticed which way they were going, and she grabbed Francis' arm.

"Station…" The request was like a punch to the gut.

"You're kidding, right?" Francis said. The streetlights passing over them, casting their faces in bright lights, and then consumed them back in shadow, like eyes blinking in the sun. "Laura, I know you think you need to carry on. And I get it. But no. I can't take you back."

"Station," Laura said, again fighting for every word. "… need to finish…" He knew how much pain she was in, and that she was still forcing herself to speak meant one thing. She would not let this go. She would not let this lie.

They had tried to call Jeremy several times. He wasn't answering, and the hotel he was staying at had searched his room, but he wasn't there. Looked like something had happened. Shattered glass and blood on the floor, but no sign of him.

"Looks like Jeremy has been spooked," Francis said. Laura scrunched her face up, hammer-fisted the car door, and didn't say another word.

Francis called the station and filled in the response sergeant on what he was thinking. The cops were now out looking for him, but not as a missing person, but as a murder suspect. The world was on fire, and whether or not he liked to admit it, Laura was the only person who could put out the flames. He had to believe in her one last time, before there was nothing left of the world other than ash and bone. "Take us to the station," Francis said to Catherine. She nodded a silent *yes,* then turned off the next exit.

No one said another word for the rest of the journey.

CHAPTER THIRTY – EIGHT

LAURA

Laura turned on the shower and let the hot water douse her. She hated the showers at the office. But she wouldn't go home. The only place she felt safe right now was in the station, surrounded by high walls, strong gates, and police officers. Lots and lots of police officers. She didn't want to be alone ever again. Francis had even gone to retrieve Bagpipe for her. She hadn't been home in so long. The poor guy must have been missing her like crazy.

The wound to her head was not as severe as she thought. A deep cut, but no cracking to her skull. The actual pain was in her neck, and she had some seriously strong painkillers to help with that. The swelling was already going down, thanks to the work at the hospital. No damaged vertebrae. No nerve damage. Dare she think she had been lucky? She had bruises, and she had trauma. Both of which she should be used to by now.

She stepped into the shower fully clothed. Almost in a trance. It was as hot as she could bare it, and then she cranked it a little hotter.

Laura sat on the floor under the downpour. She brought in her knees and held them there tightly. How much could one person take? How much could she fight to stay alive? When all this was done, what would be left of her?

Would she even recognise herself in the mirror? Why did Gabriel want her? Why was he doing this? Playing her like a pawn, only to track her down and try to kill her?

The forensics team would do tests on the blood. Maybe they would come back with something this time? Maybe. Every time she thought they were getting closer, and they were winning, he was already two steps ahead. Playing his game felt like chess. Every time you captured a piece, the board would flip, and the game would start anew. Meanwhile, you'd be left scrambling for your own pieces all while he continued playing. The blood from her head and face ran into the water, turning it a diluted crimson. She placed her head on the back of the shower cubical. The steam enveloped her, like she was stuck on a ship in the middle of a thick fog. She stared into the mist. The pouring water around her bringing back memories she would rather forget, but they came anyway. The scent of salt water in her nostrils. The sound of crashing waves. The steam morphed before her unblinking eyes.

She was back on the ship. South Africa. The sky breaking in half with the cracking of lightning and the ear shattering rumble of thunder. She lay on the bow of the ship, being drenched by the rain that pounded her. Puddles of water forming around her. She heard his screams as the sea took him.

Her eyes snapped open as the cold air hit her. The steam sucked out of the shower cubical, and someone was standing there. Laura went to scramble. To move. He had found her again. He had come to finish her off.

Francis moved into the shower. Not saying a word. He crouched under the downpour with her, and pressed his back against the cubical, holding Laura in his arms. She stayed rigid, but not out of fear of Francis. She was afraid that if she moved, she would have to get back to work.

He held her under that shower for an unknown amount of time. Laura began to sob. He ran his hands through her hair and pressed his head to her crown. Laura let go of her legs and reached for Francis' drenched shirt. They sat in silence, comforted by the white noise. No thoughts, just heat. A space between breaths and reason. They both knew what they needed to do next. So much said without uttering a syllable. Laura sucked in a staggered breath, and her tears fell like rain.

CHAPTER THIRTY – NINE

LAURA

Laura dried off. Francis left without saying a word. She found fresh clothes laid out for her. Ones from her home. Some dry shampoo. Some makeup. Other bits that he had grabbed. By the looks of things, he had grabbed whatever he thought she might need. She could tell he was single by his choices. He didn't bring her any fresh underwear. He would have been too embarrassed to go through her knickers. Thankfully, she kept a fresh set of clothing at the office in case of emergencies or a double shift.

She dried off and queried the bottle of dry shampoo he had brought her. There was no chance in hell that would go near her with a head wound. He had even brought her some sanitary pads and a toothbrush. She laughed to herself. He was hopeless. But she liked it.

She got dressed and made herself look remotely human. The bruising around her neck had bloomed a deep purple. It would get much, much worse.

She checked her phone. No missed calls. The MIU had set up a link to her phone should Gabriel call. Something they did so not to miss anything.

She made herself feel human. After brushing her teeth, she dried her hair and tied it up in a bun. It resembled a fox's tail. She straightened out her clothes as she looked in the locker room mirror. A white shirt and a pair of jeans. The whites of her eyes were still full of broken blood vessels from being choked, and although her throat hurt like a bitch, she could force her words out easier. The hot steam must have helped. Or maybe she was still high on the painkillers she had been given. Either way, she was thankful.

Instead of heels, she threw on a pair of trainers that she had in her locker. She didn't care about appearances. The blood in her eyes would draw any attention away from whatever she was wearing. She looked like a demon of some kind, and part of her, dare she admit, liked it.

Gabriel believed him to be an angel. A messenger from God. Well, now he would face the Devil. And the Devil was not a furry half man, half goat, with hooves and a serpent's tongue. No. She was five foot nine, had abs you could grate cheese on, red hair and a bad fucking attitude.

She was going to catch this mother fucker. He tried to take her life, like so many others. They had all met their end, one way or another. She wouldn't let him ruin her clean record.

In the MIU, Laura was greeted by the sound of keys rattling and the smell of coffee. Faces looked up to greet her as she walked in. She saw him then, running to her. Bagpipe. She reached down and ran her fingers through his fur, and he purred fondly, weaving between her legs like a velvet shadow. Laura buried her fingers in the fur on his head. His ears flickered with the scratching. His little fangs poked from his lips under his small pink nose. When he opened his eyes, those bright yellow orbs greeted her with a love that only animals knew.

"I tried to do that," Francis said, raising his hand. Laura could see the distinct scratch marks that all cat owners knew too well.

"He does that," Laura said. Her throat still sore, but much better.

"You look well," Francis said. He had changed his clothes too. The look on his face, happy about the moment they had shared, yet neither of them needed to say a word about it.

On his computer he had cell site data up. A map of the country, triangulating the different cell masts, trying to pinpoint where the last call had come from Gabriel.

Laura moved to her chair and took a seat. A black coffee was waiting for her. She surveyed the office. Burnell was sitting in the corner with the superintendent. They were discussing movements, officer placement, and the press.

Politics, Laura thought. *They do the politics. We catch the fuckers.* Just the way she liked it. Catherine was sitting there and staring at the computer screen. Her face devoid of expression. It had been a rough ride for her, and Laura had so much to say to her, but couldn't find where to begin. Her friend, who she had betrayed worse than humanly possible, and now the blood of her lover was on her hands, and no matter how much Laura tried, she knew she could never scrub it off.

"Where are we up to?" Laura said, addressing the room. Francis looked up. His face grave. He looked at Laura. "What is it?" She said.

"We've had the forensics back on the blood." Laura's heart stuck in her throat.

"Go on…" Laura said, waiting for the answer. Did they have him? Did they know who he was? Anything right now could help them find him. She checked her watch. It was nearly dawn. He might call her soon. If they could find out who he was, then Laura could get the upper hand. Something she desperately needed.

Francis shook his head.

"No matches," he said. Laura clenched her eyes shut. He almost killed her. She had hoped it might have been worth it if it got her ahead of him. To make her own rules in this game. But it had been for nothing. They were no further on, and Laura was barely alive because of it.

"Fuck!" She ground out. Her throat seared with pain, and she grabbed it. Laura took a long drink of her coffee, and the heat soothed it away. "Okay," she said, trying to keep a lid on it. "Any news on Jeremy?"

"We're still looking," Francis said. Laura felt the familiar rush of heat.

"What exactly *do* we know?" She said.

"Not much," Francis said. "No forensics. No M.O. No vehicles, cell site data, or top up data. The Butcher is a ghost."

You're taking the piss.

"He nearly killed me, and we have nothing to show for it," Laura said.

"I know," Francis said. "But we need to –"

"We need to find him!" Laura bellowed, thrashing her hand along her desk, sending the cup of coffee flying along the room. Her throat screamed with pain, and she massaged it, her eyes brimming with pain. All eyes fell on her. A moment of silence as Laura pressed her hands into her face and leaned back in her chair. She took a moment and let out a long breath.

"Okay," Laura said, pressing the word out slowly, trying to keep her head on a level. "Okay." She raised her hand out. "Has anyone tried calling Jeremy?"

"I don't think that's a good idea," Catherine said. Laura slammed her fist into the desk.

"Just," she hissed, her mood borderline hostile. "Just do it." Catherine took out her phone and fumbled with it. She wanted to prove Laura wrong. Wanted to show her it wouldn't work. She put her phone to her ear.

"Anything?" Laura said, impatiently.

The call connected, and Catherine's face turned into abject horror. She turned to Laura, all eyes now on her. Laura feeling like she was having her feet held near a fire. With trembling lips, Catherine uttered the next words that made Laura's jaw tighten.

"It's *him*," Catherine said. "He has Jeremy's phone."

CHAPTER FORTY

LAURA

THE OFFERING

Laura looked at the ovens. Her throat was in agony. Head was pounding from the pain. The stitches were coming loose from the exertion. What was she doing here? One of them was a murderer. Jason was dead. Laura could see the pool of dried blood around him. A large swelling of red around his chest had turned a dark brown. His skin pasty. He was already beginning to rot. Which meant that it was Jeremy. He *had* to be the killer. All signs pointed to it. That was what Gabriel wanted him to confess. Confess to the killing of his wife.

Laura raced to the furnace door and tried to pull the lock open with all her might. The blood rushed to her head, and she felt the glue in her skull beginning to tear open. Peeling away. Prying apart like a fleshy, sealed mouth. She released the handle, gasping fiercely. Jeremy was on the other side, sitting there as naked as the day he was born. His body had been brutalised. His flabby skin pressed against the thick glass window. The sound of the incinerator coming alive. A large hum. The fans whirring into action. Jeremy's screams were barely audible over the racket.

"Get me out of here!" Jeremy screamed, hammering his fists on the glass. Laura stared into his eyes. She had never seen so much fear. So much terror. A man who was staring at death, and nothing he could do about it.

"I'm going to get you out!" Laura shouted, ignoring the agony in her throat. She moved away from the window, and Jeremy hammered even louder. The clock above the oven counting down. Less than four minutes left.

Laura could see the oven begin to glow a dull red and feel the heat coming from it. She desperately looked around to find some release switch, some kind of emergency override. A wrench. A hammer. Anything she could use to pry the doors open.

There are two murderers in this room. Confess your sins.

"I killed Celine!" She shouted. "I am one of the killers!" It couldn't be Jason. He was dead. Gabriel was cruel, but there was always a method to his games. So, it had to be her, which also meant it also had to be Jeremy. Laura rushed to the window. Jeremy was red. His body sweating profusely. Thick globs of liquid poured from his face. "Jeremy!" Laura said. "You have to tell me what happened to Mary!" He looked at her, the desperation turning to horror.

"Nothing!" He said. "You killed her! You murderer!" Laura looked like she was chewing on glass.

"Jeremy," she said, tapping on the glass with her finger. "Jeremy, listen to me." She turned and looked at the timer. Two minutes gone. Three left. The big red numbers counting down. The fans getting louder. "Jeremy, you are going to die," she said. "Whatever happened, we can talk about it. But you have to tell me what happened to Mary. I didn't kill her. You know I didn't, so tell me the truth before it's too late." Jeremy shook his head and pointed to the furnace Jason was lying dead in.

"It must have been him!" He screamed. He looked up to the heavens, searching for some kind of absolution. Holy intervention. Anything. Anything that would save his skin from the flames. "It was him! He killed my wife! He killed her and then pinned the death on Laura! He hid her clothing in the boot of her car, disposed of the body, and burned the evidence in the shipping container! Let me out!" Laura's eyes snapped wider.

"Shipping container?" She said, barely audible. Jeremy looked around, wanting the door to open. To feel the cold breath of the wind on his heated skin. But the door stayed shut. "I didn't know anything about a shipping container..." Laura's eyes turned hard. "So it *was* you!" Laura snarled, pressing her teeth an inch from the glass. Jeremy turned to her, his face frantic. "It was you! You pinned it on me! You were going to let me go down for murder!" Jeremy shook his head.

"Laura," he said, a desperate laughter escaping his lips. "You know me. I wouldn't do that. I loved my wife. Twenty years together! You can't just turn your back on that. It was him!" He screamed again. "Let me out. Come on. I'm telling the truth. Let me out!" Laura turned and looked at the clock. Three minutes gone. Two left.

With a *whoosh*, flames appeared at the back of the furnace. Thousands of tiny yellow and red flames, creeping slowly towards Jeremy. He turned and saw the flames and began banging on the window furiously, a snarl on his face. "Laura!" He screamed. "Laura, open the door! Open the door right now!"

"You're lying," she said. "You're lying, and he knows it. He knows the truth. He knows what you did. Tell the truth, or you're going to burn!"

The sight of the flames fractured Jeremy's mind. Rows and rows of them appeared, moving closer towards him. Immolation was only a few feet away. One of the flames seared his foot, and he snapped it closer to him with a yowl of agony. "Confess!" Laura screamed. Her breath was ragged. Her throat seared with white-hot pain like someone was placing it on a grill. The hot air was drying it out. The shouting causing it to swell again. She had a little left in her before she couldn't speak over the blasting of the fans. "You have to tell the truth!" Jeremy's face turned from anguish to guilt. Tears streaming down his face, marred with sweat and soot. He looked at Laura through that small porthole. He saw it in her eyes. He was done. He had nowhere left to run.

"I did it," he said, just louder than a whisper. "I killed her," he said in a stifled whimper. He raised his head, shouting the heavens, "I killed my wife!" Laura felt her heart sink. His face turned to hers. He moved to the iron walls. Tears streaming down his face, carving through the soot that had matted with his sweat. "I lost my mind when I caught her cheating. Oh, God … the things I did to her body. I tried to cover it up. Make it look like one of the other murders. I cut out her tongue. Removed her teeth and destroyed the evidence. Took off her hands … Gouged out her eyes…" Whatever strength was holding him together left him with every breath. He sat there, quivering in that destitute heat. A shell of a man. A man who knew that he had nothing to live for anymore.

"Okay," Laura said, the lump in her throat growing larger. But not out of anger or pain, but of remorse. Fierce remorse and pity. She had more questions, but they would wait. He could answer them at the station. Laura looked around the crematorium chamber. "He confessed! He killed his wife. I murdered Celine. Now let him out!"

No answer. Nothing from the radio, and the counter continued to count down. One minute left. Sixty seconds and counting.

Despite the heat, Laura felt the cold run through her blood. Laura snatched the radio, and she screamed into it.

"Gabriel!" She bellowed. "He confessed! I confessed! What sick game is this!? Let him out! Unlock the door!"

Flames continued to grow. Jeremy screamed louder, banging violently on the glass. He lay on his back, slamming his feet into the sealed door, over and over again. The sound bouncing around the room. The radio stayed silent. Laura felt debilitated. She grabbed the handle and with all her might and pulled so hard she thought she was going to snap her wrists. She released the handle. Her breath was ragged. Bloody tears falling from her face. She looked through the glass. Jeremy was now pressed against the wall. The flames were now inches from his skin.

"I can't get it open," she cried. "Jeremy," she banged on the window. "I can't get it open. I'm sorry. I'm so sorry."

Jeremy was shouting something. Begging. Pleading again and again. His thin, grey hair was frazzled. His body scoured red. His hands were bloody from banging so hard, smearing soot and crimson onto the window.

3…

"Laura, Laura, please!"

2…

"It's so hot!" A wail of despair.

1…

"I don't want to die. Oh God, I don't want to die!"

"I'm sorry, Jeremy." The radio came to life.

"You failed."

The timer hit zero.

The flames rose, becoming flaming geysers that engulfed Jeremy's body. He fell to the ground, thrashing, screaming fiercely. Laura knew she would hear nothing but those screams as the flames devoured him. Her eyes fixated on him, unable to pull them away. The image of him burning searing itself into her brain like a hot brand. He writhed in the liquid fire ate him alive. All Laura could do was watch it happen. The image of the man she had worked with for the last few years. The man who she had fought with. Laughed with. Admired and despised, was consumed by an inferno a few inches from her, and there was nothing she could do about it. The smell hit her then, The stench of burning meat and boiling blood.

Jeremy shot up and slammed against the glass. His face was raw, skin burned away. His eyes bubbling, leaking down his face. His scalp chewed away. A strained death rattle escaping his torched throat. He slipped down the door, leaving a long streak of sizzling blood on the glass.

Laura collapsed to the floor, holding herself. Whimpering to herself on that cold ground.

"I confessed," she cried. "I confessed. He confessed. We did as we were told. We played the game. We did what we had to do. Why? Why did you do that to him…" Hot tears found her mouth. Her voice dying away. The strain on her damaged voice rendering her cries into a strangled gurgle.

The flames died away, and the fan soon after, leaving Laura in a silent and cold tomb. The wound on her head was fully open, pouring scarlet onto her. She fell into the darkest corners of her mind. Her body devoid of energy. She could lie here, and this be her grave. An exhaustion only the dead knew.

She opened her eyes at the sound of something metallic unlatching. A figure in front of her, drenched in dried blood. A face that looked familiar. A face of a man she thought was dead.

Jason stood above her. The furnace door to his oven open. He stretched himself out. Laura wanted to fight. To run. To scream. But she was too fatigued. All she could do was watch. Watch as he smiled at her. As he touched the large, flashy scar on his cheek, in his hand a small radio.

"You got me good," he said, touching the wound on his

face. "I thought I had you. But you're tougher than I thought." He took a small voice box from the radio and tossed it onto the ground. Then, in a voice she recognised, "the offering to the Lord is complete. The sinner's body cleansed by flames." He turned and stepped away, moving to the door of the crematorium.

Laura moved her arms. Willing herself to get to her feet. She stumbled. Her legs shaking. Her body on the brink of collapse.

"We confessed," she croaked. It's all she could say. Shock ravaging her. Jason got to the door. He paused and turned to her.

"*He* confessed," he said. "But you?" He said, shaking his head. His eyes bore into her. Eyes that she didn't recognise. Eyes that were cruel. Malevolent. "But you still hold that secret deep in your wretched heart." He stepped back and grabbed the steel door. Laura forced herself to move. She stumbled to her feet. Fought to stay upright, using the walls for support, inching her way over to the door. He was going to close it. He was going to lock her in, and he was going to get away and continue his sadistic crusade. Just a few more steps. Just a few more. Jason grabbed the door, his arm taut, ready to slam it shut. "You almost had me, Laura," he said. "But this is not how, or where, this ends." He reached his hand to the light switch. Laura tried to run, but her legs failed her. She fell to the ground and reached out her hand in desperation. Fingers splayed, willing that door to stay open, and for those lights to stay on. "Until the next offering," he hissed. "Until *our Reckoning* is complete."

Jason slammed the door shut, and Laura Warburton was left alone in the dark, with only her failures and nightmares to keep her company.

Order the final, dramatic conclusion to Detective Laura Warburton's story by heading to Amazon / Jay Darkmoore

If you enjoyed this title, please leave a review. Reviews are how indie authors make a name for themselves and are able to keep releasing content for you hungry readers to eat up.

Thank you for taking the time and spending it reading my work. I thoroughly hoped you enjoyed it.

For my other books, social media and for a free novella from my website, visit here –

https://linktr.ee/Jaydarkmoore

Jay Darkmoore is a UK-based author with a background in crime and investigation. He is a huge fan of all things dark - exploring the macabre, demonic and darker aspects of the human psyche.

Jay likes putting his characters in terrible situations and then turning out all the lights. To date, he has self-published novels of horror, crime and dark fantasy dystopia. His inspirations are Stephen King, Keith C Blackmore and Nick Cutter.

When not at his desk, Jay spends his free time making YouTube videos to help writers in their craft, promoting other books he has enjoyed, as well as hitting the gym and taking wild cold plunges with ducks.

He is a single parent to his son Joe who is his biggest fan.

Printed in Dunstable, United Kingdom